KISS SHOT

....

(Dublin Mafia:
Triskelion Team, Book 2)

ZARA KEANE

Beaverstone Press LLC
Switzerland

KISS SHOT
Copyright © 2016 by Sarah Tanner.
Published 2016 by Beaverstone Press GmbH (LLC).
Cover Design © 2016 by Okay Creations.
All rights reserved. No part of this publication may be reproduced, distributed or transmitted in any form or by any means, including photocopying, recording, or other electronic or mechanical methods, without the prior written permission of the publisher, except in the case of brief quotations embodied in critical reviews and certain other noncommercial uses permitted by copyright law. For permission requests, write to the publisher, addressed "Attention: Permissions Coordinator," at the address below.

Beaverstone Press
CH-5023 Biberstein
Switzerland
www.beaverstonepress.com

Publisher's Note: This is a work of fiction. Names, characters, places, and incidents are a product of the author's imagination. Locales and public names are sometimes used for atmospheric purposes. Any resemblance to actual people, living or dead, or to businesses, companies, events, institutions, or locales is completely coincidental.

Book Layout ©2016 Beaverstone Press LLC

Ordering Information:

Quantity sales. Special discounts are available on quantity purchases by corporations, associations, and others. For details, contact the "Special Sales Department" at the address above.

Kiss Shot/Zara Keane. -- 1st ed.

ISBN: 978-3-906245-34-8

ONE

Kilpatrick, Dublin

Shane regarded Olga's bare arse with an indifference borne of many years hanging around his father's strip club.

"So what do you think?" she asked, staring at him upside down through her opened legs. "Should I bleach it?"

What she should do, in Shane's opinion, was get the fuck away from his brother, Greg, her alleged boyfriend. "I dunno," he said in a bored tone. "Does anal bleaching hurt?"

After whipping her long ponytail back over her shoulder, Olga straightened her back and yanked up her crystal thong. "My friend Petra burned the arse off herself doing it, but she said she had an allergic reaction to the cream."

Shane shuddered. "Jaysus. If her experience was bad, why are you thinking of bleaching yours?"

"Greg likes the idea." Olga wound a strand of dark hair around her index finger and batted her fake eyelashes. "He thinks it looks sexy."

And what Greg liked, Greg got. His older brother was a mean son of a bitch to everyone, but utterly vile to his girlfriends. "If you want to do it, go for it, but make sure you're doing it for you and not for my brother."

"You're sweet." Olga placed a hand on his arm and brushed her impressive cleavage against him. "Are you seeing anyone at the moment?" she asked in a sultry whisper. "If you're ever lonely, you know where to find me."

Yeah, he knew where to find her—stripping at his father's lap dancing club and fucking punters on the side. Hell no. Shane was no saint, but the appeal of screwing around with the girls at Valentine's had worn off by the time he was out of his teens. His father and older brothers considered the female employees of Valentine's to be their never-ending supply of blow jobs. Shane preferred women to sleep with him of their own free will, and not because he controlled their livelihood.

In Olga's case, she was more out of bounds than the other girls. Every once in a while, Greg played the girls off one another, eventually picking one to be his official live-in girlfriend and temporarily removing her from circulation at the club. Olga was his most recent acquisition, although Greg had yet to seal the deal by inviting her to quit her job and share his apartment.

It would never last. Fickle was Greg's middle name. Soon, Olga would find herself out on her bleached arse, probably with a broken jaw or swollen lip as a souvenir of the relationship.

Shane removed Olga's hand from his arm. "I don't think meeting up would be wise."

She pouted, making her look like a sulky teenager wearing a bucket of makeup. Which she probably was. Shane's father didn't look too closely at the paperwork of the girls who applied to work at his club, and the probability that Olga's papers were fake was high.

"Okay," she demurred, turning the pout into a come-hither smile. "But if you're ever at a loose end..."

He liked to live dangerously at times—his rival Adam Kowalski's on-off girlfriend was one of his regular hook-ups—but a smart man didn't crap in his backyard. And Shane was smart, apart from a weak spot for damsels in distress. "Listen, Olga, remember what I told you last week?"

"Yeah. So Greg gets a bit rough at times." The girl shrugged. "Some of the punters do as well. I'm used to it."

"His parting gift to his last girlfriend was a broken jaw and a dislocated shoulder," Shane said gently. "That's a lot more serious than 'a bit rough.'"

Olga stared at him through her heavily made-up eyes. "Greg has never hurt me."

Not yet, but he would. Shane sighed. There was no getting through to the girl. She'd been a lost cause the moment she'd set eyes on Greg's Porsche and flash-with-the-cash swagger. "If you're ever in trouble, give me a call. Not to hook up," he added hastily, noting how her face had lit up, "but if you're ever in need of a friend, you know where to find me."

In other words, he'd be willing to help when, not if, Greg beat the crap out of her.

Olga's pout returned, and she tossed her hair over her shoulder in a dismissive gesture. "You don't know what you're missing."

He had a fair idea—practiced sex moves designed to appeal to the average paying client. He'd bet Olga was good at them, too.

However, Shane preferred to be the seducer, not the seduced. Only once in his life had he dropped his guard and allowed a woman to call the shots.

It hadn't ended well.

He winced at the memory, as corrosive today as it had been the morning after. Even after all these years, he tasted the bitter dregs of regret whenever he thought of her.

Or maybe that was just the gap in his mouth where the tooth she'd knocked out used to be.

Ruthie Reynolds, the girl with the iron fists. The only person who'd ever succeeded in beating Shane to a pulp in the boxing ring. Happy days.

Shane left Olga sulking in the corridor and ambled toward his father's office. One of Frank's eejit security guards loitered outside the door, looking tough in an ill-fitting suit. "Hey, Mark," Shane said in a breezy tone. "Is my dad in?"

Mark gave a slight inclination of his neckless head and jerked a thumb at the closed door. "He's in a foul mood today. Just as a warning."

Shane suppressed a laugh. When was Frank *not* in a bad mood these days? A visit from his least favorite son was unlikely to improve his temper, especially when Shane came bearing bad news. He rapped on the door and opened it without waiting for permission to enter.

His father sat behind his desk, glowering at the computer screen. Funny to think he'd once been considered handsome. Years of cigarettes, alcohol, and hard living had taken their toll on Frank "Mad Dog" Delaney, and left him puffy-featured and acid-tongued. He glanced up when his son came in and drew his bushy eyebrows closer together. "What the fuck do you want?"

Frank never bothered to feign affection for his youngest child. When Shane was a kid, his father's dislike of him had nagged at him, prompting him to try to please Frank. At nearly thirty, Shane was all out of fucks to give.

"Hello to you, too, Dad. You asked me to stop by, remember? You got Greg to call me." His father's avoidance of modern technology never failed to amuse him. Judging by the expression on Frank's face, he was no more comfortable with his new computer than he was with mobile phones. Shane flopped into a chair across from his reluctant parent and rolled up the sleeves of his shirt. "Holy crap, it's hot in here. I don't know why you won't install air conditioning. The place is a furnace."

"It's not worth the investment. We're in the middle of a heat wave, but it won't last." Frank pressed a key on his laptop and swore.

Shane settled back in his chair and grinned. "Problem?"

"Damn thing keeps crashing." A beat passed. "Would you have a look at it for me?"

Shane smiled sweetly across the desk. "Don't tell me you're asking for *my* help? I thought I was wasting my time screwing around on computers."

Frank's nostrils flared, but he kept his annoyance in check. "Please."

His father being polite? That was a first. Shane's smile widened. "No problem."

The last time Frank had experienced a computer crisis, he'd forgotten to plug it in. Shane had taken great pleasure in his father's humiliation.

He got up and scooted behind the desk to take a look at the laptop. "What buttons are you pressing?"

Frank blinked. "Dunno. I hit a few keys, the way Greg showed me."

What Greg knew about computers didn't extend beyond looking up porn on the internet. Shane's fingers flew over the keyboard. "You keep hitting restart. It should work now."

His father grunted something that might have been akin to "thank you" had Shane not known better. "Want a drink?" Frank muttered.

It wasn't a serious question. Shane was getting a drink whether he wanted one or not. Frank extracted a half-empty whiskey bottle from his desk drawer and sloshed two generous servings into chipped mugs. He shoved one across the desk to Shane. Given his father's slurred speech, this wasn't Frank's first drink of the day.

Shane reclaimed his seat and picked up his mug, eyeing his father warily. Any moment now, he'd ask him for an update on The Lar Situation—capitals intended. Shane hadn't a clue what to tell him. Whatever his father had been hoping to uncover on his wayward nephew, Shane was pretty sure it wasn't Lar selling out Frank and their family. If Shane revealed that his cousin was—or had been—an informer, Lar would go for a swim in the River Liffey, wearing a pair of cement shoes. That was how Frank rolled. "Why did you want to talk to me, Dad? I'm assuming my summons to your office wasn't for the love of my company."

Frank glared at his youngest son. "You know why you're here. What's Lar up to? You installed bugs in his house weeks ago. Are you telling me you have nothing interesting to report?"

"So far, the recordings have given me a few leads to follow, but nothing concrete." Total bollocks, but Frank didn't have the brains or the technological know-how to check up on him.

"Nothing concrete?" His father's voice was pure ice. "Are you sure about that? You wouldn't be lying to me to protect your cousin, now would you?"

Maybe, whispered a voice in Shane's head. "No," he said out loud, meeting his father's piercing gaze head on. "If I knew what to look for, it would help. Do you have any particular reason to suspect Lar's up to something that could harm the family? From what I can see, he's genuinely working hard to set up his new business in such a way as to honor the terms you and he negotiated. We talked about it at length during the Triskelion Team's launch party last week."

This much was true. What Shane failed to add was the info he'd uncovered regarding the deal Lar had brokered with Irish intelligence in return for an early release from prison. A searing heat burned his chest. Lar had lied to him—repeatedly. He was going to make damn sure his cousin paid for his disloyalty, but he'd do it his way, not Frank's.

His father's piercing gaze didn't falter. "I want you to keep looking. Dig deeper, dammit. And while you're at it, check out a rumor I heard about Lar clipping Jimmy Connolly."

"What the fuck?" Shane jerked to attention. Jimmy Connolly, one of Frank's rivals in the tits and arse trade, had been gunned down a couple of weeks ago in what the police presumed was part of a series of Dublin gangland killings. "Why would Lar kill Connolly? He never had much to do with the man."

Frank's smirk grated on Shane's nerves. "Let's just say he had a motive."

"Are you sure? I didn't hear anything about a dispute between him and Connolly." And Shane "heard" things. Keeping tabs on all the wheelings and dealings that occurred in and around Kilpatrick was one of his talents. "Besides, Lar's been busy with his new girlfriend and getting the Triskelion Team off the ground."

His father's lip curled. "The Triskelion Team. What sort of name is that? Lar always had notions."

In Ireland, having "notions," or aspiring to better oneself, was subject to derision.

"I think it works for a private security firm." Shane didn't add that the name referred to his and his cousins' matching triskelion tattoos. No point in giving Frank more ammunition to sneer at them.

His father took a generous gulp of whiskey and slammed the mug down on his desk, causing papers to go flying. "I want you to look into Connolly's killing," he growled. "Find out who knows what. And I want a full report on Lar's comings and goings on my desk in one week. Is that clear?"

"Crystal." Why was his father convinced Lar was behind Connolly's murder? As far as Shane knew, any hits Lar carried out were well paid and occurred abroad. If he'd taken out a man who lived nearby, his motive had to be personal. Shane opened his mouth to voice this observation, but his words were cut short by a loud knock on the office door.

His favorite uncle, Malachy, peered his gray head around the door and winked at Shane. "Greg said you were in, Francis. I need a word."

Malachy was the only member of the Delaney clan who referred to Frank by his full name. He was the only person who dared. The media referred to Frank as "Mad Dog Delaney", a moniker his father accepted with pride.

"What do you want?" Frank demanded. "Now's not a good time."

Unperturbed by his brother's unenthusiastic greeting, Malachy cleared papers from the seat beside Shane's and sat down with an air of a man under no pressing time constraints and a quiet but steely determination to stay. As the priest scanned the office, his lips twitched with amusement. "I see you haven't found a replacement for Susie."

Kiss Shot

Susie, Frank's former secretary, had quit a few weeks ago following a presumed-but-never-confirmed run-in with Greg. Since the efficient Susie's exit from his life, Frank's office had devolved into a perpetual state of chaos. Papers were piled everywhere, willy-nilly. Folders that belonged in filing cabinets were stacked all around the room. Even Frank himself looked more disheveled than usual, as if taking his cue from his surroundings.

Frank narrowed his eyes at the priest. "You don't usually come to see me at the club, Malachy. What's up?"

His uncle adjusted his dog collar and smiled at Shane. "Do you mind giving us some privacy?"

Shane glanced at his father, but Frank was staring at Malachy, a guarded expression on his face.

"Sure thing." Shane met Malachy's eyes but could read little from their pale blue depths. "Let me know if there's anything else you need me to do, Dad."

Frank's only response was a grunt.

"Come by the house one of these days, Shane," Malachy said, his expression softening. "I miss our games of chess. I'll have Mrs. Cryan make us her cottage pie."

"Yeah, okay. I'll send you a text after Max goes back to Berlin."

"Siobhan mentioned he was staying with you for a few days."

Shane exchanged an amused glance with Malachy. Max's mother was less than thrilled that her younger son had chosen to spend his days in Dublin crashing on Shane's sofa rather than staying with her. Mother and son had had a falling out on Max's last visit home—something to do with Max's father and Siobhan's ex-husband. Shane didn't know the details, and Max had been disinclined to share.

Happy fucking families, eh?

"Bye now, lads. Don't go too wild with the ladies, Malachy." Shane's smile of farewell for his uncle was heartfelt, and a world away from the curt nod he gave his father. Not for the first time, he wished the men could trade personalities, but this was as unlikely as Malachy suddenly deciding to swap the church for a lap dancing club.

Outside the club, the sun beat down on Kilpatrick, one of Dublin's less salubrious suburbs. Men perspired through their T-shirts, and some had opted for the bare-chested look. Women wore summer dresses and had traded their fake tans for the real deal. Shane laughed to himself. What the Irish considered a heat wave was nothing in comparison to the hot summers he'd experienced in Australia.

He hopped on his bike and revved the engine, his mind drifting back to the strange atmosphere in his father's office. What was so urgent that Malachy would visit Frank at Valentine's? The priest never came near the club. Whatever the reason, at least his uncle's interruption meant he didn't have to come up with more lies and excuses regarding his traitor of a cousin.

The now-familiar burning rage he experienced every time he thought of Lar swelled in his chest. His hands tightened around the handlebars of his bike, turning his knuckles white. Showing up to work at the Triskelion Team's new offices was hell, but every day he forced himself to act as normally as his poor acting skills allowed.

Tonight, he didn't have to worry about running into Lar and losing his cool, thank fuck. Shane was meeting an old pal for a drink and had deliberately chosen a pub that wasn't among his cousin's usual watering holes. Man, he needed something to take the edge off his week and get his thoughts far away from everything related to the Delaney family.

But first, he had to do more internet digging. Lar wanted him to search for info for a Triskelion Team assignment, and Frank wanted him to dig for dirt on Lar. How fucking ironic.

Shane's jaw hardened. Then he flexed his shoulders, revved the engine, and pointed the bike in the direction of home.

TWO

After four vodka shots, selling one's soul to the devil felt pretty damn good. It was a temporary high in an otherwise shitty situation, but Ruthie Reynolds would take any rays of sunshine audacious enough to penetrate the storm clouds looming over her life. With a smile tugging at the corners of her mouth, Ruthie examined the balls on the pool table and lined up her next shot.

She'd persuaded two brawny eejits to teach her to play pool. After showing her the basics, they'd agreed to an extortionate cash prize for the winner of this game, assuming the girl with the diamond stud earrings was good for it and confident she'd lose. *Fucking clowns.* She'd show them not to make assumptions.

Carefully angling her cue stick, Ruthie nudged the white ball into motion. In a perfect kiss shot, it hit off a ball, changed direction, and rolled toward her real target: the striped ball located just outside a pocket. The barest contact sent the striped ball into the basket. "Yes!" Ruthie cried, beaming at her companions.

Eejit One stared at her with open-mouthed amazement and exchanged a significant glance with Eejit Two.

"I'm a quick learner," she said in what she hoped was a husky tone. "And you're great teachers."

She needed to allay their misgivings fast, or the fight she planned to incite would break out sooner than she wanted. Ruthie smiled at the men, leaned over the pool table to draw their attention to her tight jeans—also purchased especially for this occasion—and deliberately screwed up her next shot. She straightened and made a moue of disappointment. "What did I do wrong?"

"You hit my ball instead of yours." Eejit One examined her carefully, his suspicions aroused. A big, bald man with a broken nose and scarred knuckles, he was what passed for the brains of the duo. Not that this was saying much.

Eejit Two was his pal's polar opposite in appearance: small, lanky, and greasy-haired. He had the twitchy movements of the habitual user, and the unnatural pallor of his skin enhanced this impression. The man's gaze was fixed on Ruthie's breasts, which were more prominent than usual in her figure-hugging tank top. His leer did nothing to improve his looks. "You'll get better with practice," he said with a smirk. "We could give you some private lessons if you like. Teach you how to handle balls."

The only thing I'd like to do to your balls is kick them. Ruthie's fake smile didn't falter. "I'm sure you know all about balls," she purred. *Seeing as wanking is probably the only action you get.*

Eejit One shot her a wary glance but didn't say anything further.

Ruthie smiled to herself and stepped back to let him line up his shot. "Good luck."

The man sneered. "No luck needed. I play to win."

Oh, she was sure he played to win. The idea of winning five hundred euros from her was a major enticement. Ruthie had barely fifty euros to her name at the moment, but he didn't know that. If she'd had money, she wouldn't be in her present predicament. Paying off the first chunk of her brother's debts had wiped out her savings account. The second chunk wouldn't be paid until Ruthie completed her stealth assignment for the Jarvis Agency.

She'd been wary of them the moment they'd approached her several months ago. It had been in her changing room in Geneva, right after she'd lost a fight. Staring at her swollen knee, Ruthie had finally allowed her doctor's words to penetrate: her problem knee was as good as it was going to get. She'd never fight at her peak again, never become the next Ronda Rousey.

Kiss Shot

The disappointment crushed her. Which was why she'd pushed past her doubts and embraced the idea of receiving training in surveillance and intelligence from the Jarvis Agency. They needed someone with her combat skills, and her knee was good enough for their purposes. Ruthie had envisioned glamor and excitement, more in the style of James Bond than Jason Bourne. The reality of sleazy undercover assignments, spying on drug smugglers and black market diamond dealers, was a rude awakening. When Travers, her handler, had informed her she'd have her first solo assignment, Ruthie had experienced a surge of excitement, a sliver of hope that she'd finally get a case where she could make a difference. And then they'd told her what she was expected to do.

Ruthie flexed her jaw. Kevin ought to appreciate her efforts on his behalf, but she didn't expect any thanks from her brother.

She focused on the pool table. Eejit One lined up another shot. He wasn't a bad player, but his ability paled in comparison to Ruthie's. Her opponent coaxed three balls in succession into the baskets. He was catching up fast. She had to hope that his next shot went awry.

It did.

The man swore when his ball ricocheted off the edge of the pool table and sent other balls flying, but none in the direction he wanted. Ruthie flexed her shoulders, limbering up for her next shot. She cast a quick glance around the bar. Shane Delaney had better show his face fast, or the game would be over before he arrived. The lads were getting antsy, Eejit One in particular. And rightly so. She was playing them for fools.

She successfully sank her first shot and deliberately fucked up her second. Sticking her cleavage out to the max, she stood back to let Eejit One do his stuff on the pool table. She glanced at her watch. Nine fifteen. Where the fuck was Shane Delaney? Her brother had said Shane was due to meet a mutual friend for a drink at nine o'clock. Unless he'd had a personality transplant over the last few years, Shane was always punctual. Ruthie scanned the crowd and her breath caught.

Shane Delaney weaved his way through the throng, cutting a meandering path toward the bar. He was taller than she remembered, but he still had the same high cheekbones and almond-shaped eyes that she saw in her dreams.

Her treacherous heart skipped a beat. Why did Shane have to look so damn good? Why couldn't he have developed a beer belly or acquired a man bun in the five years since she'd last seen him? Anything to lessen his sex appeal. Instead, Shane had added muscle and a sinfully sexy beard. Ruthie didn't need to see underneath his T-shirt to know he had rock-hard abs. The memory of their one and only make-out session clouded her vision. She took a deep breath and forced herself to concentrate. She'd spent too much time planning this encounter to screw it up at the last second.

Eejit One took his next shot, sent the ball wide, and swore at his ineptitude.

"Your turn, little lady." His words were laden with more than a hint of a threat.

Eejit Two blinked in confusion, his friend's menacing tone alerting him to the fact that something was off about this game. The men looked at one another, and then turned their bloodshot eyes toward her. A fight was brewing, and Ruthie intended to make sure it broke out soon. Brandishing her cue stick with a flourish, she treated Eejit One to a cheeky grin and shot the eight ball into her chosen pocket. "Well, what do you know? You owe me five hundred euros."

"You said you couldn't play," Eejit Two growled, outrage written all over his gaunt face.

"She's a fucking hustler, Dec," said his slightly smarter friend. "She played us for fools."

Ruthie erupted with laughter. "You *are* fools. The easiest pair I've ever hustled, but a deal is a deal. Now pay up."

"No fucking way." Eejit Two got up in her face, the smell of alcohol on his breath a pungent reminder of the danger she was in. "You're not seeing a red cent of my money."

"I'm not interested in cents, red or otherwise." Ruthie twirled her pool stick between her fingers. "I want the five hundred euros you and your pal promised to pay me if I won the game."

"I'm not paying you anything," Eejit One said, his nostrils flaring. "Go fuck yourself, cunt."

"Now that's no way to speak to a lady." Ruthie sidled up to him and stuck her hand into his shirt pocket to grab his wallet.

"Hey," he roared, slapping her hand away. Here was the moment Ruthie had been waiting for. She drew back her right arm and delivered a sharp left jab, right cross that sent Eejit One flying. Eejit Two was on his feet in an instant, teeth bared and fists at the ready. He flew at Ruthie and crashed into a table when she sidestepped him at the last second. Eejit One regained his footing and lumbered toward Ruthie, fists at the ready.

"That's enough," said the gravelly voice that still had the power to make Ruthie go weak at the knees.

THREE

Shane Delaney emerged from the shadows, grabbed Eejit One, and hurled the man onto the sofa beside the pool table.

Eejit Two's jaw dropped at the sight of Shane and he practically threw himself onto the seat beside his friend. "We didn't know she was with you, Delaney."

"She wasn't, but she is now." Shane turned his gorgeous blue eyes on Ruthie and riveted her to the spot with the intensity of his gaze. The floor seemed to shift beneath her. Maybe knocking back that fourth vodka shot hadn't been the smartest move. Here was the moment she'd been waiting for since she'd returned to Dublin, and all she could do was gawk at him.

"I didn't think you went in for hustling, Delaney," Eejit One muttered. "Your girl tried to fleece me out of five hundred euros."

"Let's call it a practical joke and move on, lads. I'll stand you a drink, and we'll forget all about it." Eejit One opened his mouth as if to protest, but kept silent when Shane held up a palm. "I was *telling* you how this was going to play out, Murph, not opening the floor for a discussion. I'll order you both pints of the black stuff with whiskey chasers, and you'll go back to playing pool with each other."

Ruthie snorted. "Probably the only ball action they'll get all night."

Eejit One leaped out of his seat, growling. Shane shoved him back down. "Stay there, and I'll get your drinks sent over."

The man muttered under his breath and shot Ruthie a filthy look. "Got no choice, have I?"

"You don't." Shane grabbed Ruthie by the arm and hauled her over to the bar. When they reached two empty barstools, he spun her around to face him. "Ruthie Reynolds. I shoulda fucking known. Only you could turn an otherwise peaceful gathering into a punch-up in under two minutes."

"More like half an hour." Ruthie's heart thumped in her chest, making it hard to think straight. "Long time no see, Shane."

He pinned her in place with his gaze, his expression inscrutable. "If this is the chaos you bring in your wake, I'd have been happy to extend the 'no see' part."

His dry delivery took the edge off his words, but they stung all the same. Ruthie widened her smile and aimed for nonchalance. "Now, don't be mean. We're old friends, after all. Aren't you glad to see me?"

For a painful moment, she thought he'd reject her, but then his face split into a wide grin. He grabbed her up in a bear hug, crushing her against his muscular chest. He smelled spicy and male and oh so desirable. She longed to lean in and never let go, to allow herself to surrender to this man in every possible way.

The embrace ended as abruptly as it had begun. Shane stood back and gave her an appreciative once-over. "It's good to see you, Ruthie, especially looking so well."

Her cheeks grew warm. She was under no illusions about her appearance. Thanks to years of kickboxing and mixed martial arts, she was more ripped than most men and preferred to conceal her bulky arm muscles and strong legs underneath long-sleeved T-shirts and combat pants. Tonight's formfitting sleeveless top and tight jeans were an anomaly. She'd bought them with hustling in mind. "You're a shameless flatterer, Shane Delaney," she said in a breezy tone that didn't match her churning stomach.

His eyes twinkled with humor. "No flattery required. When did you get back? Last I heard, you were gallivanting around Europe."

"Hardly gallivanting," she said dryly. "I did the amateur MMA circuit for a while." *In addition to other less-than-salubrious lines of work...*

"You've bulked up since I saw you last." Shane's smile widened, and he squeezed one of her biceps. "Impressive."

"All part of the job." The feel of his fingers on her skin made her heart beat a little faster, and his words reignited her self-consciousness over her looks. A betraying warmth crept up her cheeks.

If Shane noticed her embarrassment, he pretended not to. "I've often wondered how you were," he said. "You haven't been back in Dublin for years."

"If you were interested, you could have gotten in touch." The words slipped out before she could stop herself. *Shit.* She hadn't intended to steer the conversation in this direction.

His smile faded. "I should never have done what I did, Ruthie. I was Kevin's mate, and you were his little sister."

Shane's candid words shredded the last of her fake-it-till-you-make-it self-confidence. "And out of bounds," she finished for him, struggling to keep her tone light. "Until I wasn't."

Their eyes locked. A tense silence stretched the seconds.

"Sorry about your tooth," she added, shooting Shane a grin.

His gaze softened. "You won the fight fair and square, Miss Ruthie, and losing the tooth was my fault. I've never forgotten to wear a mouthguard since." His posture shifted. "I need to order Murph and Dec their drinks. What are you having?"

"A vodka shot, please." Inviting her to join him for a drink was a good sign. With alcohol loosening his inhibitions, she'd salvage the situation and inveigle an invitation to a Delaney family event.

Shane nodded to the barman and ordered. While he was busy paying and organizing the delivery of Murph and Dec's drinks, Ruthie slid her phone out of her pocket. Her hands wouldn't stop shaking as she typed a text message. She'd played this scenario out in her head many times, but she'd failed to take into account the effect Shane Delaney had on her equilibrium. Finally, she deleted the long, typo-ridden message and sent one that was short and to the point.

He's here. Proceed as planned.

A moment later, Shane's phone beeped. He glanced at the display and frowned. "Looks like I've been stood up."

"Hot date canceled?"

He laughed, drawing attention to the smile lines around his eyes. "Hell no. Do you remember Lenny Keogh?"

Sure, Ruthie remembered Lenny; she'd seen him three short hours ago when she'd paid him one hundred euros to arrange to meet Shane for a drink and cancel on him at the last minute.

"He was supposed to meet me here," Shane continued, "but something's come up. Typical Lenny.

The guy doesn't contact me for months, and then he bloody well stands me up."

The barman shoved two drinks across the counter to them: a vodka shot for Ruthie and a whiskey for Shane.

"Lenny was never the most reliable of souls," Ruthie said, picking up her glass. "*Sláinte.*"

"*Sláinte.*" A muscle in Shane's cheek flexed. "I'm sorry about how we left things, Ruthie."

"Sorry that you walked out on me in the middle of the night and legged it to Australia? All you had to do was tell me you weren't interested in sleeping with me. Switching hemispheres was an extreme reaction." The words tumbled out unfiltered, shattering any illusions she'd had of steering this engineered meeting into one that would provide her with an "in" to spy on the Delaneys. *Fuck.* What was wrong with her? She'd kept her shit together in other undercover situations. Why was she screwing this one up so spectacularly?

But she knew the answer to her questions, and he was standing right next to her.

Shane's cheeks darkened underneath his tan. "I'd already planned to go to Australia. I didn't leave because of you."

"No?" She arched an eyebrow. "You didn't say goodbye."

"I wanted to come over," he said gruffly, "but I didn't feel welcome at your house."

"Your argument with my brother had nothing to do with me. You could have called me before you got on the plane. You could've—" *Crap, crap, crap.* Ruthie took a deep breath. She needed to pull herself together before she screwed up the entire operation. With a single throat-burning swig, she tossed back the vodka and set the glass on the counter. "Thanks for the drink. I'd better make tracks."

"Ruthie—" he began and reached for her hand.

Despite her best efforts at self-control, she trembled at his touch. "It's fine, Shane. Let's forget what happened. It was a long time ago."

"I shouldn't have brought it up," he said. "I wanted to get that part of the conversation out of the way, seeing as we'd have to have it eventually. I see now that it was a mistake."

He hadn't let go of her hand. The intimacy of his fingers entwined with hers made her light-headed. Unbeknownst to himself, Shane had thrown her a lifeline to fix this encounter and turn it to her advantage. She'd be a fool not to avail of the opportunity. Ruthie drew in a slow breath. "No, you were right," she conceded. "It needed to be said. I could have tracked you down before you left instead of waiting for you to come to me."

"I should have called you. At the time, staying away seemed like the smartest move, but I realize now how badly I fucked up. We were friends before I lost my head and kissed you."

They'd been more than friends, at least as far as she'd been concerned. Shane's rejection had shattered her heart, but his disappearance had cut the ground out from under her feet. However, if she wanted to be Shane's plus-one at the next Delaney family gathering, she needed to play it sweet. Ruthie plastered on a smile. "Apology accepted."

Shane released her hand and took a sip from his glass. "What are you doing in Dublin? I thought you lived in Germany now."

"Switzerland. And I'm back to visit my family."

A frown line appeared on his forehead. "Is something wrong? You haven't been back to Ireland in years. Why now?"

"Have you been keeping tabs on me?" she teased.

"Not exactly, but Kilpatrick isn't big. Word gets around."

"Better late than never. My dad isn't getting any younger."

He snorted with laughter. "Your father is fit as a fiddle. Big Mike pounds the bags at Dan's gym. I've seen him in action."

"Guess I take after him." Ruthie flexed her arm in a subconscious movement that immediately drew his attention to her muscles, and then to her chest.

Kiss Shot

Shane's gaze lingered on her breasts for a second before meeting her eyes. "You look nothing like Big Mike."

Ruthie's nipples hardened underneath the thin material of her top. God, how she wanted him. "I haven't seen much of my father over the last few years," she said quickly. "It's good to spend time with him again."

"How long will you be in Dublin?"

She dropped her voice to the husky tone she'd adopted for the pool players. "That depends. I might not leave."

"Surely you're not thinking of staying?" Shane frowned. "There's nothing for you in Kilpatrick."

"You know how to make a girl feel welcome," she drawled.

Shane's cheeks reddened. "I didn't mean to be rude. I just think you're better off out of Kilpatrick and away from Dublin altogether."

"If it's so bad here, why did you come back from Australia?"

He shrugged. "I guess I'm a home bird after all. I missed the craic and the Irish sense of humor. It's hard to be the only foreigner in the bunch, you know?"

"I do know. It's even more difficult when you move around a lot like I did."

Shane jerked a thumb in the direction of the pool table, where Eejit One and Two, armed with their whiskey chasers, were engaged in a drunken game of pool. "Why were you fighting with Murph and Dec? Surely you're not so hard up for money that you need to hustle those fools?"

If only he knew just how hard up I am... "Nah. I thought riling them up might be fun."

Shane shook his head. "You can take the girl out of Dublin, but you're still the same old Ruthie."

Actually, a lot had changed over the years, but she wasn't in a position to tell him exactly what. Perhaps she should feel more than the small prick of remorse that nagged at her conscience for using Shane in this way, but he'd had no qualms about humiliating her five years ago. Whatever she thought of him, she needed the money. If Kevin didn't pay his debts, the Kowalski brothers would kill him.

She shifted her weight from one leg to the other. It was time to up the ante in this exchange. Ruthie placed her hand on his arm, a finger touching his wrist. "I'm glad I bumped into you, Shane. I was starting to think I'd be stuck with those eejits all evening."

"Given that you were in the process of beating them up, I don't think that would have been an issue."

Was it her imagination, or had his voice deepened a notch when she'd touched him? His gaze met hers, and her pulse quickened. No way was she imagining the desire in his eyes. Another woman—one skilled in the art of flirtation—would use this to her advantage. What better way to get info out of a man than pillow talk?

Kiss Shot

Pillow talk... If she slept with Shane, he'd know her secret. She was excellent at faking bravado, but pretending to be sexually experienced? That went far beyond her area of expertise. She swallowed hard as a vision of the enormous debt her brother owed loomed. All she needed to do was dig for info on Shane and his family. Easy, right?

Ruthie skimmed a fingertip over his pulse and heard his sharp intake of breath. "Want to get out of here?" she whispered.

His eyes widened, then darkened with a desire that reflected her own. "Ruthie, you're killing me."

"Got someplace else to be?" She trailed a finger down the front of his shirt. "Or someone expecting you?"

"No," he said hoarsely. "There's no one expecting me tonight."

"In that case..." Her finger paused just above his waist. "Your place or mine?"

FOUR

Outside the pub, Shane hailed a taxi and rattled off the directions to Ruthie's house on autopilot. After all these years, he still remembered the house number. Before he'd fallen out with Kevin, he'd regarded the Reynolds' house as his second home, but it had been a long time since he'd visited 24 Clondale Terrace.

Beside him on the backseat, Ruthie sat stiff and nervous and so fucking beautiful that Shane wanted to rip her clothes off and have her here and now. He reached for her hand, marveling at the softness of her skin. Her hand trembled in his, the self-confidence she'd displayed in the pub no longer in evidence.

What the hell was he doing? Agreeing to go home with Ruthie was insanity. If Kevin caught them together, he'd go ballistic. And as for Big Mike... Lar and Dan would be seriously pissed if Shane lost them one of their most loyal clients.

Kiss Shot

Shane squeezed his eyes shut and bit back a curse. He wanted her so damn much, but he'd never have suggested spending the night with her had it not been for the whiskey he'd ordered in the pub, and the two shots of schnapps he'd had with Max back at his apartment before they'd both gone their separate ways for the night.

Just as he was on the verge of telling Ruthie he'd escort her to her door and then get the taxi to take him home, she moved position and one of her generous breasts brushed against his chest. He sucked in a breath. A sly smile curved her lips. She danced her fingers down his torso and playfully teased the hem of his shirt, and her touch sent a tingling awareness through his body. When he made eye contact, her sexy wink melted the last of his reserves. He leaned down and kissed her, softly at first, then growing more insistent. Yeah, sleeping with Ruthie was a lousy idea, but right now, he didn't care.

By the time she broke the kiss, they were both breathing hard. She placed a finger on his lips. "We don't want to scandalize the taxi driver."

"I'm sure he's seen worse." Shane ran his fingers through her long hair, stretching a strand to its full length. Despite the darkness in the back of the taxi, the lights from outside gave him a good view of her hair color—a rich black that people paid a chunk of change to achieve. In Ruthie's case, her raven tone was natural. "You grew your hair."

"Yeah. I got tired of needing to get it cut all the time. With long hair, I can just tie it back and forget about it." She touched it self-consciously. "I don't usually wear it loose."

"It suits you." All the changes time had wrought on Ruthie's body were favorable. She'd been a pretty teenager, if gawky, but she'd grown into a beautiful woman. Her breasts were bigger than average, but Shane would bet money that they were real. She was a few kilos heavier than when he'd last seen her, and she'd added the extra weight to all the right places. And if her muscular arms were any indication, the rest of her curvy body was fit and toned.

When the taxi pulled into Ruthie's street, she leaned forward and addressed the driver. "First house on the left." As the taxi drew to a halt, she shoved a twenty-euro note at Shane. "You paid for the drinks. I'll take care of the fare."

He cupped her chin and dropped a kiss on her gorgeous upturned nose. "No way. This is on me. If my cousin weren't crashing at my place, we wouldn't have needed a taxi."

Before she could object, Shane slipped the twenty into the back pocket of her jeans. Feeling her tight backside turned his groin to granite. He bit back a groan.

"You're killing me, Ruthie," he whispered into her ear. "I can't get us out of this taxi fast enough."

Her slow-burn smile warmed him from the inside out. "You deal with the fare while I deal with the house alarm." She drew a fingertip across his bearded jaw, turning his mouth into a desert.

With a parting wink, Ruthie slid out of the taxi and strode to her front door. Her gait was purposeful, and the subtle sway of her hips owed more to her feminine shape than to a deliberate attempt to draw attention to her body.

Shane paid the taxi driver with his own money and followed Ruthie into the house, closing the door behind him. They stood staring at one another for ten long seconds. Finally, Shane wrenched his gaze away from her and took in his surroundings. The walls were painted an off-white shade that gave the narrow house the impression of being wider than it was. The polished wood flooring had become popular in Ireland over the last decade, but it had been an unusual choice back when the Reynolds had decided to get rid of their carpets in deference to Kevin's allergies.

"The place looks the very same." The very same as it had the day he'd almost had sex with her, fought with Kevin, and exited their lives forever.

A twinkle of amusement appeared in her eyes. "Dad doesn't go in for interior design. I doubt he notices what the house looks like."

Shane closed the space between them and touched her arm. His breathing grew shallow, and his pants felt uncomfortably tight. "Are you sure about this, Ruthie? I can call a taxi and head home."

For an instant, hesitation flickered across her face, but she soon masked it with a grin. "I wouldn't have suggested you come home with me if I wasn't sure. The question mark in this sentence is *you*, Mr. Delaney. Do you want to spend the night with me?"

A vision of Ruthie naked and riding him danced through his mind, making his balls throb with desire.

When she ran the tip of her tongue over her upper lip, Shane's breath caught. He pulled her to him and lowered his mouth to hers, teasing her with a fluttery kiss. "I'm sure," he whispered against her neck. "I've been sure since I set eyes on you punching Murph."

Ruthie's laugh tickled his neck. "You find women who get into punch-ups a turn-on?"

"Only ones who can throw punches as well as you do." He smoothed a palm down her side. His heart rate accelerated when he skimmed the edge of her breast. Beneath the thin material of her top, her nipples were rock hard. He touched one pebbled orb and rolled it between his thumb and index finger, sending a jolt of raw need shooting through his body. "You're so sexy, Ruthie. The only thing holding me back from taking you here and now in the hallway is the idea of being interrupted by your dad or brother." He glanced around the hallway as if Big Mike or Kevin would charge through the walls at any moment.

"You're the one who suggested coming back to my place, mister. I said we should go to yours."

He gave a rueful smile. "Only because Max is crashing at mine for the weekend. I can't guarantee we'd be alone. Can you?"

"It won't be a problem," she told him, running her hands over his back. "I told you, Dad is away on business and Kevin is at a friend's. The only company we'll have are the china dolls in my room."

Shane threw his head back and laughed. "Do you still have those? And the doll's house?"

"Oh, yes." She tugged on his hand. "Want to come up to my room to check them out?"

"I'd much rather check *you* out."

"You can do that as well."

With a grin, he placed a hand on the small of her back and propelled her up the stairs. On the landing, Shane's gaze lingered on the closed door of Kevin's bedroom. He'd spent many afternoons in there during their teenage years, listening to music and reading comics.

Ruthie toyed with his belt buckle, yanking him back to the present. When she slipped a hand beneath the hem of his shirt, he groaned. "I saw the direction of your gaze," she said in an amused voice. "Stop worrying and just go with the flow. Kevin rarely comes home before morning."

Her sexy half smile made him ache in all the right places. "I can't help it, kid. Overthinking is what I do when it comes to you. You bring out the protective side in me."

She took his hand and placed it on her breast. "I haven't been a kid for a long time, Shane."

He gave her an appreciative squeeze. "I've noticed."

"And I don't need protecting. Besides..." She trailed a hand down his side, pausing to run a finger beneath the waistline of his jeans. "You want this just as much as I do. So what are we waiting for?"

What, indeed? He put his arms around her shoulders and claimed her mouth with his. Ruthie wrapped her arms around his back and pulled him closer, deepening the kiss. The sensation of her lips under his sent him whirling back through time to the days when he'd had a crush on her but couldn't act on it for fear of destroying his friendship with Kevin.

As abruptly as the kiss began, it ended. Shane trailed kisses across her cheek to her ear. "Want to take this into your room?"

"Hell yeah." She took his hand and led the way.

When they entered the pastel paradise, Shane looked around in wonder. "It looks exactly like I remember it. Right down to the posters on the wall."

"I left Ireland soon after you did. I guess Dad never bothered to repurpose my bedroom."

Kiss Shot

He turned to her and smiled. "Of course he didn't. You're his only daughter. He'd want to keep the room ready for you in case you came back."

They stood there for a moment, each taking in the details of her bedroom. The girly pink and pastels; the elaborate doll's house and china doll collection; the antique dressing table. Kevin had once told Shane that Big Mike had redecorated all the kids' rooms soon after his wife had died. He'd wanted to give his children the best. Kevin and Brian had loved their new bunk beds and Star Wars-themed rooms, but it had never occurred to Big Mike that the fussy and feminine décor he'd chosen for his daughter's room didn't suit Ruthie's personality.

"Go on," she said beside him. "Laugh. You know you want to."

He turned to her and grinned. "The only part of this room that's truly *you* is your choice in posters."

"Yeah. Dad meant well, and I didn't have the heart to object. He thought a girly room was just what I needed. He even gave me my mother's dressing table."

"Families, eh? There's so much we keep in for fear of upsetting someone." Shane drew her into his arms and dropped a kiss on her forehead. He inhaled the fresh scent of her perfume. Or was it shower gel? Ruthie didn't strike him as the sort of woman who owned perfume.

"Dad loves me, but he's inept around women and..." She trailed off, her cheeks turning a becoming shade of pink. "Sorry. I'm babbling. I didn't expect to be nervous. I was fine a minute ago."

"But now we're in your room," he added for her, "and right next to your bed. And we're both remembering what almost happened in that bed the last time we were together."

She nodded and her eyes met his.

Shane reached out and cupped her face in his hands. "I want you. Here and now and in every position."

"I want you, too," she whispered, her voice laced with an enticing mixture of hesitation and desire.

Shane eyed the dressing table, which was covered with graphic novels and other assorted odds and ends. "I can think of another way to use that dressing table. How about it, Miss Ruthie?"

Before she could react, he'd picked her up and plunked her on top of the dressing table. Ruthie laughed and wrapped her legs around his waist. "Now this is a position I could get used to," he said and kissed her again.

The sensation of her mouth against his felt so good. He deepened the kiss, his tongue meeting hers in an erotic dance. He ran his fingers through her hair, marveling in its texture. She drew him closer, wanting and needing the intimacy with a ferocity that matched his own desire.

"Ruthie," he groaned when they came up for air. "You're killing me."

Kiss Shot

"Shane, I—" She swallowed whatever she'd been about to say, then slipped off the dressing table and stood before him.

Ruthie was tall for a woman, having inherited her father's height, but her head barely skimmed Shane's nose. He traced her face with his fingertips, soaking in the details: naturally dark lashes framed rich brown eyes; high cheekbones offset a narrow chin. Ruthie wasn't conventionally beautiful, but Shane had always found her face fascinating.

This time, he kissed her with an intensity that turned his already hard body to cement. Within seconds, he'd tugged off her tank top and let her unbutton his shirt. Underneath her top, Ruthie wore a black sports bra. For a man who'd grown up around fancy lingerie and topless women, the sight of Ruthie's practical bra was a major turn-on. He fingered the strap. "You're so fucking sexy, Ruthie."

"You're joking, right? There's nothing sexy about a sports bra."

"I disagree. It's simple, functional, and shapes your breasts nicely. What's not to like?"

She eyed him skeptically, then smiled and reached for his belt. Shane groaned when she unbuckled it and undid the buttons of his jeans one by one. The instant she touched him through his underwear, he shuddered with anticipation.

"You need to get naked, Miss Ruthie."

She laughed and kissed him again, teasing him with her tongue, making him so hot he thought he'd burst. He'd reached for her bra strap when the door to the bedroom burst open. They whipped around to see Kevin standing in the doorframe, wild-eyed and breathing heavily.

"Kev—" Ruthie began, then gasped. Shane caught sight of a glint of silver at the same moment she said, "Oh, God, Shane. He's got a knife."

FIVE

Ruthie's stomach lurched. What a moment for her brother to have one of his "turns." "Put the knife down, Kevin. You don't need it."

"He's in here," Kevin said, his eyes darting wildly around the room. "He followed me home, but I was too smart for him. I hid downstairs when I heard him come into the house."

"You probably heard us in the hallway," Ruthie said gently. "Just me and Shane. No one else is here. Now please put down the knife."

Kevin gave a violent shake of his head and took a step closer, clutching the knife. Shane tried to move in front of Ruthie, but she sidestepped him.

"I'm telling you," Kevin said, "*he* followed me home."

"Who's he?" Shane whispered to Ruthie.

"The man in the black cloak," Kevin said, reacting to Shane's question but not appearing to register his presence. "He follows me everywhere. I can't get away from him."

Ruthie squeezed her eyes shut, the well of helplessness and despair that she'd felt for days threatening to overwhelm her. "No one is following you, Kev. You need to go back to Dr. Jameson."

"All he wants to do is lock me up." Her brother's nostrils flared, and he gripped the handle of the knife with such force that his knuckles turned white. Sweat beaded on his pale forehead—from fear or as a result of whatever substance he'd imbibed, she couldn't tell. While drugs exacerbated Kevin's symptoms, they weren't the only cause.

"Let me put you to bed," she said, close to tears at the sight of what her once-vibrant brother had become. "We can talk in the morning."

Kevin appeared to deflate before her eyes. Blinking, he stared at the knife in his hand as if seeing it for the first time. Then he let it fall to the floor, crumpling in on himself and hugging his bony chest with his thin arms. Shane stepped forward and kicked the knife out of Kevin's reach.

Ruthie took a step toward her brother. "Come on, Kev. You're tired. Let me put you to bed."

Shane bent down to retrieve the knife. When he rose, he slipped it behind his back and mouthed, *I'll be downstairs.*

Kiss Shot

Ruthie nodded her understanding. She grabbed up her discarded top and placed a hand on Kevin's arm before coaxing him out of her room and down the hallway to his bedroom.

Her brother's frail body shook and his teeth chattered. "I'm sorry, Ruthie. I don't know what came over me."

"Don't think about it now. Just get some sleep."

Kevin allowed her to help him undress, and he raised no objection when she gave him a glass of milk to drink, even though he must have known she'd crushed a sedative into it. Once she was sure he was settled, Ruthie closed her brother's bedroom door behind her and slipped down the stairs to the kitchen.

Shane sat at the kitchen table, two steaming mugs before him. When Ruthie took the seat opposite, he shoved a mug over to her. She inhaled deeply and sighed. "Hot chocolate. Thank you."

"I thought you could do with something sweet." He scanned the kitchen. "It's just as I remember, right down to the joke magnets on the fridge."

In spite of her exhaustion, a smile crept over her face. "Like I said, Dad doesn't notice his surroundings." Ruthie took a sip of her hot chocolate and met Shane's gaze over the rim of her mug. Sitting here with him felt... right. Comforting. It shouldn't have. She should feel embarrassed, given the moves she'd put on him in yet another failed attempt to lose her virginity.

And how would she have dealt with the issue if they had gotten as far as having sex? Hoped he didn't notice? Most men were clueless, but not Shane. If anyone were to notice she'd never had sex before, he would.

Among the steady stream of friends her brothers dragged home, Shane stood out from the pack. From the first moment she'd set eyes on him at the age of eight, Ruthie had known that Shane Delaney was different. He was five years her senior and in the same class as her brother Kevin. Unlike the other boys, Shane listened to her and always made a point of chatting with her when he visited her home. And here he was, in her kitchen, helping her when she felt her most vulnerable.

Shane leaned across the table to take her hand in his. His hand felt strong and warm around hers. He'd ask her about her brother. How could he not? Ruthie trembled slightly, as she did whenever she was nervous or uncomfortable, hence her tendency to shove her hands into her pockets at every opportunity.

"What happened to Kevin?" Shane asked gently. "I'd heard he was using, but this isn't just a drug problem, is it?"

Ruthie dropped her gaze to the cocoa foam coating the inside of her mug. Her shoulders ached from a weariness that was both physical and emotional. "No," she said after a long pause. "This isn't just drugs."

Kiss Shot

"What's going on? Is Kevin's—" he broke off, as if searching for the right word, "—situation the reason you came back to Dublin?"

A bitter laugh rose unbidden and rumbled in her throat. If Shane only knew the extent of Kevin's "situation". "Yes, I came back to help Kevin." She gave him a wan smile. "As you can see, my being here hasn't done much good."

The concern in his eyes slew her. Ruthie closed her eyes as guilt burned a path from her stomach to her throat. Another guy would have left skid marks in his haste to flee from the house after Kevin pulled the knife, but not Shane Delaney. He'd even made her hot chocolate, for heaven's sake. And here she was, plotting her way into his life to dig for dirt on him and his family.

"What's wrong with Kevin?" Shane asked.

Ruthie opened her eyes and bit her lip. "My brother has what are politely described as mental health issues." Issues...such an innocent-sounding term for a condition that had destroyed his life.

"They must be bad to have an effect this extreme."

She exhaled in a whoosh. "My brother is on the bipolar spectrum."

"Jaysus." His jaw dropped. "How long have you known?"

"For years. Kevin got the diagnosis when he was eighteen, but the signs were there before."

Shane leaned back in his chair, frowning. "I knew Kev was moody and a bit weird, but we were geeks. Weird was a way of life."

"He played a good game for a long time," Ruthie said with a sigh. "He managed to keep it together at school and with friends, but the cracks showed at home. And after a while, even his best efforts at self-control couldn't stop him from unraveling. He started taking drugs to self-medicate, but they make him worse. When he's high, he gets paranoid. The guy he thought was following him home was probably just one of our neighbors."

"Is he in treatment? Because if he isn't, he needs to be."

"He's supposed to see a doctor regularly. As you can probably guess, he's off his meds at the moment."

"Can't your father force him into treatment?" Shane demanded. "I can't imagine anyone saying no to Big Mike."

She gave him a wobbly smile. "Kevin is over eighteen, and my father is unwilling to take the steps necessary to put him in a psychiatric hospital against his will."

"Whatever Big Mike's reservations, this can't continue. Kevin has to have treatment, for his sake and yours."

She sighed. "I know. I'm trying to persuade Dad, but it's not easy. He's a proud man. It's hard for him to admit his son is mentally ill."

Kiss Shot

"Kevin needs help. As his next of kin, it's your father's responsibility to make sure he gets it. Apart from anything, Big Mike has been living with Kevin on his own for years. That has to have taken a toll on him."

"That's part of the reason I'm back." Ruthie took another sip of hot chocolate and gathered her thoughts. "Dad wants to help Kevin, but he's not convinced that taking away his freedom is the answer. With one son already in prison and his own past, Dad doesn't want Kevin locked up."

"A psychiatric hospital is different to a prison. From what you're telling me, Kevin on medication is a different guy. If the docs get his illness under control, he might be allowed home."

"I know all that, but Dad's not reasonable on this topic. He feels he let us down after Mum left. Despite his reputation, Dad's a mush when it comes to his kids. He'd do anything to protect us, and he sees having Kevin committed as the ultimate betrayal."

Shane leaped up and went to her side of the table. Leaning down, he pulled her to his chest and wrapped his arms around her. Ruthie leaned against him and snuggled close, relishing his warmth.

"Thanks, Shane."

"Thanks for what? I didn't do anything. I only wished I could do something to help."

"You were here when I needed you. That counts for a lot in my world."

He stroked her hair, and her scalp tingled at his touch. "Anyone would have done it, Ruthie."

"'Anyone' wasn't here. *You* were."

"Would you like me to stay until morning?" he asked. "In case Kevin wakes up?"

She shook her head. "Thanks for the offer, but there's no need. With the dosage I gave him, he'll sleep until late morning, and Dad's due home before lunch."

Shane squeezed her arm. "I'm sorry our evening took a crappy turn. Seeing you again has been great. I hope it won't be the last time I see you while you're in Kilpatrick."

Butterflies tickled her stomach at the sight of the wicked glint in his eye. Ruthie took the hint. "That depends on you," she said. "You know where I live, and now—" she whipped a notepad and pen off the kitchen counter and scribbled on it, "—you have my number."

Shane tucked the piece of paper into his breast pocket with a bone-melting grin. "I'll call you," he said when she accompanied him to the door. "Maybe we can go out to dinner and have a proper catch-up."

Guilt wrapped itself around her heart and squeezed, but she forced the words out. This was too good an opportunity to miss. "I'd like that," she said carefully, "and I'd like to catch up with your family. It's been too long."

"I'm sure we can arrange a get-together." He grinned and pointed to the place where Ruthie had knocked out his tooth. "Siobhan always asks after you. She loves the idea of a woman taking me down."

She chuckled. "Your aunt is bloodthirsty."

"So are you, Miss Ruthie. That's why we get along." He brushed back her hair. "Try to get some sleep."

"You, too."

And then Shane brushed her lips one last time and disappeared down the garden path.

SIX

At six o'clock the next morning, Shane rolled up to Dan's gym for a kickboxing session. He was bone tired and demoralized after a fruitless Internet search session that had uncovered precisely nothing. Courtesy of his father's demands, he was obliged to divide his research time digging into Lar's past, as well as looking for information on the massacre at his father's Boston club, The Lucky Leprechaun, that had claimed the lives of his oldest brother, Con, and Lar's younger brother, Tony five years ago. Given that he had to produce results on the Boston case within a time frame that wouldn't arouse Lar's suspicion that Shane was working a side job, caffeine-fueled late nights were the logical solution.

He climbed off his bike and rubbed his eyes. They felt like they'd been sandpapered. Between work stress and family tensions, seeing Ruthie and Kevin Reynolds had done a number on his equilibrium. He shouldn't have gone back to her place, however tempting the prospect of sex with her was. He didn't do commitment. Never had. Ruthie deserved better than a guy who swam in the murky waters of legal and moral gray zones. She needed a man who'd be there for her one hundred percent, particularly with all the crap she had going on in her life at the moment. He'd known Kevin had a drug problem, but he'd had no idea his old friend had severe mental health issues.

Shane reached the back door of the gym and opened it with his key card. What he needed was an invigorating workout to punch out the stress. A session at the bags never failed to switch off his mind, albeit temporarily.

Unfortunately, he wasn't the only Delaney with the idea of an early morning session. Dan and Lar were already at the bags. Judging by the sweat rolling off them, they'd been at it for a while.

Shane changed into his workout gear and pulled on his gloves. When he joined his cousins at the bags, they were having a water break.

"How's it going?" Dan asked in his usual gruff manner, and mopped sweat from his brow. "Had the same idea as us, I see."

Lar nodded in greeting. "Hey, Shane. Max not with you?" His cheery smile and genuine pleasure at seeing Shane cut him to the core, bringing forth the surge of rage he experienced every time he saw his cousin these days.

Shane drew in a deep breath. Losing his temper with Lar would achieve nothing. It wouldn't bring him any closer to understanding why his cousin had failed to confide in him, and it would jeopardize the job he'd agreed to do for his father. "I'd say Max is snoring on my sofa. He only came home when I was leaving."

Dan rolled his eyes and Lar laughed. Max's ability to party was well known.

"He'd better have his arse in gear by this afternoon," Dan said firmly. "I'm driving him to the airport after lunch."

"Max is leaving so soon?" Lar asked, frowning. "Isn't he sticking around for your mother's birthday party?"

"Yeah, but he has a job to do in Berlin. He'll fly back to Dublin on Friday." Dan turned to Shane. "Want a sparring partner? Lar and I were about to go into the ring, but I can have a go with you first."

"Nah," Shane said. "I'll stick to the bags this morning."

A rare grin broke through Dan's grumpy countenance. "Need to work off some frustration? Mum said you'd been to see your father yesterday."

Of course, Aunt Siobhan knew he'd been at Valentine's. Olga had probably mentioned seeing him. And naturally, Siobhan had shared this info with her oldest son. "You know my dad," Shane said in a breezy tone. "Never a dull moment with Frank."

Dan didn't press the matter. An instant later, he stepped into the ring with Lar and started sparring.

Shane chose a bag facing away from his cousins and got to work. While he'd never rival Dan as a boxer or kickboxer—few people could—Shane could hold his own in a fight.

Jab. Hook. Right cross.

In the background, Lar laughed at something Dan had said. Shane cranked up the volume on his earbuds to drown them out. In truth, Shane didn't begrudge his cousin the opportunity for his freedom. The part that hurt was the personal betrayal. Why hadn't Lar confided in him? Why hadn't he told him the truth? Shane would've understood.

If he could turn back the clock, he'd have told his father to stick his surveillance equipment up his arse. He'd have remained in blissful ignorance, never knowing that Lar had lied to him repeatedly. And yet a niggling doubt remained. If he'd been in Lar's situation, would he have acted any differently? Locked up for a crime he didn't commit, facing several more years in jail...under those circumstances, a deal with the spooks would be tempting.

Unfortunately, erasing the last couple of weeks was impossible. Shane knew more than he wanted to about Lar and his girlfriend, Gen. He knew enough that would get them both killed if he were to tell his father. Which was precisely why he'd remained silent so far. Yes, Lar was a lying bastard, but Frank had screwed him over. It should have been Greg doing time, not Lar. But because

Lar was still a minor, he was the chosen fall guy for the murder of a security guard during a botched robbery.

Shane kept at the bags for almost an hour. By the end of his session, he was dripping with sweat. Grabbing his towel, he padded toward the showers. Lar had dressed and was ready to go by the time Shane emerged from the shower.

"Is something up, Shane?" Lar asked, his forehead creased in concern. "You seem on edge lately."

"I'm grand," Shane said, more abruptly than he'd intended. "I guess the research is taking its toll. I'm not having much luck finding info we didn't already know about The Lucky Leprechaun."

"Are you getting enough sleep?" Lar asked. "Is your insomnia acting up again?"

Having Lar express concern was jarring and contradicted the mental image Shane had formed of his cousin as a traitor with no genuine feelings for Shane or the rest of the family. "Seriously, I'm fine. Don't worry about me."

"What did Frank want to talk to you about?"

The question wasn't unnatural. Lar knew Shane only went to see Frank when he was summoned. "He's impatient with my lack of progress. Implied I wasn't competent to do the sort of research required to get to the bottom of the case."

"That's a load of bollocks. You're a skilled hacker. If anything relevant is online, you're the man to find it."

Kiss Shot

A muscle flexed in Shane's cheek. Oh, yeah...he knew all about digging up dirt online. He just hadn't expected to uncover what he had on Lar. "You know Dad," he said in a neutral tone. "He doesn't think I'm capable of anything."

Lar snorted. "Frank is a fool. He's always underestimated you and overestimated your dumb-arse brothers."

Shane stepped into his underwear. Now was as good a time as any to question Lar about Frank's accusation. "According to my father, you offed Connolly. Any idea why he'd say that?"

Lar's expression turned curiously blank. "No."

He was lying, Shane was sure of it. But why would Lar clip Connolly? He wasn't stupid enough to agree to a hit job in his own neighborhood, so it had to be personal. "I don't believe you," he said, struggling to keep the hurt out of his voice but failing. "Whoever took out Connolly was a pro."

"I'm not the only pro in Kilpatrick." Lar's jaw jutted in defiance. "The place is fucking teeming with ex-paramilitaries. Jimmy pissed a few people off in his time. I guess someone decided to get even."

"I guess someone did." Shane held Lar's glare until his cousin averted his gaze.

"Look, just drop it, okay? I can't talk about it, and you're better off not knowing."

"So there is something to know after all?" Shane pressed. The instinct he'd had in his father's office that Frank was telling the truth crystallized. "What happened?"

Lar closed his eyes and sighed. "I promise it's not what you think, but I'm not in a position to talk about it."

"Well, now. Isn't that a surprise?" Shane shoved his workout clothes and old underwear into his sports bag and slung it over his shoulder. He made to move past Lar to the exit, but his cousin blocked his path.

"What the fuck is wrong with you, Shane?" Lar demanded. "You've been moody for weeks. Is it because I'm serious about Gen? I'm not going to dump my friends because I have a girlfriend. Surely you know me better than that?"

"I sometimes wonder if I know you at all," Shane said.

"That's cryptic, even for you. Come on, man. Spit it out. What is going on?"

He'd said too much already. Lack of sleep. Stress. Confusion over Ruthie Reynolds blasting back into his life. Whatever the cause, he had to pull himself together. "I'm frustrated with my slow progress. I've never had as many problems accessing information as I've experienced with the Boston case."

As part of Shane and Lar's exit strategy from the family "business," they'd struck a bargain with Frank. They each had to fulfill a job in order to leave the family "firm" without inciting a war. Shane's job was, officially at least, to use his internet skills to trace the people behind the attack on his father's club in Boston five years previously.

"You'll get there. I've never known you to fail yet." Lar's grin turned sly. "I hear Ruthie Reynolds is back in town and all grown up. Have you seen her yet?"

Shane's shutters slammed down. "Why do you ask? I haven't been friends with Kevin in years."

"I know, but Ruthie isn't Kevin. Something happened between you and her, didn't it?"

"Actually, no." That had been the damned problem. The last time he'd seen her before he'd left for Australia, they'd shared the most memorable kiss of Shane's life. Memorable until he'd belatedly developed a conscience and had been on the verge of leaving when Kevin had walked in on them and freaked out.

"Just saying. Ruthie is a much better bet than banging Adam Kowalski's girlfriend on the sly."

"What do you care? I don't interrogate you about all your past hook-ups."

"I'm not interrogating you, man. Just expressing interest. You were always sweet on Ruthie."

"Concentrate on your own love life," Shane snapped, "and let me concentrate on mine."

"All right. Keep your hair on. I was only wondering. I hear she's turned into a looker. Who'd have thought it? I remember her being plain and gangly with braces on her teeth."

"Ruthie was always pretty," Shane said. "It just took the world a while to wake up to that fact."

Lar eyed Shane closely. "You've been on edge lately, and I don't think Ruthie Reynolds is the cause. Is there anything we need to say to one another?"

"I don't know," Shane couldn't resist saying. "Is there?"

Lar's expression darkened. Before he could respond, Dan came over. "Would you guys stop yapping? The punters are starting to arrive, and you're scaring them off."

"I was about to make tracks." Shane slapped Dan on the back. "If you're looking for an early morning sparring partner, I'll be here at six tomorrow."

Dan cocked an eyebrow. "Since when did you start training before dawn?"

"Since sleep decided it didn't like me. Better than tossing and turning or looking at porn."

His cousin threw his head back and laughed. "So sparring with me is preferable to having a wank. You sure know how to deliver a compliment."

"It's a talent of mine."

"Will I see you at the office later?" Lar asked, one eyebrow arched. "You owe me your report on the Donnelly assignment."

Shane gritted his teeth. He could just as easily email the report to his cousin, but he had no wish to antagonize Lar. Not yet, at any rate. "I'll come by at three.

I need to update you on The Lucky Leprechaun investigation as well."

With a parting salute, Shane sauntered out of the gym and headed for the side lane where he'd parked his bike. Before he entered the lane, laughter floated out to greet him, followed by the pitiful sound of an animal in pain. He quickened his step. Four boys in their early teens had cornered a mangy-looking puppy and were throwing rocks at it. Judging by the smell, they'd doused the poor creature with gasoline. Sure enough, one of the boys slipped a cigarette lighter from his pocket and held it up with a smirk.

Shane's heart lurched in his chest. Without a second's hesitation, he barreled into the boy and held his wrist tight. "No, you little fucker. Drop it now."

The boy yelped in pain and let go of the lighter. His pals took one look at Shane and read murder in his eyes. Without waiting for their fallen friend, they turned and fled.

Shane hauled the kid to his feet. "Derek O'Malley, isn't it? I know your dad and I'll be having a word with him."

O'Malley spat on the ground. "Go ahead. Dad doesn't care what I do."

"He'll care by the time I've finished with you. Now get out of my sight before I do something you'd regret."

The kid took to his heels, leaving Shane and the bedraggled puppy alone in the deserted lane.

Shane bent down and held out a hand. The animal whimpered and cringed away from yet another human who might hurt him. "It's okay, little guy. I mean you no harm." He scooped the creature into his arms, not caring if the gasoline stained his clothes. The puppy struggled to get free, but Shane held tight. He needed to get the animal clean and check his wounds, and the closest place was Schneider's.

When Shane reentered the gym, it was starting to fill up with the early morning clientele. The men's eyes widened when they clocked Shane and his smelly new friend.

Dan and Lar ambled over and regarded the puppy with matching expressions of horror. "What the hell happened to him?" Dan demanded.

"He was tortured by that little shit Derek O'Malley and his cohorts. They were planning to set him on fire. Fucking psychos."

"The O'Malleys are all nuts," Dan said with a grimace. "They make Frank look sane."

Lar moved closer to the puppy and recoiled at the smell. "Jaysus. That's got to be the ugliest dog in creation. What is it, anyway? Did a sausage dog mate with a squirrel?"

"Fuck off," Shane said. "He's prettier than you."

"You sure it's a him?" Dan asked, eyeing the dog dubiously.

Shane turned the animal over. "Yeah, it's a him all right. Can I use the kitchen to give him a bath? I need to wash the petrol off him."

"You sure you want to do that?" Lar asked, deadpan. "Leaving it on for a while might help him get rid of a few fleas."

"Fleas?" Dan's eyebrows shot up to his hairline. "I can't have a dog with fleas in here. Health and safety will close me down."

"I'll be five minutes, tops," Shane said. "I want to give him a rinse and check if he needs to see a vet."

"An anti-contamination facility might be more appropriate," Lar said. "That thing looks like the lone survivor of a radioactive spill."

"The pair of you have no heart," Shane said with dignity. "Don't listen to them, Patches."

Dan's jaw dropped. "He has a name? Jaysus, Shane. You're not thinking of keeping him, are you?"

"I'm not chucking him back outside to be finished off of by Hannibal Lecter's protégés."

"Seriously," Lar said, "Patches? As in 'flea-infested patches?' Or are you referring to his mottled fur?"

"Go fuck yourself," Shane said but without rancor. Maybe he did need to rethink the dog's name. "I'll clean him up and find a vet. If he has an identity chip, we can track down his owners."

Dan snorted. "No one in their right mind will lay claim to that dog."

Shane looked down at the pathetic bundle in his arms and felt oddly protective of the broken little creature. "Someone, somewhere, loves you," he said to the puppy. "And we're going to find them. In the meantime, let's go and get you cleaned up."

SEVEN

Ruthie checked the address on her phone. Yeah, this was the place her dad had mentioned. A simple sign proclaiming Schneider's Boxing Gym hung over the entrance of the modern building. Judging by the plaques that framed the door, the upper levels were comprised of offices and residential apartments, while the two lower floors belonged to the gym. She checked her reflection in one of the shiny plaques. The lip gloss she'd applied at the last second before leaving her father's house had disappeared, but the rest of her looked presentable. Back in her safety zone of combats, boots, and T-shirt, she felt less exposed than she had in last night's more revealing outfit, and better equipped to tackle the task ahead. Joining Dan's gym would give her an excellent opportunity to dig for information on the Delaney family, and allow her a chance to run into Shane again.

A shiver of desire coursed through her body. Despite the awkwardness of the other night, she longed to see him again, and not just to pump him for info. But lustful thoughts of Shane Delaney were best left for a later time. Right now, Ruthie had a job to do...and dirt to unearth. She took a deep breath, squared her shoulders, and stepped inside the gym.

Schneider's was a temple of testosterone. Half-naked men lounged on benches, watching other half-naked men train at the bags or in the rings and commenting on their form. Two guys were in a ring, sparring. Ruthie squinted. The one in the red shorts was Dan Schneider-Delaney, Shane's cousin and the proprietor of this establishment. Dan's opponent was Jack Cotton, her father's neighbor. They were both good, but Dan was clearly the pro to Jack's competent amateur.

The men nearest to Ruthie registered her presence and stared her up and down with matching expressions of incredulity. She itched to give them a withering put-down, but if she intended to become a regular at Schneider's, antagonizing the clientele wasn't the way to begin. Ignoring their stares, she strode up to the reception desk. A young man clad in boxing gear sat before a computer, frowning at the screen. He glanced up when Ruthie approached and his jaw slid south.

"Hey. I'm Ruthie Reynolds. I'm looking for a place to train, and my dad recommended Schneider's."

The receptionist blinked several times. "You're Big Mike's daughter?"

Kiss Shot

Ruthie knew what he was thinking—how did a bruiser like Big Mike produce a skinny thing like her? "Yeah, he's my father. Do you have a registration form I need to fill out?"

The receptionist gestured to the ring where Dan was still throwing and ducking punches. "If you want to join, you'll need to talk to the boss, but he's occupied at the moment. Want to take a seat at the bar while you wait?"

"Sure." She flashed him a smile, and his expression softened.

"Here." He shoved a brochure and a plastic chip across the counter. "Use this token for a free drink."

"Thanks." Ruthie pocketed the chip and headed for the bar. When the men already perched on barstools caught sight of her, a hushed silence descended. Ruthie rolled her eyes. She slung her sports bag onto the floor and glared at them. "What's the matter? Never seen breasts before?" So much for her intention to keep her mouth shut.

The guy beside her turned tomato red. "We don't usually see women in here."

"Well, you're seeing one now." Ruthie claimed a free barstool and ordered a mocha-flavored protein shake. While she was sipping her drink, she scanned the gym. It was a large, open-plan arrangement that had been cleverly divided into four half levels. The reception area and bar overlooked the boxing rings. A short flight of steps led up to the training area with bags. According to the brochure, the weights room, exercise machines, and showers were located on the lower levels.

The door behind the bar opened. Shane Delaney emerged, clutching the ugliest puppy she'd ever clapped eyes on. It had the long body and stumpy legs of a dachshund, combined with huge, floppy ears and a bushy tail. Shane's face lit up when he saw her, displaying none of the awkwardness she felt after last night's drama. "Hey, Ruthie. I didn't expect to see you here."

But she'd known she'd see him...or at least hoped she would. She struggled to ignore the butterflies in her stomach and concentrated on the cowering puppy in Shane's arms. "What's with the dog? Is he yours?"

"A few local brats were abusing him outside in the lane. I chased them off and cleaned him up. I'm about to take him to the vet." He cradled the little dog to his chest. "What are you doing here? Is your dad training?"

"No. *I'm* here to train."

Shane shook his head. "Not today. Women's hours are on Tuesday and Thursday evenings."

"Only two evenings a week? That's bullshit." Ruthie glowered at him. "Dude, I don't know if you've noticed, but your dick plays no part in a boxing match."

"It's not about being sexist. Dan only has one shower area, and it's open plan. He doesn't want any trouble, so he makes sure the gym is women's only two evenings a week."

She shook her head. "Twice a week isn't enough. Not for me."

"Can't you find another place to train? A regular gym with kickboxing classes, or whatever they call it in fitness studios?"

She gave him a withering smile. "If you're referring to tae-bo or boxercise, I'm a little beyond them. I have to practice six days a week to maintain my form, and I need access to a gym where people have a clue about professional boxing."

Indecision flickered across his face. She was wearing him down. "All right," he said with a sigh. "Gen—Lar's girlfriend—sometimes joins him and Dan for a training session early in the morning, before the gym officially opens. Let me talk to Dan and see what we can arrange. But right now, I have to take care of this little guy." He stroked the puppy's fur, and the animal trembled with fear. "Besides, Dan is best approached alone. He's grumpy at the best of times, and there's some strain between his mother and brother at the moment."

Ruthie beamed at him. "Thanks, Shane. I'd rather train here than trek across the city to find another boxing gym."

"I can understand that, but you have to see Dan's point of view." Shane dropped his voice a notch. "Look around you. Kilpatrick isn't the best neighborhood, and this gym attracts a rough clientele."

Ruthie snorted. "Do you honestly believe women are only in danger from guys with rough backgrounds?"

"Of course not." His expression softened. "I just wanted you to understand that it can get rough in here at times. I don't want you to get hurt."

Her stomach churned. His concern for her welfare brought all her guilt about using him to the fore. She sucked in a breath and forced a smile. "Thanks for your concern, but I'm asking to train at a boxing gym. Of course I'm going to get hurt."

"You know what I mean." Shane's expression darkened. "Some of the guys won't like to hear 'no' as an answer."

"They'll have to get used to it," she said. "Unless, of course, I say 'yes.'"

This drew his full attention. "Who would you want to say 'yes' to?" he asked, his eyes darkening.

"I don't know, Shane," she teased. "Can you recommend someone to me?"

Shane gave a rueful grin. "I'm no matchmaker. Hell, I can't even find the right woman for myself."

She stepped closer to him and had to strain her neck to look up at him. "I didn't think you wanted to find the right woman. You strike me as the sort of man who likes his space."

His eyes twinkled. "I do. But certain activities are best enjoyed with a partner."

"Sounds intriguing. Care to elaborate?"

Whatever Shane might have said was interrupted by a whine from the dog. Despite the puppy's matted fur and unfortunate appearance, there was something about his pitiful expression that tugged at Ruthie's heartstrings. She held out a hand and let the dog sniff her. After deciding she wasn't about to hurt him, he treated her to a quick lick before cowering back.

"Poor little guy," she said, gently touching the dog's ripped ear. "He's been through the wars. Do you have a vet in mind? If not, I can recommend Dr. McGrath on Griffith Avenue. He looks after Dad's greyhounds."

"Thanks." A long pause. "I don't know much about dogs."

Their eyes met and Ruthie's heart skipped a beat. How did he manage to look sexier every time she saw him? She darted a glance around the gym. Dan was still in the ring. No possibility to schmooze him for a while. Maybe she could use the chance encounter with Shane to her advantage. "I'm no expert on dogs," she began, "but I know a little, even if Dad's greyhounds were always kept in kennels outdoors. Kevin's allergies, you know."

"Of course," he murmured, and then gave her a sly grin. "No chance of foisting the puppy onto you, then?"

"Absolutely none. You're going to have to find a home for him. Maybe the vet can suggest a good animal shelter."

"Speaking of the vet..." His sheepish expression made her smile. "Are you here by car? I took my bike this morning. I wasn't expecting I'd need to transport an animal."

"And you'd like me to give you and your new friend a lift to the vet," Ruthie finished for him, seizing the opportunity. "All right, but on one condition."

"That sounds ominous."

"But not unexpected. You persuade Dan to let me train here five days a week. I don't mind coming in early if that's what it takes. I'll even agree to shower at home."

Shane appeared to consider her proposition for a moment. "Fair enough," he said finally. "I'll talk to Dan this evening and let you know what he says."

"Thanks, Shane." Ruthie beamed at him and stroked the puppy, earning her another lick. "Now let's get this guy to the vet."

* * *

When Shane and Ruthie walked into the vet's waiting room, the place was packed. A squawking budgie and a howling dalmatian battled for attention. A harassed-looking mother comforted a screaming toddler, who'd received bad news about his gerbil, while his younger sibling took the opportunity to make a bid for freedom.

In the midst of this cacophony, the puppy quivered against Shane's chest. He stroked the animal on autopilot. "You sure you want to hang around?" he asked Ruthie. "The receptionist said it could take a while."

Kiss Shot

Her warm smile sent prickles of awareness down his spine. "No problem. My only plan for this morning was getting in a session at your cousin's gym. Seeing as that's not happening, I might as well wait and give you and your new pal a lift home."

"I appreciate the offer, but he won't be coming home with me. I'm hoping the vet can recommend a good animal shelter that can find him a family. Maybe one with kids and a garden for him to run around." He scratched under the puppy's chin and was rewarded with a lick. "You'd like that, wouldn't you?"

Ruthie gave the dog a pitying look. "You seriously think anyone will..." At the sight of his raised eyebrow, she trailed off. "Never mind. Look, the lady with the kids is leaving. Let's grab their seats."

They claimed the newly vacated chairs and found themselves wedged between the squawking budgie and a carrier basket filled with mewling kittens. The puppy burrowed deeper into Shane's chest and whimpered. Shane stroked his back and whispered soothing words. He hadn't owned a dog since Greg had run over Shane's new puppy, Bosco, on Shane's tenth birthday. Frank, annoyed by all the weeping and gnashing caused by Greg's carelessness, had declared that no more pets would enter the Delaney household. And Frank was a man of his word.

Ruthie cocked her head to the side and a grin spread across her pretty face. "No way are you giving him up."

"No way am I keeping him," Shane replied. "My apartment building has a strict no-pets policy."

"You two look pretty comfortable together. Seems a shame to break you up."

"Ruthie," he said in a drawl, "this dog is not coming home with me. I'm not a pet person. Besides, I live in a fifth-floor apartment that's most definitely not pet-friendly, even if the building didn't have a no-pets policy."

She grinned at him. "Whatever you say, Delaney."

Shane settled back in his chair. Despite the awful din going on around them, the puppy's eyes fluttered shut and he was soon snoozing against Shane's chest.

Ruthie drummed a restless beat on the arm of her chair. In the few minutes since they'd taken their seats, she'd crossed and uncrossed her legs several times. Even as a kid, Ruthie had been a fidgeter—always impatient to be on the move. Shane smiled to himself. Age and maturity might have improved her looks, but they hadn't instilled a sense of Zen in Ms. Ruthie Reynolds.

After a few minutes, she leaped to her feet. "I'm parched. Want a drink?"

"A mineral water would be good. Flat, please."

"Coming right up." She sailed across the room, neatly dodging an escaped kitten and sidestepping its owner. As she moved, the gentle sway of her hips drew Shane's attention to her pert backside. Who'd have thought combat pants could be sexy?

Kiss Shot

Shane's mouth grew dry and he blinked away an X-rated vision of a naked Ruthie—under him, on top of him, on her knees before him. He blew out a breath. Getting horny in the middle of a crowded waiting room wasn't his usual modus operandi, but then, Ruthie wasn't his usual kind of woman. Football...yeah, he'd think of football instead.

Ruthie punched numbers into the vending machine and bent down to retrieve the water bottles from the tray at the bottom, providing him with a tantalizing glimpse of bare skin between the waist of her pants and her T-shirt. A stab of lust hit that was so visceral he could sense it in every cell. Shane bit back a groan. All his efforts to distract himself from having imaginary sex with her had been in vain. How in the hell had little Ruthie Reynolds grown into such a sexy piece?

She strode back to their seats and handed Shane his bottle. When he reached to take it from her, their fingers touched. A frisson of awareness brought his gaze to hers. Hot damn, but she was gorgeous. In the depths of her brown eyes, he read a desire that matched his own. He swallowed hard. Man, he had to pull himself together.

"Mr. Delaney? The vet will see you now."

The nurse's words broke through Shane's X-rated reverie. He wrenched his attention away from Ruthie and focused on the stocky nurse wielding a clipboard. "So soon? Are you sure it's our turn?" He cast a glance around the packed waiting room. Several pairs of resentful eyes stared back at him.

"Come along now," the nurse said in a brisk tone. "Dr. McGrath is waiting for you."

Shane glanced at Ruthie. She shrugged. "What's that they say about not looking a gift horse in the mouth?"

"Want to come with me?" he asked on impulse, the words tripping off his tongue before he had a chance to register their significance.

Ruthie's beam lit up her face. "Sure. I've known Dr. McGrath for years."

They trailed after the nurse, who led them down a dimly lit corridor and into a bright examination room. The vet, a dapper man in his late forties, leaped to his feet and treated them to firm handshakes. "I'm sorry to have kept you waiting, Ruthie. Had I known you were here, I'd have seen you at once." The man punctuated his sentence with a one-shouldered shrug and turned to Shane. "I've treated Big Mike's greyhounds for years. We're old pals."

Insofar as anyone could be pals with their loan shark. Shane's lips twisted into a cynical smile. So it wasn't terror of the Delaney family that had prompted Dr. McGrath's enthusiasm to bump them up the queue; he was scared shitless of Ruthie's dad.

Whatever vices the vet had that had led him to borrow money from Big Mike Reynolds, he proved to be an efficient and competent vet. He soon had the puppy

Kiss Shot

examined, vaccinated, and dispatched with a nurse for a thorough bath and detangling. "No identity chip," the vet said after the nurse had escorted the squirming animal out of the room. "Not that I expected to find one. Are you planning to keep him?"

"I was hoping you could recommend a shelter for him. One that arranges adoptions."

The vet's handlebar mustache twitched. "To be frank, Mr. Delaney, there's no way that dog will find a home."

Shane shot a glance at Ruthie, who mouthed, *I told you so*. "If he doesn't find a home, will he be put down?"

"I'm afraid so. People are all for adopting rescue dogs these days, but only the cute ones." The vet shook his head regretfully. "That dog isn't pretty, but he's a healthy little chap. Such a shame to see him destroyed."

Shane pictured the dog's squashed face, long body, stumpy legs, and ridiculous bushy tail. *Aw, hell.* "No one is destroying him," he said firmly. "He's coming home with me."

EIGHT

After the visit to the vet, Ruthie drove Shane to a pet shop, where he stocked up on what the shop owner assured them were just a few puppy essentials: food, bowls, travel cage, basket, and toys.

"That's a lot of stuff for one puppy," Ruthie said as she slowed the car to a halt outside Shane's apartment building. "You sure keeping him is a good idea?"

"Hell no, but there was no way I was leaving him to be put down."

"What will your landlord say?"

"He won't be impressed." Shane wrapped the wriggling puppy into his jacket and grinned. "Guess it's time to look for another place."

"Don't you mind? I thought you liked your bachelor pad."

"I do. Doesn't mean I can't like another. It's just a place to sleep. Besides, I've been thinking of buying a house. Now is as good a time as any."

Kiss Shot

Hesitation flickered across Shane's face, an accurate reflection of her own emotions. Without the alcohol to soften their inhibitions, neither knew how to act around the other. Despite their physical intimacy last night, they weren't a couple, yet they'd made out. It was hard, if not impossible, to segue back into the "friends" category.

Shane appeared to make up his mind. He leaned over and brushed her cheek with his lips. "Thanks for your help today, Ruthie. I owe you one."

His lips felt soft against her skin, making it difficult to think straight. "I was happy to help. All you owe me is a word with Dan about me using the gym."

"I won't forget." Shane opened the passenger door and got out. Before he closed it, he leaned in again and gave her a bone-melting smile. "Want to meet me for a drink later this week? Preferably without Murph, Dec, or Kevin making an appearance."

Her heart performed a slow thump and roll. And it wasn't purely because her plan to use Shane as her "in" with the Delaneys was working. "Sure," she said, striving for calm and collected. "You have my number. Give me a call."

"I will."

He flashed her one last smile and was gone. Ruthie paused for a moment before starting the engine. God, he was gorgeous. And just as nice a guy as she'd remembered. Her efforts to get close to him were paying off, but she couldn't shake the guilt. Shane had nothing to do with Kevin's situation, yet she was about to betray Shane and his family in return for cash.

She wiped her damp palms on the front of her combats and blew out a breath. Whatever happened, she needed to keep her cool. The last thing she needed was to lose her heart to Shane Delaney all over again. Which didn't rule out having sex with the guy...

She gave herself a mental shaking and gunned the engine. Dad was expecting her for dinner. "Dinner" in the Reynolds household was what other people called a hot lunch. Big Mike worked nights and insisted on cooking a warm meal at lunchtime. Her father was more of a gourmand than a gourmet, but he'd always made sure his kids ate at least one solid meal a day that included all the food groups. Even though it was just him and Kevin living at home, Big Mike hadn't altered his routine.

Her dad lived a few streets away from Shane's newly built high-rise apartment block, but it might have been a different world. During the boom years of the late nineties and early two thousands, Kilpatrick had aspired to rival the upmarket areas of Dublin through the construction of fancy office and residential buildings in a spot previously occupied by warehouses. With the collapse of the economy, the construction boom ceased. Many of the offices and apartments were unoccupied, and Ruthie suspected Shane's rent was reasonable. In contrast to the affectations of Carlisle Street, Clondale

Kiss Shot

Terrace looked just as it had when she was a child: a respectable working-class street with no pretensions.

Ruthie's dad had parallel parked in front of their house. She pulled up behind his car and got out.

After letting herself into the house with the key she still kept on her keychain even though she hadn't lived with her dad in several years, Ruthie slung her sports bag on the floor and walked into the kitchen. Her father was at the stove, stirring an enormous pot of stew. Big Mike Reynolds was a large man, both in height and in girth, but he was solid muscle. Wearing an apron with his sleeves rolled up to reveal arms covered in tattoos, he looked incongruous yet adorable.

Ruthie squeezed his arm. "Hey, Dad. How was your trip?"

"Successful." Big Mike beamed. "I should go to the Donegal races more often."

She leaned over to sniff the pot. "That smells good."

"I hope it tastes good. You need a decent meal to put some flesh on your bones." Her father eyed her up and down with a twinkle in his eye. "Have they no food in Switzerland?"

Ruthie slumped into a chair and smiled at her father. "They have great food, and I eat plenty. I just work out a lot."

"All the same..." Her father let his sentence trail off and turned his attention back to the stew.

"Maybe you can come visit me, and I'll prove to you that it's possible to get a proper meal outside your kitchen."

Big Mike grunted. "You know me, Ruthie. I don't do travel. I have no idea why people want to go gallivanting all over the world when we live in such a lovely country."

"Different strokes, I guess. I like seeing the world beyond Ireland." The thump of music from her brother's room brought a frown to Ruthie's brow. "How's Kevin today?"

Her father shot her a knowing look. "He told me about you and Shane Delaney if that's what you're wondering."

Ruthie's cheeks grew warm. "There's nothing to tell."

"From what I heard, only because Kevin showed up at an inconvenient moment." Her father's expression of concern reignited her feelings of guilt for not confiding in him, but she knew him well enough to know he'd go ballistic. And pissing off the Kowalski brothers wouldn't be a smart move, not even for a man like Big Mike Reynolds.

"You don't need to worry about me, Dad. I can look after myself."

"I know you're all grown up," her father said, dishing three generous portions of Irish stew into bowls, "but I'll always worry about you. It's what dads do."

Tears stung Ruthie's eyes but she blinked them back. Her getting weepy would embarrass both of them.

Kiss Shot

Instead, she set the table and was busy filling their water glasses when Kevin entered the kitchen. He looked like he'd been dragged through a hedge backward.

"Did the smell of food lure you downstairs?" she asked, keeping her tone light. She hadn't seen her brother since she'd put him to bed last night. Difficult to know what he remembered—nothing, she hoped.

Kevin glared at her. "Is Delaney with you?"

So much for that hope. "Shane is at home."

"How do you know that?" Her father placed bowls of steaming hot stew on the table and eyed his daughter with suspicion. "Did you see him this morning?"

"He was at Dan's gym."

Her father's expression darkened. "I don't want you seeing Shane, love. Those boys are magnets for trouble."

"And we're pillars of the community?" Ruthie rolled her eyes. "*You* recommended I join Dan Schneider-Delaney's gym. You knew his cousins trained there."

Big Mike took the seat across from her and Kevin, his frown lines deeper than usual. "I've got nothing against Shane personally, but there's...stuff...going on in Kilpatrick. I don't want you mixed up in any shenanigans. You're better off getting back to Switzerland and living your life."

His enthusiasm to get rid of her stung. "'Stuff' covers a lot of ground, Dad. Care to be more specific?"

"Jimmy Connolly got gunned down a few weeks ago," Kevin supplied. "Rumor has it the Delaneys were involved."

"There are a lot of Delaneys. Does rumor have it that Shane was responsible?"

"No," her father conceded, "but all the same..."

"All the same nothing," Ruthie said with emphasis. "Kilpatrick has more than its fair share of career criminals. There's no reason to suppose Shane is responsible for Connolly's murder. I'd have thought that was more in Lar's line."

"It is," her father said, "but Lar's not stupid enough to kill a man in his own neighborhood."

"Neither is Shane."

"Maybe not, but the atmosphere doesn't sit right with me." Her father shook his bald head. "Something is up in Kilpatrick, and I want no part of it."

Ruthie resisted the urge to steal a glance at her brother. Big Mike had spent years navigating the choppy waters of the Dublin criminal underworld, careful to make enough money to take care of his family and equally cautious about not rising too high to be seen as a threat by the big players. If Dad found out about Kevin's debt to the Kowalskis, he'd throw years of caution and common sense to the wind. All the more reason for her to make sure he remained in blissful ignorance.

"Eat your stew, Dad, and let's change the subject." She plastered a smile on her face. "How are the dogs?"

Kiss Shot

Her father took the hint and spent the rest of the meal regaling her with stories of his greyhounds' racing prowess. He deflected all questions about his work and social life, but this was nothing new. Dad had always avoided talking business and personal stuff with his daughter, preferring to focus on their family life—or what was left of it.

Kevin was monosyllabic and picked at his food. He only spoke when asked a direct question. Suddenly, mid-meal, he stood and shuffled out of the room. A moment later, they heard the front door close. Ruthie forced herself to swallow the food in her mouth. Her dad's delicious stew now tasted like sawdust. Big Mike refused to meet her gaze. They both knew what Kevin was doing: going out in search of his next hit.

In silence, Ruthie helped her father clear up after lunch and fixed them two large mugs of coffee.

"Dad," she finally began in a cautious tone, "Kev should have treatment. He barged into my room last night with a knife."

Her father stared at her in horror. "Did he hurt you?"

"No. He was in one of his paranoid phases and convinced he was being followed.

Unseeing, her father dumped two heaped spoonfuls of sugar into his coffee.

"I'm serious," Ruthie said, more forcefully this time. "You have to take steps to have him hospitalized."

Big Mike's head jerked up and pain flashed through his dark eyes. "You know I don't want him locked up. Why did you come home, Ruthie? And don't give me that bull about feeling homesick. If you just wanted to see us, you could have stayed a few days. Are you home because of Kevin?"

No point in denying the obvious. "He needs help, Dad."

"Do you think I don't know that?" Her father's expression crumpled. "I've tried everything. Bar chaining him up at home, there's nothing more I can do."

"Kevin should be in the hospital," she repeated.

A flash of belligerence crossed over his face. "How many times do I have to tell you I won't lock my son up? I have one son in prison. I'm not having the other incarcerated."

"Kevin is out of control," she insisted. "He's a danger to himself and others."

Her father bristled. "We don't know that. He's been in a few fights, yeah, but no more than other lads."

"He's a ticking time bomb, and you know it."

Her father shoved his chair back and stood, breathing heavily. "I'm delighted to see you, love, but if locking up Kevin is your reason for coming home, you should leave."

His words cut her like a lash. "Dad, please..."

But Big Mike was gone. He didn't slam the back door behind him as she would have done had their roles been reversed—that wasn't his style. Instead, he'd retreat outside to his beloved greyhounds and put the entire ugly conversation out of his mind.

With shaking hands, Ruthie placed her mug on the table. Getting through to her father was impossible. Even if she stayed home for months, he'd never force Kevin into psychiatric care. And if he knew about Kevin's debt to the Kowalskis, he'd get into a fight he couldn't win.

Big Mike was a turf accountant and moneylender of dubious legality, but the loans he gave out were on the small side. There was no way he could afford to pay back the kind of debts Kevin had accumulated. Confiding in Dad would accomplish nothing except run the risk of him losing his temper and going after Adam and Reuben Kowalski to fight a war he couldn't win. In the hierarchy of Dublin's criminals, they were several tiers above Big Mike and could counter her father's hired thugs with a veritable army of their own.

Ruthie massaged her aching temples and finished loading the dishwasher. A painkiller would take the edge off her headache. She'd just slipped her hand into her bag to get a Tylenol when her phone rang. At the sight of the Unknown Caller message flashing on the display, she tasted bile. She knew only too well who it would be. With frozen fingers, she hit Connect. "Hello?"

"Ms. Reynolds." The sardonic English drawl made her skin crawl.

She shot a glance through the kitchen door into the backyard where her father was occupied with his dogs. "I have no news, Travers," she said without preamble. "I've established an 'in' through one family member, but I've yet to learn anything of significance."

"That's unfortunate," Travers said in a voice dipped in sarcasm. "We'd hoped you'd work faster."

She could picture him sitting behind his enormous mahogany desk, a sneer on his face. During her months of training, she'd grown to loathe the man. "I've only been back in Dublin a few days. Worming my way into people's confidence takes time."

"Time," Travers said, "is a luxury we don't have. I'll give you two days to give me concrete information."

He seriously expected her to dig for info on what the Delaneys knew about the attack on The Lucky Leprechaun and produce valuable intel in *two days*?

"Two days won't cut it." She deliberately left out the "sir." "The Delaneys are a tight-knit bunch and disinclined to confide in people outside their small circle. If I barge in and start asking questions, they'll clam up."

"I credit you with more finesse than that," Travers said in a steel-dipped tone. "I trained you, after all."

Yes, he had, but why? The entire case intrigued Ruthie. Why was the Jarvis Agency interested in the Delaneys? And in Lar Delaney's girlfriend, Genevieve McEllroy? Why should an international intelligence agency care about them digging for information about the attack on Frank Delaney's Boston club five years ago? Unless, of course, they had something to hide.

"Five days," she countered. "Give me five days to come up with useful information."

"Seventy-two hours," Travers said without missing a beat, "and not a second more. I'll be in touch."

Before she could haggle further, he disconnected. *Prick.*

When the agency recruited Ruthie, they'd shown her papers that proved they were an international intelligence agency, affiliated with various nations and empowered to work together for the common good. The papers had looked legit as far as Ruthie could see, and the amount of money they were prepared to pay her was enticing.

During her months of training, both at the agency's headquarters in Geneva and in the field, she'd seen nothing to indicate they weren't exactly what they claimed to be—a legitimate, albeit secret, intelligence agency that specialized in matters of international importance. And yet...something was off, a piece of the puzzle that didn't quite fit. It was nothing she could put her finger on. No snatches of overheard conversation had aroused her suspicions. It was merely a feeling—an ominous undercurrent she could sense but not see. At the point when Travers had approached her with the Delaney assignment and offered her a generous bonus if she were successful, she'd been on the verge of quitting. However, Kevin's situation made leaving a well-paid job impossible, especially after she'd calculated that the proffered bonus would more than cover the second chunk of Kevin's debt.

In her hand, the phone vibrated for the second time. Ruthie glared at the Unknown Caller message flashing on the screen. Had Travers decided to dick her around again? Maybe cut the seventy-two hours they'd negotiated back to forty-eight? What a wanker. She hit Connect.

"Ms. Reynolds." Reuben Kowalski's heavily accented drawl was unmistakable. Unlike his brother, Reuben had never shed his Warsaw accent, despite years of living in Ireland.

"What do you want?" she asked in a resigned tone. "Have you let my brother run up more debts he can't afford to repay?"

Reuben's laugh made the hairs on the nape of her neck stand to attention. "Not exactly. It's more a dispute over an existing debt."

Ruthie sighed. "We've been through all of this. I told Adam—"

"I have Kevin," Reuben said, throwing a grenade into the conversation.

"What do you mean?" Her heart hammered against her ribs. "I saw him just a few minutes ago."

Kiss Shot

"A few of my men picked him up outside the chip shop and escorted him to a meeting with me."

Ruthie gritted her teeth. "Where is he?"

"My warehouse," Reuben said, as if she should know exactly where that was. "And Ms. Reynolds? Bring twelve thousand euros with you if you'd like your brother to keep all of his fingers. You have thirty minutes."

With these chilling words, Reuben Kowalski cut the call.

Ruthie stared at the phone in her hand. The floor seemed to move beneath her feet. She blinked and dragged oxygen into her lungs. Where was Reuben's warehouse? And how the hell was she supposed to conjure up twelve thousand euros in less than half an hour?

Outside the window, drizzle soaked the yard. Her father fed the dogs, leaning down to pet each one in turn. Ruthie's stomach twisted. Asking him for help was out of the question. Which left her only one option: Shane Delaney. His sister was married to Reuben Kowalski. Surely he'd know the location of Reuben and Adam's warehouses? With a last glance through the rain-splattered window into the yard, Ruthie grabbed her father's car keys from the kitchen counter and ran.

NINE

Shane paused in front of the steps of St. Patrick's Church and stared up at its imposing façade. As a child, the church had terrified him. Its high ceilings and funny smell convinced him horrors lurked in every recess. Before she'd taken off for sunnier climes, his mother had been an avid churchgoer. Not, Shane suspected, out of religious conviction, but more because she liked to be seen. As the wife of one of Kilpatrick's most notorious residents, an air of infamy had preceded Chantelle Delaney's every public appearance, and she'd relished in the attention. Unfortunately, Chantelle hadn't been quite as enthused about the reality of being married to Frank "Mad Dog" Delaney. She'd packed her bags and hit the road during one of the lean years when Frank was doing a five-year stretch in Mountjoy Prison, leaving her children in their aunt Siobhan's care. Shane had neither seen nor spoken to his mother in over twenty years.

Kiss Shot

The puppy snuggled against his chest, and Shane stroked him gently. In the few hours since he'd become a pet owner, he'd coaxed the creature to trust him a little, but they still had a long way to go. After Ruthie had dropped them home, Shane had found himself in an empty apartment, save for a new puppy with a penchant for chewing on cables. Max was already at the airport, but he'd left a bottle of Shane's favorite German chocolate syrup as a thank-you gift.

After he'd fixed himself a cappuccino liberally laced with chocolate syrup, Shane had gone through the motions of finishing the report he was due to give to Lar by tomorrow. It was for a new client—a wealthy private bank that didn't want its good name associated with hacking into a rival's files in search of evidence of insider trading—but Shane found it hard to focus. Two wasted hours later, he'd decided to unburden himself to Malachy. Even if he didn't tell his uncle everything about the Lar dilemma, a chat over coffee would do him good.

Shane shoved open the heavy door and entered the church. The place was deserted. He made his way to the back of the church and knocked on the sacristy door.

"Come in."

He opened the door and stepped into the room.

Malachy sat behind his enormous oak desk, surrounded by books. When he looked up and saw Shane, his craggy face split into a smile. "Hello, Shane. What brings you here?"

"I called by your house, and Mrs. Cryan said you were here. I hope you don't mind me bringing the dog. He howled when I tried to leave him behind, and he's already wreaked havoc in my apartment."

"Lar just left," Malachy said. "He said you'd acquired a dog."

Shane's mood plummeted at the mention of his cousin. "I'm sure he added a few choice adjectives to his description. Flash might not be pretty, but he's a sweet dog." At these words, the puppy snuggled closer, farted, and began to snore. Both men laughed. "Yeah...like I said, he's not quite house-trained yet."

"Take a seat, lad," his uncle said, gesturing to the armchair across from his desk. "Can I offer you a latte?"

"I'd love one. Do you still have that caramel syrup?"

His uncle smiled. "I do. I bought a new bottle just for you." A couple of minutes later, Malachy set a tall latte macchiato in front of Shane. "Strong and sweet, just as you like it."

"Thanks."

Shane doubted his father remembered he preferred coffee over tea, never mind his preference for strong and sweet. Unlike Uncle Patrick, Lar's father, Frank hadn't moved in a mistress or remarried, preferring the freedom that being a separated and then divorced man offered him. With his wife gone, Frank's tendency to pick on Shane increased. He wasn't physically abusive, but he took pleasure in belittling his youngest son and comparing him unfavorably with his sporty older brothers. Being bookish wasn't a trait considered worthy of anything but derision in Frank's household.

And so Shane sought refuge with his Uncle Malachy, spending as much time with him as he dared. Unlike Frank, Malachy encouraged his reading. And even though Malachy had neither interest nor talent when it came to computers, he'd bought Shane his first PC and let him use a spare room in his house to tinker with electronics. The bond between uncle and nephew continued into adulthood.

"Now, lad," Malachy said, taking a seat opposite. "What's up?"

"Straight to the point as usual."

Malachy laughed. "I've known you all your life. I can tell when something's bothering you. Is it that wee creature you have in your arms that brings you here?"

"No. I rescued him a few hours ago, and he seems to have moved in with me."

Malachy nodded with approval. "It'll do you good to have a pet."

"I doubt my landlord will feel the same way. I'll need to find a new place that's pet-friendly."

His uncle eyed him knowingly. "If you didn't come here to talk about the dog, what's the matter?"

Shane took a sip of his coffee and weighed his next words with care. "I recently found out some information about a family member, and it's been troubling me."

Was it his imagination, or did Malachy turn pale at his words? Was Malachy aware of what Lar had done to secure an early release from prison? His uncle cleared his throat. "How did you come by this information?"

"I tapped his phone and placed surveillance bugs in his house."

Malachy slow-blinked. "That seems...extreme."

"It's part of my exit strategy from the family 'business.' I made a deal with my father to run surveillance on this person in return for him not making a fuss about my leaving to pursue my own career."

His uncle scrutinized his face. "Francis asked you to spy on one of us?"

"Yeah."

Malachy swore beneath his breath. "That was below the belt, even for Francis. He knows you and Lar are close."

Shane jerked to attention. "How did you guess it was Lar?"

"Lar has gone to a lot of trouble to make sure Francis can't siphon off funds from the Triskelion Team." Malachy's smile was wan. "Let's just say Francis didn't take Lar's defection from the family 'business' well."

Shane weighed his next words with care. "Did you know about Lar's deal to secure an early release from prison? If he confided in anyone, it would have been you."

Malachy held up a hand to stop him. "I guessed something like that had happened, but I don't want to know the details."

"He's a fucking traitor," Shane growled. "Don't you care?"

"Why is he a traitor?" Malachy suddenly looked older than his sixty-two years. "His father and Francis shafted him over that bank robbery. Lar had every right to be upset."

"He lied to us all, including me. He's supposed to be my friend."

"If he did what I think he did, he couldn't have told you, Shane. He'd have signed a legal agreement not to breathe a word about what he was up to and, on a personal level, sharing info with you would have put you in danger if Francis ever found out." Malachy took a sip from his coffee mug and drew his bushy gray eyebrows together. "I'm guessing you haven't told your father."

Shane shook his head. "He'd kill Lar. Don't get me wrong. I'm mad as hell over this. But I'm not prepared to see my cousin killed. I need to know more about what, exactly, he discovered and passed on to the spooks."

"Leave it alone, Shane. Stay out of it. You don't want to go hacking into top-secret files."

This made Shane laugh out loud. "What do you think I've been doing for years, Malachy?"

His uncle shook his head. "You're playing with fire, son. Leave well alone. You're a smart lad. Why don't you find a legit job where you can put your hacking skills to good use?"

"I didn't just come because of what I found out about Lar. My father gave me another job, one that's connected."

"Oh?" Malachy raised an eyebrow. "Why do I get the impression it's not an assignment you want to carry out?"

"It's not so much reluctance on my part as confusion. Dad is under the impression that Lar killed Jimmy Connolly. Now, I keep my ears open. There's not much that goes on in Kilpatrick that I don't know. The identity of Jimmy's killer is one, and finding a link between Lar and Jimmy is another. I mean, I know Lar didn't like the man, but who did? It's not like Lar to take on a hit job in his own neighborhood."

"I'm assuming you haven't mentioned any of this to your cousin."

Was it his imagination, or had his uncle gone unnaturally pale all of a sudden? Even if Lar hadn't killed Connolly, there was a good chance Malachy knew who did from hearing confessions.

"No, I haven't said anything to Lar yet. I wanted your advice first. You hear even more than I do about what goes on around here. Have you heard anything about Lar clipping Connolly?"

Malachy's mouth drew into a hard line. "No. But what I can tell you is this: Lar didn't kill Jimmy Connolly. Of that I'm certain."

"Something you heard in the confessional?" Shane asked, noting his uncle's certainty in his words. "Do you know who did it?"

"Let's just say I know Lar didn't do it. And with that information, you'll have to be satisfied."

"Dad wants me to look into the killing. I'm to try to ferret out what happened."

Malachy snorted. "Francis doesn't like the idea of a Kilpatrick kingpin being gunned down on his own property. He's worried it'll become a trend."

"Dad excels at looking out for numero uno. I guess Connolly's killing alarmed him. I have no idea why he'd link Lar to it, apart from the fact that it was a professional job."

"So the newspapers said." Malachy drained his coffee cup and nodded toward Shane's almost empty glass. "Do you want another?"

"Nah, I'm good, thanks." Malachy was skilled in bringing conversations to a close without outright telling people to leave and let him get back to his work. Shane got the message. He stood and shook hands with his uncle, an old habit they'd gotten into when Shane was a boy. The Delaneys didn't go in for displays of physical affection, particularly not the men, and the handshake was half joke, half serious. This time, Malachy held onto his hand for longer than usual.

"I'm serious, Shane. Quit digging up other people's dirt and concentrate on the present. With your skills, you'd easily find a job in the computer industry."

"Maybe I would, but I have enough Delaney blood in my veins not to want to work for a company."

"Then set up on your own, something more respectable than what Lar proposes to do with the Triskelion Team."

"Something boring, staid, and respectable, you mean?"

His uncle pinned him in place with the intensity of his gaze. "If you need start-up capital, just say the word. I don't have much savings, but I have a bit put by."

"Thanks, Malachy," Shane said, genuinely touched, "but I'll be okay. I'm not cut out for the sort of job you'd like me to have. When I'm not discovering shite about people I care about, I like what I'm doing for the Triskelion Team."

"And the job for Francis? Do you like that?"

Shane grimaced. "You know I don't, but it'll be over soon."

"What are you going to tell Francis about Lar?"

"I haven't decided yet. Depends on what else I turn up."

Malachy sighed. "Don't jeopardize your friendship with your cousin. You two are as close as brothers."

Kiss Shot

"Were—past tense. And the brother analogy doesn't work on me. Greg and Tom are shits, and Con wasn't much better."

"Bad analogy, fine. But you know what I mean. Lar's your best friend. Don't throw away a friendship lightly."

"I have no intention of doing so. He's the one who lied."

Malachy's smile was tired. "By omission and not by choice."

"I can't believe you're defending him."

"I'm not. I can understand that you feel betrayed, but you need to look at the big picture here. How does this change anything? It doesn't negate all the good times you two have shared, or all the occasions when you helped each other out."

"But it makes me question how much any of that was real."

"You have to decide what matters most—what you found written on a few pieces of paper, or all the years of shared experiences and friendship. And another thing: how do you think Lar would react if your roles were reversed? Do you think he'd understand if you'd taken a deal to get out of prison for a crime you didn't commit? He was very young when he agreed to take the fall for Greg. He had no idea what he was facing. I'd imagine the realities of prison life wore him down and made him realize that his father and uncle had taken advantage of him. Why should Lar remain loyal?"

Truthfully, Shane had no idea how Lar would react if their positions had been reversed. He suspected his cousin would take his side, but there was no love lost between Lar and Frank. "Thanks for the coffee and conversation. I'll let you get back to work."

"Shane..." Malachy began, then appeared to think better of it. "Just promise me you'll be careful."

He snuggled the wriggling puppy close and smiled. "I always am."

Shane left the sacristy and strolled down the church, clutching the dog against his chest. Talking to Malachy had helped, as it always did, but he still had no clear idea of how he should approach Lar. He was halfway down the aisle, brooding over his options, when the church door flew open and Ruthie Reynolds burst inside.

TEN

"Thank God," Ruthie said between gasps. "I called by your apartment and your neighbor told me you were here. I tried your phone, but it went to voicemail."

"I switched it off while I was talking to my uncle." Shane surveyed her damp hair and rain-splattered clothes. "What's wrong? Has something happened to Kevin?"

"Yes." She shivered and hugged herself, whether from cold or fear or both, he couldn't tell. "I need your help. The Kowalskis have taken him."

Shane's blood ran cold. "What's Kevin done?"

"I'll explain on the way. You've got to come quick." Her eyes pleaded with him. "I don't know who else to turn to. I can't tell my dad or he'd go ballistic. When you didn't answer your phone, I jumped in Dad's car to find you." She bounced from one foot to the other, her gaze sliding to the door.

Shane swore under his breath. When he, Lar, and Dan had negotiated their exit deal from the family "business", they'd promised Shane's father they'd stay away from the Kowalskis. Frank didn't want the Triskelion Team forming an alliance with his rivals, or worse still, pissing them off and bringing trouble to his doorstep. Still, this situation had nothing to do with the Triskelion Team. With a bit of luck—okay, a lot of luck—he and Ruthie could clear up the mess without enraging either Kowalski brother. He took her by the arm and led her outside. "Of course I'll help you. Where have they taken Kevin?"

"Reuben said they were in their warehouse," she said as they descended the steps. "Do you know where that is?"

"Yeah. Is that your car?" He indicated the Land Rover parked behind his black BMW.

"It's Dad's."

"We'll take mine." Shane pressed his key to unlock the doors. "I know where to go."

"Thanks, Shane."

"There's no need to thank me. You don't know if I'll be any help yet." He opened the passenger door for her and gestured for her to get in. After he'd loaded the puppy into the carrier cage in the back, he went to the driver's side and slid behind the wheel. Seconds later, they were on the move, heading south toward the industrial estate where the Kowalskis owned several warehouses.

"Want to tell me what's going on?" Shane asked when they eased to a stop at a set of traffic lights. "Why did the Kowalski brothers take Kevin?"

She sighed. "It's a long story."

"Then you'd better start talking. We'll reach the industrial estate in about ten minutes, depending on traffic."

"It's...embarrassing."

Shane slid her a glance and smiled. "My father runs a strip club-come-brothel—pun intended. You'll have to try real hard to embarrass me."

"Kevin owes the Kowalskis money," she blurted. "Gambling and drugs."

"Shit." Given the state Kevin Reynolds had been in last night, Shane wasn't surprised. "Adam and Reuben aren't guys you want to owe anything to. How much debt did your brother run up?"

"Twenty-five grand," Ruthie said, then added, "and that was just the first installment. I have to pay back the second half of his debt before the end of the month."

"Fifty grand in total?" Shane whistled. "Wow, Ruthie. What a fucking mess."

Owing any form of debt to the Kowalskis was a risky endeavor, but fifty thousand euros was a hell of a lot to owe to a pair of psychos.

Ruthie's rigid posture crumpled, and all signs of the plucky bravado she'd displayed earlier evaporated. "Despite our agreement, Reuben called me today, saying he was holding Kevin hostage and wouldn't release him until I paid him twelve thousand euros."

Shane drew his brows together. "'Our agreement?' This is Kevin's mess. Let him sort it out."

"Kevin isn't in a position to sort out his troubles. We look out for one another in my family. If circumstances were different, he'd do it for me."

In other words, a sane and sober Kevin might stick up for his little sister. However, given his almost constant state of inebriation, that would never happen. Shane ached for her. Lar's face loomed before him, a harsh reminder of what it was like to be let down by a family member. Although Ruthie's situation was different, he recognized the hurt of not being able to rely on the people who should be there for you one hundred percent.

"I don't understand why Reuben changed the plan," she said, frowning. "Adam gave me until the end of the month to pay the second installment."

Shane shot her a glance. "So what's the deal? How are you planning to come up with twenty-five grand to settle the balance?"

She crossed her arms over her chest, regaining some of her confident poise. "That's my business."

Kiss Shot

"Can't your dad help? In his line of work, Big Mike must have a fair amount of cash stashed away."

Ruthie's eyes widened in alarm and she shook her head. "My father can't know anything about this, Shane. I'm serious. Promise me you won't breathe a word to anyone."

"Why? Your dad is a loan shark, for heaven's sake. He has to have enough money to pay off Kevin's debt."

"My father isn't as wealthy as people seem to think. He gives small loans. Nothing on the scale of what Kevin owes the Kowalski brothers. Besides, if he knew the Kowalskis were putting the screws into Kevin, he'd lose his shit. Dad doesn't have the manpower to back him up, and the Kowalskis most assuredly do." Her voice rose in panic. "They'd kill him. I can't let that happen. I've already lost one parent. I can't lose Dad."

"Okay, calm down." He placed his hand over hers. "I see your point. This is why you came home, right? To help Kevin?"

She nodded and took a shuddery breath. "My brother called me a few months ago when he first had money problems."

"Where did you get the money to pay back the first installment? Twenty-five grand is a hell of a lot of money."

"Like I said, that's my business." She bristled visibly at his question.

Shane sighed. "Come on, Ruthie. You can tell me. I'm not going to judge you."

She paled beneath her tan and opened and shut her mouth wordlessly.

"Surely it can't be that bad?" he prompted. "Want me to regale you with all the insane things I've done over the last few years?"

Ruthie grimaced and slumped into her seat. "I threw a few fights for money."

"On the MMA circuit?"

"Yeah. I'm not proud of what I did, but I didn't have the full twenty-five thousand in savings. Nowhere near it, unfortunately."

"I'm sorry," he murmured. "I know it must have been hell for you to do that. It's not fair that you have to take on this burden on your own."

"Life's not fair. It is what it is."

Shane rolled the car to a stop at another set of traffic lights. "What's the plan? If you don't have the cash to pay Reuben, how are we going to handle this?"

She averted her gaze and twisted the rings on her fingers. "I need to liquidate a couple of assets. It takes time. Once that's done, I'll have the cash to pay them the rest of the money Kevin owes."

"What happens the next time he runs up debts?" he asked softly. "You can't keep bailing him out."

She shook her head. "There can't be a next time. However I manage it, Kevin is going to get help."

"That's why I think you should confide in Big Mike. You need his cooperation to get Kevin the help he needs."

"Yeah, but I want to do it without mentioning the mess with the Kowalskis."

Shane sighed. "You're making a mistake."

"That's the story of my life."

He reached across the car and squeezed her knee. "I admire you, you know."

She flushed to the roots of her dark hair. "What do you mean?"

"You're loyal. You don't even get on with Kevin, yet you dropped everything to come to his rescue."

"There's nothing to admire. The fallout if the Kowalskis kill Kevin could wipe out my whole family. I'm not prepared to take that risk."

"Families, eh?" His laugh was low and bitter. "All that blood-is-thicker-than-water nonsense. It's the people who care about you and are loyal to you who count, regardless of whether you have shared DNA."

"True, but it's hard to shake off old bonds. Kevin and I were close as kids, despite our age difference. Brian was so much older that he didn't have much interest in me, but Kevin took the time to play with me and read me stories."

"He was always fond of you, Ruthie. That's why I kept my distance—or tried to. He was fiercely protective of you."

In spite of her fear, she grinned. "Goodness knows why. It wasn't like I had guys queuing up to date me."

"Only because they were scared shitless of Kevin and your dad."

She laughed. "I'm not exactly the sort of woman men ask out, even now."

"You scare them away. You exude a 'don't fuck with me' attitude. That's why I knew you had to be hustling those eejits at Power's Pub. You *flirted* with one of them."

Ruthie grinned. "Maybe I developed killer flirting skills during my time abroad."

He shook his head. "Not you. People change, but not that much."

"A damning conclusion," she said dryly.

"But accurate in my experience. Sometimes, of course, people turn out not to be what you thought they were, but that's a different matter entirely."

She eyed him sharply. "Are you referring to someone in particular?"

Ruthie had always been perceptive. It was one of the traits he admired about her. "Nothing I feel like discussing. Just one of those things."

"Why can't life go from A to B without taking a million detours?" she asked with a sigh. "Why does it have to be so complicated?"

He laughed. "If it always went smoothly, life would be very boring."

"Frankly, boring sounds like bliss to me right now."

Kiss Shot

"I just don't like the idea of you having to deal with this pressure all on your own," he said, frowning. "It's not fair."

"In case you haven't noticed," she said dryly, "I'm a grown woman. I can handle tricky situations."

"Until you can't," Shane said.

A pink stain crept up her cheeks. "I appreciate you providing backup for me today."

"Not a problem, Ruthie. I'm happy to help, but don't thank me yet. We still have to get past Reuben and his rottweiler bodyguards. Which brother have you been dealing with over the money?"

"Adam mostly, which was why I found it odd that Reuben called me today."

"Nothing that involves Reuben is good news." An understatement of epic proportions. "Do you remember my sister, Kaylee?"

Ruthie inclined her head. "Vaguely. She's a couple of years older than you, isn't she? She went to my secondary school, but I think she was in her final year when I was in my first, so our paths never crossed."

"Kaylee is married to Reuben Kowalski."

"I heard." She wrinkled her nose as if the idea of marriage to Reuben was as repulsive to her as it was to him. "How does Frank feel about having Reuben as his son-in-law?"

"Not happy, but Kaylee was already pregnant when they got married. Our father gritted his teeth and accepted the situation, even if he's not exactly thrilled. For Kaylee's sake, he tries to avoid coming into conflict with the Kowalskis."

"How do you get on with Reuben?"

"I don't." Breaking the prick's nose frequently featured in his fantasies.

"That's...succinct."

"I've never liked him," Shane said with venom. "He treats my sister like shit."

"Why does she stay with him?"

"I don't know. Kaylee says she loves him, and they have two small kids. She doesn't want to break up the family."

"That's a crap reason for staying. Is Reuben violent?"

"I'm not sure. He's definitely emotionally abusive. Since she married him, Kaylee's become a recluse. Keeps to her house, and we don't see much of her or the kids." Shane stopped at another set of traffic lights and turned to her. "Are you sure about this, Ruthie? There's still time to change your mind and call the police."

"A *Delaney* is suggesting I call the police?" She threw back her head and roared with laughter. "Things have changed in Kilpatrick."

He gave a rueful smile. "I'm no fan of the Guards, but the Kowalskis won't just hand Kevin over to us. I can't call my cousins for backup because we have a deal with my father that we stay clear of the Kowalski brothers." A deal that included all interaction with the Kowalski

Kiss Shot

brothers—friendly or hostile. Frank was more concerned by the potential threat of his son and nephews joining forces with his rivals than of their personal safety. If Frank knew that one of Shane's regular booty calls was Adam Kowalski's on-off girlfriend, he'd blow a gasket.

The light changed to green, and Shane hung left and entered an industrial estate dotted with factories and outlets. "The place I think they're holding Kevin in is that red building on the left."

Ruthie swung in her seat, straining to get a better look. "How do we do this? We can't walk up and knock on the door."

"Do you have a better suggestion? We want to parlay, not break in and spark a gunfight."

Ruthie patted her jacket pocket. "I have a gun. And I know how to use it."

Jaysus. The last thing they needed was Ruthie shooting up the place. "No guns," he said firmly. "Our only chance at getting them to cooperate with us is to show them we're unarmed. If they see any sign of a weapon on us, they'll attack. I'm pretty good at martial arts, but this is real life, not an action film. I can't beat the crap out of eight equally well-trained fighters."

"Right about now, shooting the fuckers sounds pretty damn good." Ruthie's voice cracked with emotion. "Okay, fine. I'll leave the gun here. I just hate what the Kowalskis are doing to Kevin. I'm well aware that my brother is a pain, but they took advantage of him. They had to have known that Kevin would never be in a position to pay back the debt on his own."

"The Kowalskis are in the 'expansion phase,'" Shane said, making air quotes with his fingers. "Squeezing your father out of a portion of his business is exactly the kind of thing they'd do."

"That occurred to me. But if they wanted to do that, why not approach Dad directly? Instead, they put the squeeze on Kevin, and he contacted me to bail him out."

"The Kowalskis don't do anything without a good reason. I'm betting there's a puzzle piece we're missing here."

"Whatever it is, I still wish I could shoot them. That'd solve the problem."

"Unfortunately, I doubt it would," Shane said with a grin. "We have a pesky legal system that doesn't take kindly to people shooting each other, however much the victim deserved it."

"It'd make me feel a whole lot better, though." Ruthie scowled. "Do you seriously want us to knock on the door and talk to them?"

"It's the smartest move. Reuben is my brother-in-law. I can use that fact to get him to talk to us. And if Adam is there, we might be able to get down to some real negotiations. Adam is less hot-headed than his brother." Shane drew up outside a high chain-link fence topped with barbed wire and cut the engine. "This is as far as we can go by car without a permit. Ready?"

Kiss Shot

Ruthie stiffened and said nothing for a moment. Then she nodded and reached for the car door handle. "I can do this."

ELEVEN

I can do this. The words echoed in Ruthie's head. What a joke. Without Shane's help, she wouldn't even have known where to find Kevin at such short notice. She could have gotten the info through the agency, but she was reluctant to confide in them about her brother's situation. That they knew about Kevin's debts, she had no doubt. They knew everything about her, including why she'd negotiated a specific bonus for this job. Still, she had no intention of appearing vulnerable. She'd complete this assignment and then quit.

Outside the sanctuary of the car, the rain bucketed down from the heavens, blown sideways by the strong sea wind. Ruthie shivered and hugged her arms around her chest. "You wouldn't think it was June today," she said, grateful for a mundane topic to try to take her mind off the encounter ahead. It didn't work.

Kiss Shot

Shane opened the back of the car and pulled out a raincoat. "Wear this. It'll be too big, but at least you'll be dry."

"Thanks," she said, slipping on the coat. "I forgot mine at Dad's house. When Reuben called, I just...ran."

"Understandable." Shane opened the back door to the car and filled the puppy's food and water bowls. The little dog greeted his new owner with an enthusiastic lick.

Seeing Shane being sweet to the ugly little creature nagged at her conscience even more than his willingness to help her. He was a good guy. He didn't deserve to be used. He didn't deserve to be lied to. Throw a fight for money? Hell no. Her skin crawled at the idea of engaging in fight fixing, but the lie served its purpose. Both she and Shane came from families that lived on the wrong side of the law. How else could she explain having access to twenty-five grand at short notice?

And then her thoughts turned to her father, another man who found it easier to communicate with dogs than with people. Much as she loved her brother, Kevin's welfare wasn't the only reason she was helping him repay the Kowalskis. If anything happened to Dad, it would destroy her. She'd already lost one parent far too young. She wasn't ready to lose another.

"The puppy looks happy. Is he settling in at his new home?"

Shane laughed. "Oh, yeah. He's already eaten my best pair of shoes."

"Have you decided on a name yet?"

"I'm debating between Data and Flash." He gave her a rueful grin. "As in flash drive."

"I like Flash. It suits him." Ruthie leaned in to pet the dog and he rewarded her with a lick. "Will he be okay out here on his own?"

Shane looked over her shoulder at the warehouses beyond. "He'll be safer out here than with us. Reuben's a violent prick, and his posse is of a similar mindset. There's no telling what he'll do if he's in one of his moods, and he's not going to be pleased you don't have his money."

"He had to have known I couldn't get twelve thousand euros in thirty minutes. He's yanking my chain. The question is why." Ruthie scanned her surroundings. Rows of warehouses stretched as far as the eye could see. "Which one belongs to the Kowalskis?"

"They own two at the back of the park. It's about a five-hundred-meter walk." After giving the dog a last pat on the back, Shane closed the car door and ushered Ruthie through a crude gap in the fence that had been pulled back in a half-hearted attempt to admit pedestrians.

Ruthie squared her shoulders and jogged to keep up with Shane's brisk pace. Under the borrowed raincoat, her damp clothes stuck to her skin.

Kiss Shot

Shane glanced over his shoulder and slowed his pace to let her catch up. "Maybe I should do the talking when we get inside. I'm not as emotionally involved as you are, and Reuben needs to keep on my good side for Kaylee's sake."

"No." She shook her head emphatically. "This is my mess to sort out. I'm sorry to drag you into it."

"Technically, it's Kevin's mess, but okay." Shane's long strides covered a lot of ground, and Ruthie struggled to keep up. "Why did the Kowalskis take Kevin if you'd agreed to pay them the rest of the money in a few weeks?"

She scowled. "I don't know what game they're playing. If this is their idea of a hostile takeover to force my father out of business, I wish they'd get to the point. I feel like a puppet dangling on a string, only ever getting part of the story before I'm yanked in another direction."

"That doesn't sound like their usual MO," Shane said, frowning. "Adam and Reuben cooperate over certain 'business ventures,' but they divide most of their jobs between them. You negotiated the deal with Adam, right?"

Ruthie nodded. "Reuben was present when I delivered the first installment, but Adam was the one in charge."

"Interesting. I wonder why Reuben called you today instead of his brother."

"I don't know, but I guess we're about to find out." And she had a feeling she wasn't going to like the answer.

Shane's pace slowed. "Listen, I have some savings. If Reuben insists on you paying up today, I can help."

His words were like a blow to her solar plexus. Guilt burned a hole in her conscience, vicious as alcohol on an open wound. "I can't ask you to do that."

"You're not asking. I'm offering."

Heat burned her cheeks. "Thanks for driving me here, but I'll take care of getting the money together." *How* was the twelve-thousand-euro question, but she'd figure out a way. She had no choice.

"Ruthie—" he began, but she cut him off.

"I'll manage. Don't worry about it. I appreciate the lift, but that's where your help ends."

Shane's mouth pulled up at one side and he shook his head. "You're the most stubborn person I've ever met. I don't buy your excuse for being in Dublin for a second. You could have transferred the money to the Kowalskis without showing up in person. You're up to something, and I'm willing to bet it has to do with a scheme to come up with twenty-five thousand euros by the end of June. Whatever it is, don't do it."

"For all you know, I could have found a legit way to raise the money."

He raised an eyebrow. "Have you?"

She dropped her gaze. "It's legit, all right."

Kiss Shot

"But not something you feel comfortable doing," he guessed, correctly interpreting the expression on her face.

"Please drop the subject, Shane. We need to concentrate on rescuing Kevin. Let me worry about getting the money to pay the Kowalskis."

He opened his mouth as if to say more but then closed it again. "All right. If you change your mind and want to confide in me, I'm here."

Her gut twisted painfully. Why did he have to be so damn nice? It made using and losing him all the harder. Ruthie swallowed past the lump in her throat and quickened her pace to a jog. "We'd better hurry. Reuben sounded impatient on the phone. Which warehouse is theirs?"

"They own the green building down on the left, and the red one opposite."

"Let's try the red one first."

The front door of the warehouse was locked and the yard deserted.

"There's a back entrance," Shane said. "I've been here before."

Ruthie followed him around to the back of the building. He rapped hard on the door, and the noise echoed inside. A moment later, the sound of scraping metal indicated someone was sliding back the bolts. The door opened a crack to reveal a huge man with a shaven head. "What do you want?" he demanded in a thick Polish accent.

"We're here to speak to Adam. Or Reuben if Adam's away."

The man's gaze swiveled to the side and he raked Ruthie with his beady eyes. If his sneer was any indication, he wasn't impressed by what he saw. Well, neither was she. "Wait here," the man barked before slamming the door behind him.

"Friendly dude," Ruthie said. "The Kowalskis sure know how to pick them."

A minute passed before the door opened again. The big man stood aside. "Boss will see you." He didn't elaborate as to which of his bosses he was referring to. "Gotta check you for weapons first."

Shane submitted to a pat-down without complaint. Ruthie cooperated—until the moment his hands strayed over her chest and lingered. Fucking pervert. She glared at the man. "Get your paws off my breasts."

He drew back his lips in a snarl but released her. "Simmer down, lady. I need to make sure you're not carrying."

"We're not," Ruthie said. "We told you that already."

The guy's beady eyes grew shrewd. "I get told a lot of things. Some of them might even be true."

A thug and a philosopher rolled into one. Who knew?

After the bodyguard was satisfied that neither of them was in a position to shoot up the place, he led them to a door at the far end of the room. He knocked twice and opened the door. "After you," he said with a smirk, his eyes lingering on her breasts.

Ruthie's hands balled into fists. One more word from the prick and she'd rearrange his face.

Shane yanked her through the door. "Leave it," he said in a low rumble that tickled her skin and turned her senses to molten lava. "He's not worth antagonizing. Focus on freeing Kevin."

She gritted her teeth and forced her fingers to uncurl. Shane was correct. Of course he was. But men who used their physical strength to harass and intimidate women were her pet peeve. Had the circumstances been different, she'd have challenged that wanker of a bodyguard to a fight. And she'd have made damn sure she won.

On the other side of the metal door was a large room, empty apart from the carefully arranged tableau in the center. Reuben Kowalski sat sprawled on an overly stuffed sofa. The rest of the room was bare, save for a stool on which Kevin perched, his hands tied behind his back and a gag in his mouth, flanked by two of Reuben's hired thugs. Ruthie's skin turned to gooseflesh at the sight of the desperate expression in her brother's eyes.

"Hey, Reuben," Shane said, his tone casual. "How's tricks?"

What the fuck was he playing at? Ruthie slid him a dark look, but he answered her glare with a reassuring smile.

Reuben's toothy grin wasn't reflected in his ice-blue eyes. Had it not been for his inner sociopath looming close to the surface, he might have been handsome. He had thick collar-length hair with a touch of silver threaded through the black strands; a strong jaw, clean-shaven to reveal the cleft in his chin; and a broad nose that had been straightened since she'd last seen the man.

Kowalski's hard gaze focused on Shane. "What are you doing here? I don't recall inviting you."

"Surely your brother-in-law doesn't need an invitation?"

Reuben's nostrils flared. "This is a private meeting. Keep out of it."

"Your 'private meeting' just so happens to be with my friend's brother." Shane nodded in Kevin's direction, then turned his attention to Ruthie. "She's keen to know why he's being held against his will."

Ruthie bristled at not taking the lead in the conversation, but Shane appeared to know how to handle his brother-in-law. Or at least, she hoped he did.

As if reading her thoughts, Reuben stood and stretched, languid as a panther and just as deadly. "I had matters to discuss with Mr. Reynolds. Matters that he hasn't answered to my satisfaction."

Kiss Shot

"How the hell is he supposed to answer if he's gagged?" Ruthie demanded. "Cut the shite, Kowalski. I'm not due to pay the next installment until the end of the month. What the fuck are you playing at?"

Shane placed a hand on her shoulder and pressed gently, indicating she should simmer down. "We'd like to take Kevin home."

Reuben threw his head back and laughed, revealing dazzlingly white teeth. "I'm sure you would. However, there's the small matter of the money he owes me, not to mention the fact that the stupid fuck launched an unprovoked attack on one of the regular punters at my club."

Ruthie's heart sank. She gave Shane an anguished look, and then turned to Reuben. "Kevin hasn't been himself lately."

The other man snorted. "Kevin is out of control, Ms. Reynolds. But what concerns me more than his behavior is the money he still owes me."

"She told you she'd pay it by the end of the month," Shane said, "and she will. Right, Ruthie?"

Ruthie nodded. "I keep my word."

"I'm sure you do, but the agreement you struck was with my brother Adam, no? For the money Kevin still owes us from the gambling debts he ran up at our casino?"

She blinked, and a sense of icy foreboding crept over her skin. "Well, yes."

Reuben's sly smile stretched across his face. "I'm talking about the twelve thousand euros Kevin owes *me*. Did he not mention that to you?"

Ruthie tasted bile. The sick dread that had crept over her skin now oozed from every pore. In his chair, Kevin squirmed, suddenly finding the dusty floor fascinating. What the fuck had he done this time? The guy was a walking, talking liability.

"What twelve thousand euros, Kevin? You told me the fifty grand was everything you owed."

Reuben's laughter echoed off the walls. "Lady, your brother owes money all over Dublin. My brother and I just happen to be the first people to put serious pressure on him to pay us back."

She sucked in a breath and drew an unsteady hand through her damp hair. She shot her brother a look of pure venom. There was no way in hell she could find an extra twelve thousand by the end of the month, never mind cough it up immediately. Her arrangement with the agency only covered the twenty-five thousand for the second installment.

Shane cleared his throat. "Ruthie has agreed to get Adam his money by the end of this month. How about she pays you at the end of July?" She squawked in protest, but Shane ignored her and added, "With interest, of course."

Of course. Christ on a bike. How the hell was she supposed to come up with the money? Sell a kidney?

Kiss Shot

Reuben's smirk widened. "I have no intention of giving this piece of shit any more time to pay me back. If his sister can come up with twenty-five grand for Adam by the end of the month, I'm sure she'll figure out a way to make it thirty-seven grand. And I expect a down payment of two thousand now to cover the interest. In cash." He turned his icy gaze on Ruthie. "Do we have a deal, Ms. Reynolds?"

Her mouth was bone dry. "I can't—"

"It's a deal." Shane's deep voice interrupted her. "You'll have the two thousand by this evening, Reuben. The usual place, I presume?"

Ruthie's jaw tightened. What was Shane doing?

Reuben's hard stare shifted from her to Shane and back again. With a smirk, he drew a key from his suit pocket. "Catch." He tossed the key to Shane, who caught it one-handed. "Locker fifty-two at the Kilpatrick bus station. I want the money put there by six o'clock this evening, and not a second later. I'm only letting Reynolds go now as a courtesy to you, Shane. Don't fuck me around."

"Got it." Shane's jaw jutted, and he jerked his head in Kevin's direction. "Now untie him."

Ruthie longed to slap the condescending smirk from Reuben's face. "If we agree to pay this extra debt, this is where it ends," she said in a voice that sounded braver than she felt. "And I expect you to give me a list of what exactly Kevin did to run up another twelve thousand euros."

Reuben erupted with laughter, clearly finding her demand hilarious. "I'm not running a fucking shop here. We don't furnish our customers with receipts. Your brother's debt to me is because he failed to hand over all the money he made on a drug deal that I set up. Still want that itemized list?"

Ruthie opened her mouth to deliver a crushing insult, but closed it again when Shane's hand closed around her arm. "We're good," he said to Reuben. "Now let Kevin go, and we'll be on our way."

Kowalski gave Ruthie a slow up-and-down and his smirk returned. "Your sister to the rescue again, eh, Reynolds? She's got more muscle than you. Maybe she's got more balls."

Ruthie placed her hands on her hips and glared at the man. "Stop screwing us around, Kowalski. Let Kevin go."

Reuben nodded to his henchmen, who unbound Kevin's wrists and ankles and ripped the tape from his mouth. He stared back at them with dull eyes and staggered to his feet.

Ruthie rushed forward. "Lean on me if you need to."

Her brother shook her off. "I'm all right," he muttered. "I can walk out of here on my own."

His tone stung, but she understood his need to show Reuben he wasn't entirely dependent on his sister. With Ruthie and Shane bringing up the rear, Kevin limped out of the warehouse. In silence, they trudged back through the industrial estate to the spot where Shane had left his car.

"Will I drop you back to your dad's house?" Shane asked after he slid behind the wheel.

"Please." Ruthie fastened her seatbelt and cast a look over her shoulder. Kevin sat on the backseat, looking glum. Beside him, Flash snoozed in his cage, oblivious to the tension around him. She turned back to Shane. "Thanks for coming with me."

"No problem. You helped me out earlier."

But not to the tune of two grand. A wave of nausea rolled over her, and Ruthie rolled down the car window for some air. How could she borrow money from a man she was spying on? The mere thought of it turned the air to lead. She dragged in a breath and contemplated her options. Bar robbing a shop between now and six o'clock, she had two choices: confide in her father, or accept Shane's offer of help.

When Shane pulled up outside the house, Kevin murmured his thanks and got out of the car. His shoulders hunched, he shuffled up the short path to the front door and let himself into the house. Ruthie lingered by the car, the passenger door ajar.

"I know what you're going to say," Shane interjected before she could utter a word, "and it's fine. I have the money. You can pay me back whenever you're able to."

She bit her lip. "That might not be for a while."

"Not a problem." He smiled at her and his blue eyes twinkled. "We go way back, Ruthie. I trust you. I know you'll pay me back when you can."

I trust you... His words burned like corrosive acid. She was the last person he should trust. Her stomach in free fall, she exhaled through her teeth. "Can you hold off for an hour? I need time to think." *Time to hope for a miracle.*

Shane reached over to squeeze her hand. "That's fine. Send me a text when you've made up your mind, but don't leave it too long."

"Thank you." She swallowed past the pain in her throat. "For everything."

"Friends help each other out," he said quietly. "You did me a favor this morning."

"Me driving you and your dog to the vet pales in comparison to you helping me rescue Kevin. Will it cause hassle between you and Reuben?"

He shrugged. "Maybe. I can't say I'm bothered if he avoids me at future family gatherings. It's not like we're close."

She hesitated for a moment and shifted her weight from one leg to the other. "I'd better check on Kevin."

Shane inclined his head in acknowledgment. "Let me know about the money, yeah?"

"Will do." She waved and was about to follow Kevin into the house when Shane called out to her.

"Hey, Ruthie?"

She pivoted on the balls of her feet. "Yeah?"

Kiss Shot

"Before I forget, I spoke to Dan. He's okay with you using the gym early in the morning as long as I'm there to let you in."

She beamed at him. This was the first good news she'd had all day. "That's fantastic. What time is early?"

"Four in the morning." He grimaced. "I'm sorry it's so extreme, but Lar and Dan usually get in a session between five and six. I figured you'd want privacy in the changing room."

Privacy from all but him. A shiver of anticipation coiled its way down her spine. "When suits you to meet?"

"Does tomorrow work for you? Call me when you get to the front door and I'll come down to let you in." His sexy half smile tempted her to kiss him, but she hung back.

"Sounds like a plan." She forced a smile. "I'll be in touch later."

TWELVE

When Ruthie entered the house, her brother was in the kitchen, fidgeting and tugging at the bands around his thin wrists. She glanced through the window, but there was no sign of their father or the dogs.

"Dad left a note," Kevin muttered, holding up a crumpled piece of paper. "He's taken the dogs out for a walk."

"Did he mention me borrowing the car without asking?" she asked and dropped onto the seat opposite her brother.

"Nah." Kevin resumed his restless fidgeting. "I gotta go out. I'm way late to my friend's house."

Friend, my arse. Drug dealer was more like it. If her brother had wanted the world to know he was jonesing for a fix, his behavior was as effective as a flashing neon sign. "We have to talk about what happened, Kev. This crap can't continue."

Kiss Shot

"I don't want to talk about it." He rocked back and forth in a jerky manner without appearing to be aware of his movements. "Don't you need to get Dad's car from wherever you dumped it?"

The Land Rover was still parked outside St. Patrick's Church, probably one of the few locations in Kilpatrick where it was unlikely to be robbed. "I'll deal with the car later. Where did Kowalski pick you up? You can't have gotten far after you left the house."

Her brother's jerky movements ceased for a moment, then renewed with vigor. "At the end of our street. Two of his guys grabbed me and shoved me into a car."

"In broad daylight? That's bold, even for Reuben."

Kevin shrugged. "The Kowalskis do what they like. They know no one around here will rat them out to the Guards."

Of course not. Her lip curled. Curtains might twitch, but their owners would look the other way once their curiosity had been assuaged. "You need to tell me how much money you owe. The real figure this time."

"I don't know." Her brother stared at his knuckles. "A lot, I guess."

You don't say. "Can you be more specific? Like, is there another notorious Dublin thug waiting in the wings to cause trouble?"

His eyes met hers, radiating defensiveness. "I don't know, okay? I owe a few guys money, but the Kowalskis are the real problem."

"I can't come up with any more cash. I'm bled dry until the end of the month. Paying off the first installment drained my savings account."

Her brother rocked back and forth. "I'm going out later. Maybe I'll get lucky tonight."

"If any other man uttered those words, I'd assume he meant sex," Ruthie said dryly. "But if it's gambling you're referring to, don't do it. Apart from the risk of running up more debts, Kowalski wants two thousand by six o'clock this evening."

Her brother shifted his attention to his scuffed boots. "Delaney said he'd loan you the money."

Ruthie's chest swelled with the searing anger that had been building since she'd entered the kitchen. "You seriously want me to borrow from Shane? Where's your pride? Shane Delaney isn't even your friend." *Anymore.* The word echoed through the kitchen, unspoken yet understood. And they both knew Kevin was at fault for the end of that friendship.

"What's the alternative?" her brother demanded. "We can't ask Dad."

"For the two grand, maybe we can, but we'd need to spin him a line."

Kevin reared back and gaped at her in horror. "No way. He'd guess something was up, and then he'd start digging."

"Do you want me to owe money to Shane Delaney? I know we said we'd keep Dad out of this, but if your

Kiss Shot

debts extend beyond the Kowalskis, I don't see how that's possible. I won't be in Dublin forever. And even if I were, I can't keep bailing you out."

"You don't get it, Ruthie. Telling Dad will kill him."

"Only if he tries to take on Adam and Reuben. Maybe there's a way we can reason with him. Even if we don't say who you owe money to, or how much, Dad needs to know your gambling is out of control."

Kevin leaped up and grabbed her hands, squeezing them tighter than was comfortable. "Please, sis. Whatever we do, our father can't be involved. I feel bad enough that I dragged you into this. I don't want to be responsible for Dad dying."

Tears stung her eyes and she blinked them back. This was the first time he'd shown true gratitude for her help over his debts. The old Kev—the sober version who took his prescribed medication on schedule—was the sweetest brother any girl could have. The drugged-up incarnation was selfish and self-absorbed, too concerned with getting his next fix to care about the shit he'd dragged his sister into.

"Our father has to know about the gambling," she said. "And it would be better coming from you."

"Seriously?" Her brother stared at her, maintaining eye contact for the first time since she'd joined him in the kitchen. "Do you want Dad to have another heart attack?"

Her stomach plummeted and an icy dread dripped through her veins. "What are you talking about? What heart attack?"

"The one he had last summer." The words tripped off Kevin's tongue in such a matter-of-fact tone that she wanted to take him by the shoulders and shake him.

"Dad had a fucking *heart attack,* and no one thought to tell me?" She felt as though the air had been sucked from her lungs, making every word an effort. How could they keep this from her?

A flicker of guilt passed over her brother's face. "He didn't want to worry you."

She could picture the scenario with vivid clarity. Her father, stubborn as ten mules, adamant that his little girl wasn't to be told. The last thing he'd have wanted was Ruthie coming back to Dublin to look after him and getting sucked into the very life he'd always wanted her to avoid. She put her head in her hands and groaned. "For heaven's sake. This family has too many secrets. Okay, out with it. What happened to Dad?"

"He collapsed in the garden last summer. I called an ambulance, and the doctors at the hospital said he'd had a mild heart attack."

Ruthie blinked back tears. "You should have called me."

"I never call you."

"Except when you want me to pay your debts," she snapped. She was done pandering to Kev's feelings, fed up with walking on eggshells in case she'd trigger an outburst or a bout of depression. Being mentally ill wasn't an excuse to treat others like shit.

Her brother ran a trembling hand through his short curls. "Look, maybe I should have let you know—"

"Maybe?" She was shouting now, but beyond caring. "Of course you should have told me. He's my father as well as yours. I had a right to know he was in the hospital."

"It was Dad's decision to make. He didn't want people knowing he was ill."

In their father's line of work, showing any sign of weakness was an invitation for his business rivals to encroach on his territory. She understood that, but she didn't accept it as an excuse for them keeping the heart attack a secret from her. "I'm not 'people'. I'm Dad's daughter. I had a right to know."

Kevin sighed. "Dad didn't want to worry you."

"I'm an adult. Worry goes with the territory. Had I known, I'd have caught the first flight home."

"That's precisely what Dad didn't want you to do. He's glad you got out of Dublin and made a life for yourself. He's proud of you." Kevin's lips twisted into a bitter smile. "He'd change his tune if he knew what you do for a living."

She was on her feet in an instant, snarling. "Fuck you. You have no idea what it is I've done to get the money to pay off *your* debt."

Her brother snorted. "Whatever it is, I'm betting Dad wouldn't approve. Where did you get the money to pay the first installment, anyway? I doubt it was by legal means."

Breathing heavily, she glared at him. "You ungrateful little shit. You can assume what you like, but know this—I'm not doing this for you. If you weren't my brother, I'd let you rot, but I don't want Dad to get himself killed going after the Kowalskis."

The mocking expression vanished from Kevin's face, replaced with a look of contrition. "I'm sorry. I shouldn't have said that. I don't know what came over me. I need—"

"Don't you dare use your addiction or other issues as an excuse to speak to me like that. You were willing enough to ask no questions when the Kowalskis were threatening to break every bone in your body."

Despite her best efforts to block her guilt, her brother's words had struck a chord. Nothing in Kevin's not-very-fertile imagination could come close to the truth of what she'd done to get the money, nor what she was about to do. Ruthie had sold out. She was willing to betray people she'd known all her life in return for cold, hard cash. An image of Shane's face flashed before her eyes. He was a decent guy. He didn't deserve to be used like this. And then she thought of her father—big and burly and gruff, but with a heart of gold. She had to push through for his sake.

Ruthie dropped back into her chair and glowered at her brother. "What's the situation with Dad? Is he still having treatment?"

Kevin stared out the kitchen window, unblinking. "He sees a specialist every couple of months and he's on medication."

The lump in her throat grew larger. The thought of losing her father was unbearable. "One of you should have told me," she insisted. "I had a right to know."

"Not if Dad didn't want you to. Look, you know what he's like. He wants to protect us. With you so far away, he probably figured there was no point in upsetting you."

"I should have been told," she repeated. "He's my father, too."

"If it had been my choice to make, I'd have told you. Dad asked me not to, and I respected his decision."

She eyed him with skepticism. Kevin thought only of Kevin. Having her home cramped his style. When he'd contacted her about his debt, he'd had no inkling she'd show up in Dublin a couple of months later. Ruthie took a deep breath and forced all uncharitable thoughts about her brother out of her mind. Kevin was family. She didn't need to like the man to love him.

As if reading her thoughts, her brother got to his feet and put his arm around her shoulders, awkwardly at first, then with a firmer grip. "I'm sorry for what I said. I am grateful for your help, sis. I don't know what I'd do without you."

Ruthie turned into his embrace and hugged her brother for the first time in a decade. It was like hugging a stranger, or the ghost of someone she'd once known. "What happened to us?" she whispered. "We used to be a close family."

"We know what happened," Kevin said in a voice roughed by emotion. "Mum died, and we all fell apart."

"If she were alive, she'd kick our arses for screwing up so badly."

"If she were alive, everything would be different," he said with touching simplicity.

"Do you really believe that?" She searched his face for clues as to his state of mind but drew a blank. "I don't know that I do."

Her brother patted her on the back and took a step back, the restless energy back in force. He ran a hand over the back of his neck. "I need to head out. Thank you for helping me today."

Heading out to buy drugs... But bar locking him in the house, what could she do to stop him? She forced a smile, determined to maintain their tentative truce. "It's Shane you should be thanking. I don't think Reuben would have listened to me if he hadn't been there."

"You should stay away from Delaney," Kevin murmured. "He's going to have a major bust-up with Rueben Kowalski soon."

Kiss Shot

"How do you know that?"

Her brother averted his gaze. "I just do."

The wheels rotated in her mind. "Over Kaylee?"

Kevin's spun on his heels. "How did you know?"

"Shane's main link to Reuben Kowalski is his sister. Why the falling out? What's Reuben done to her?"

"He doesn't treat her right." Her brother's expression hardened. "She deserves better than that son of a bitch."

"That Reuben is a crap husband doesn't surprise me, but I'm more concerned with our problems than the state of his marriage."

Kevin shuffled to the kitchen door. "Just think about what I said. I don't want you having anything more to do with the Kowalskis than necessary."

After her brother had left, Ruthie sat at the kitchen table and poured herself a whiskey. The alcohol did little to calm her nerves, but she relished the burning sensation as it snaked down her throat. She blew out a breath. Every bone in her body ached with weariness. She'd thought—no, she'd hoped—that the debt was the only issue she needed to sort out. Now that she was back under the same roof as her brother, the strain their father was living with was palpable. No wonder he had heart problems. Whatever happened, he couldn't know how serious the situation with Kevin had grown. She hadn't come so far, hadn't made a deal with the devil, just to drag her father down with her.

Ruthie squared her shoulders and blew out an invisible smoke ring, the one aspect she missed from her short-lived days as a smoker. She was on her own, but she'd make good. One way or the other, she always did. At least she could take her frustration out on the bags tomorrow morning.

Shane's face swam before her eyes, and guilt burned through her. She reached for her phone and wrote him a text accepting his offer of a loan. Her finger hovered over the display. He trusted her, and she was about to betray him and all the people he held dear in return for cold, hard cash. She hit Send.

THIRTEEN

At a quarter to four the next morning, Shane let himself and Flash into Dan's gym. Barking with a ferocity surprising for one so small, Flash scampered across the floor and headed straight for the back of the gym. The puppy's bushy tail and wild fur appeared fluffier after yesterday's bath at the vet's. Shane stifled a laugh. The dog bounded along on his stumpy legs, resembling a hairy footrest.

"Hey, wait up," he called, his pace hampered by the dog's travel cage.

The puppy ignored him.

*Yeah...*he had to sign them up for a local obedience class. If Flash was to be a permanent fixture in his life, the dog needed to learn discipline—or, at the very least, stop chewing up Shane's apartment.

Flash skidded to a halt in front of the changing room. He barked twice, unsure of himself, and sat, panting, waiting for Shane to catch up.

"What are you barking at?" Shane bent down to pet the dog and Flash responded with a plaintive whine. "Or should I ask, whom?"

Dan and Lar were lounging by the changing room lockers—Lar sported a grin, and Dan wore his early morning grumpy look. Gen, Lar's girlfriend, sat on a bench lacing up her shoes. She shot Shane a look of bemusement. "So this is the infamous rescue puppy."

"Yeah." Shane swung the travel cage onto the bench beside Gen, followed by his sports bag. "What are you all doing here so early? I thought you'd arranged to meet at five."

"We had," Lar said cheerfully, "but we didn't want to miss the opportunity to see your new girlfriend in action. I hear she's talented."

Girlfriend...he made a lousy prospective boyfriend. Ruthie deserved a guy without a fucked-up family and with a steady job. Shane unzipped his sports bag and removed his boxing gear before responding. "Ruthie is not my girlfriend," he said finally. "She's an old pal."

"Bollocks," Dan said. "You hate early mornings. No way would you get your arse out of bed for an 'old pal.'"

"The dog needed to go out," Shane offered lamely, "and I figured I might as well stay up and get in a session."

Lar's gaze dropped to the puppy. His grin grew wider. "Is it my imagination, or is he bushier than yesterday? Are you seriously keeping that hairball?"

Kiss Shot

"'That hairball' has a name," Shane said with dignity. "And yes, I'm keeping him."

Gen kneeled down to let the puppy sniff her hand. "He's kind of cute, in a weird sort of way. What did you decide to call him?"

"Flash. As in flash drive." The dog responded to his new name instantly and bounded up to Shane as fast as his stumpy legs could carry him, then rolled onto his back, revealing his privates to the world.

Lar gave a hoot of laughter. "More like Flash as in flasher."

Flash responded with a woof, rolled over again, and gave everyone an excellent view of his arse.

Shane's cousins erupted with laughter. Flash, unsure of their intent, pawed at Shane's leg and whined to be picked up. "Don't listen to those eejits," he said as he scooped up the puppy. "You're smarter than the pair of them combined."

"Why's he here, anyway?" Dan asked, eyes narrowing with suspicion. "What's he done to your apartment?"

"What you're really asking is what's he about to do to your gym. Nothing—as long as I keep an eye on him. It's when I don't pay attention that the trouble starts."

"If he chews on anything he's not supposed to, he's out on his tail," Dan warned. "I'm serious, Shane. I can't have him pissing all over the place."

"I'll make sure he behaves. I brought his cage in the hope he'll snooze."

Dan eyed the dog warily. "He looks wide awake to me."

"When's Ruthie due to arrive?" Lar asked, bouncing back and forth in a boxer shuffle. "Because we don't want to cramp your style. Five's a crowd and all that."

"Five's a crowd...and yet you made sure to be here."

"Unless you *want* us to stay," Lar added slyly. "Seeing as she's just an old pal..."

"It's Dan's gym. You can do what you like." Shane pulled on his gloves and headed for the bags, Flash at his heels.

"Tell you what," Lar said, bringing up the rear. "Dan and I will go into a ring and spar for a bit while Gen goes to the weight room. That'll give you and Ruthie some privacy."

"We don't need privacy. I'm hardly going to bone her with you three prowling the premises."

"So you have considered it?" Lar punched his palm and beamed with delight. "I knew it. A much better choice than Adam Kowalski's ex."

Shane bit back a nasty retort. His irritation with Lar was only partly to do with the teasing over Ruthie and the dog. Looking his cousin in the eye was hard to do these days, yet he had to maintain a semblance of normality in their interaction.

"Hey, do you want to watch a film or something this evening?" Lar asked. "Gen is meeting Emma for drinks, and I'm home alone."

Kiss Shot

"And you find yourself at a loose end." Despite his efforts to keep his tone neutral, Shane registered the irritation in his voice.

Lar met his eye. "I'm sorry I've been busy lately. With starting the company and Gen moving in, I haven't had a chance for downtime."

Shane took the steps up to the area that housed the training bags. Lar followed him.

"Come on, man. What's up? You've been moody for weeks."

Shane stiffened, and a surge of fury burned his chest. He wanted to rant and rave at his cousin, but he needed to keep his cool for a while more. Just long enough to find out what information Lar had passed on to the government. "I'm okay," he said, "really."

"Bollocks. It's not like you to be surly and uncommunicative."

"We can't all be as charming as you," Shane said dryly. "In case it's escaped your notice, I'm always quieter than you are."

"Yeah, but with outsiders. Never with family and friends. Is Frank giving you a hard time for joining the Triskelion Team?"

"He's not pleased." This statement was true but it wasn't the reason for Shane's aloofness.

Lar sighed and shook his head. "I'm sorry, cuz. Breaking away from Frank's influence is bound to be harder for you than for Dan and me. Why don't you come round to my place later? I'll stock up on whiskey and we can watch a shite film and have a laugh."

"Not tonight," Shane said quickly. He wasn't ready to be alone with his cousin, faking sociability.

"Ah-ha." Lar grinned. "Are you meeting Ruthie?"

"Yeah," Shane replied, seizing on the excuse. "I'm cooking her dinner."

"Are you now?" asked a very familiar female voice. "What's on the menu?"

Shane and Lar spun around. Ruthie stood at the top of the steps, clad in workout gear and wearing a knowing smile. Shane's heart skidded and thumped against his ribs. She looked so damn sexy in her boxing shorts and the tight tank top that showed off her firm upper arms. Had circumstances been different, he'd have shoved her against the wall and kissed her, long and hard. And then he'd have stripped her out of those shorts and taken her right there and then and screw the consequences.

"You know he's a lousy cook, right? You'd better stock up on indigestion tablets." Lar slid into charm mode, flashing Ruthie the killer smile that had seduced countless women over the years. Shane wasn't even sure his cousin was aware of his natural charisma, but he was painfully aware of his lack thereof. All through their teen years, girls had flocked to Lar and ignored his geeky sidekick. Shane had gained confidence over time, but there were moments he still felt overshadowed by his confident cousin.

Kiss Shot

In contrast to just about every other instance of Shane and Lar talking to the same woman, Ruthie's eyes slid toward Shane's. She held his gaze for a long moment, and then a sly smile tugged at the corners of her mouth. "No need to worry. I've agreed to give Shane a cooking lesson."

Shane's body tightened. She managed to make it sound like a lesson in a lot more than cooking.

"Shane is learning to cook?" Gen climbed up to join them, glanced curiously at Ruthie, and smiled. "Hi, there. I'm Gen, Lar's girlfriend."

"Ruthie Reynolds. I've heard a lot about you."

Had she? Not from him. Big Mike must have mentioned Lar's new girlfriend.

"If you're in Dublin for a while, I'm sure we'll run into each other again," Gen said smoothly, shooting Shane a mischievous glance. "Maybe even next Saturday."

Jaysus. Gen didn't do subtlety. Although inviting Ruthie to Siobhan's party had crossed his mind...

A grin suffused Ruthie's face. "Once I've taught Shane to cook, maybe he can cook us all dinner."

"Haha. Very funny." Not that she could know, but dinner with Lar was the last thing Shane wanted to do. He ran a hand over the back of his neck. *Shit.* It was too early in the morning to deal with all these people, especially ones who stirred up strong emotions. "Want to get started?" he asked Ruthie.

She nodded. "Sure."

An amused smile tugged at the corners of Gen's mouth, but she took the hint. "Let's leave them to it, Lar. Will you be at the office later, Shane?"

He grunted his assent. "Gotta hand in a report."

"I'll see you then." Gen nodded at Ruthie. "Nice to meet you."

Lar's gaze moved from Ruthie to Shane and back again. "We'll leave you two to punch each other's lights out in preparation for your romantic evening together. I can see it now—matching black eyes to go with the lovey-dovey expressions."

Shane's cheeks grew warm. "Get screwed."

Lar's laughter echoed back at them as he descended the stairs. "I'll leave that pleasure to the two of you."

"Don't mind him," Shane said after Lar and Gen were out of earshot. "He's a dork."

Ruthie raised an eyebrow. "Did I sense an edge to that exchange?"

She was too sharp for his own good. "It's... complicated."

"And you'd rather not talk about it," she finished with a grin. "Got it."

"How did you get in? I didn't hear my phone ring."

"I knocked on the back door on the off-chance you'd hear me and Dan let me in." She cocked her head to the side. "So...were you serious about dinner?"

"Assuming you don't have plans, sure."

She flashed him a cheeky grin. "I'm not sure how great a teacher I'll be if you want to learn how to cook. I can just about boil water."

He laughed. Man, having Ruthie around even made mornings bearable. "How about takeout?"

"That sounds like an excellent plan."

Shane checked his gloves. "Ready to get to work?"

"Definitely. I haven't had a good workout since I got back to Dublin. I've gone jogging, but it's not the same. There's something cathartic about practicing my punches."

"It's a great stress reliever." And stress relief was what he'd needed over the last few weeks.

"I know what you mean." She grabbed a bag, then got her fists into position. "Okay. Here goes. Thirty minutes or bust."

Once they started, conversation ceased. For the first few minutes, Shane was hyperaware of Ruthie's presence, but the familiar rhythmic pounding and the sound of their footfalls bouncing back and forth eased him into a state of extreme focus. Flash snuffled around the room for a while before he settled onto his blanket and fell asleep.

Thirty minutes became forty and then fifty. Gen and his cousins called goodbye when they left, leaving Shane and Ruthie alone in the gym. After they'd been working out for a solid hour, they were both covered in sweat and flushed from their boxer's high.

"Gosh, I needed that." Ruthie mopped her brow with a towel. Even wet with sweat, she was hot as hell. "But now I need a shower."

A vision of Ruthie naked turned his mouth to ash. Her eyes met his and darkened with a desire that matched his own. He took a step toward her, noting her intake of breath. "Want help with your shower gel, Miss Ruthie?"

"Oh, yes," she said, her voice a husky whisper that made him throb with need. "But on one condition."

"What's that?"

She smiled and drew a fingertip down his torso, pausing just above the waistline of his shorts. "I get to help you with yours."

FOURTEEN

Shane dragged her toward the shower room and pushed her against the wall. When he claimed her mouth with his, the last vestiges of Ruthie's self-control shattered. *Oh, God, yes.* He deepened the kiss, turning her world into a kaleidoscope of physical reactions. She ran her palms down his chest, pausing to tease first his nipples and then his navel.

"You're gorgeous," he murmured. "So beautiful."

His touch sent a ripple of desire through her body. She stared, mesmerized, at his muscles. He was strong and well built by nature, but hours of training at the bags had added to his bulk.

She traced a tattoo of a mermaid. "I like this one," she said. "It's new since I first saw you with your shirt off."

"I've added a few tattoos and piercings since then, but I have a long way to go before I catch up with Dan."

"New piercings?" She tweaked his nipple rings. "I didn't notice any."

His rough laugh had an aphrodisiac effect, especially when coupled with him touching her bare arm. "That's because we didn't get far enough last time for you to see them. I'm happy to model them for you now."

Her mouth grew dry and her body ached with need. She'd wanted Shane all those years ago, but the intense desire she felt now made those tentative feelings pale in comparison. "I'm more than happy to let you put on a private 'modeling' show for me, Shane Delaney. Dare I hope it involves you getting naked?"

His laughter intensified. "It would be hard to show you all my piercings if I didn't." He tugged at her top and pulled it over her head. Underneath, she wore her sweaty sports bra.

"I wasn't planning on being seduced," she whispered.

"You look beautiful, Ruthie. You're perfect as you are."

"I'd have preferred to wow you with sexy underwear."

"Nah," he said and tugged at her bra strap. "It suits you better than latex or lace."

"Latex?" Ruthie shuddered. "I can't imagine wearing latex underwear."

He grinned. "Like I said before, I'm used to seeing lingerie at my father's club. It takes all sorts, I guess. But right now, the only woman's underwear I'm interested in is yours...and my main concern is removing it."

Kiss Shot

Ruthie took a deep breath. *I can do this. He doesn't need to know.* She reached behind her and snapped her bra open.

Shane eased the straps down over her shoulders until she let it fall to the floor. "You're perfect, Ruthie," he said in a hoarse voice. "Absolutely perfect." And then he bent down and claimed one of her nipples with his mouth. She gasped and pressed her head back against the shower wall. God, it felt good. His beard tickled the soft skin of her breast while he suckled her, and his free hand roamed over her torso to tickle her belly and massage her other breast.

Ruthie's breathing changed in tune with her arousal, and by the time Shane claimed her other nipple, she was achy with need. A thought danced through her mind. *I should tell him. I should warn him that I've never...*

A new sensation jolted her back to reality. Shane had trailed kisses over her abdomen and was now teasing her inner thighs with his lips and skimming his thumbs underneath the sides of her knickers. She should tell him to stop, say they needed to talk, but stopping was the last thing she wanted him to do. He tugged her knickers over her hips and down her legs. When they reached her ankles, she kicked them off, her stare never leaving Shane's face. As he raked her naked body with his eyes, his pupils dilated. "You're gorgeous, Ruthie."

Her cheeks burned and her heart beat a little faster. *Here goes.* She straightened her back, stuck out her chest, and resisted the urge to hide her naked body. "There's only one problem with this scenario," she said, enjoying watching him watching her. "You're still dressed."

Shane grinned. "Not for long."

Ruthie's reached out to touch his chest at the precise moment Shane dropped his pants. Her gaze dropped southward.

And she sucked in a breath.

His smooth shaft was already hard. And much bigger than she'd anticipated.

She exhaled in a whoosh as all her old fears flooded back. She couldn't do this. She'd waited too long to lose her virginity. Who was still a virgin at twenty-five? Ruthie squared her shoulders and slammed her insecurities back in the mental drawer where they belonged. No way was she letting her lack of experience chafe at her self-confidence today. Even if Shane wasn't sexy as sin, she had a job to do.

He closed the space between them. A wicked smile tugged at his lips. "Time to get wet, Miss Ruthie."

She blinked in confusion. "What—?"

Before she could register his intent, he'd reached behind her and switched on the shower. Warm water cascaded over her body, washing away the sweat from her workout.

He raised one eyebrow and held up a bottle of shower gel. "Want me to get to work?"

"I..." Her mouth grew dry, her breathing shallow. "Yes."

He started on her arms, massaging the shower gel onto her skin. He worked it into a lather on her back, and his hands moved to her front. By the time he touched her breasts, Ruthie's knees had turned to mush. Shane caressed her breasts with a sinful reverence that made her ache for him in all the right places.

"They're perfect," he murmured, rolling her nipples between his thumb and forefinger. "You're perfect."

"My turn," she whispered. "I want to soap you."

His broad smile brought a twinkle to his eyes. He handed her the shower gel. "Be my guest."

Ruthie started on his torso, working the gel into a lather while tracing the lines of his tattoos. "A triskelion," she murmured, pausing at one.

"I got it when I joined the Triskelion Team. That's the name of Lar's new private security firm."

"Dad mentioned it." And even if he hadn't, the name was included in the agency files she'd read before traveling to Dublin. Her head spun in a whirlwind of conflicting emotions. She wanted this. She wanted him. But how much of her willingness to push past her fears was down to her need to get into his confidence—and better still, his computer?

Shane took her into his arms and kissed her. In the heat of his searing kiss, Ruthie's doubts evaporated. She melted against his chest, relishing the sensation of his wet, soapy skin against hers. Before her brain registered what her hands were doing, she was stroking his erection. Silky-smooth skin contrasted with rock hardness. Her movements were tentative at first, but curiosity soon won out over shyness. Ruthie explored his balls, laughing when he groaned in pleasure. She drew her hand up his shaft to tease the tip.

"You're killing me," Shane grunted. "I don't know how much time we have until the guys start arriving to train."

She trailed kisses along his bearded jawline, sighing when it tickled her skin. "In that case, we'd better make the most of the time we have."

"I couldn't agree more," Shane said and slid to his knees.

Ruthie's heart skipped a beat. "What are you doing?"

He grinned up at her, a wicked twinkle in his eyes. "Something you'll like." Shane started with her toes, teasing each one in turn before shifting his attention to her ankles, calves, and behind her knees.

"Shane, where are you going?"

"Some*where* you'll like. Now shush and relax." He continued his torturous path of kisses past her knees and up her inner thighs. Her chest rose and fell with each rapid breath. Would he kiss her...there...or keep going? An insistent throb between her legs told her exactly how her body felt about this prospect.

Shane paused at the top of her thighs and placed his hands on her behind before resuming his trail of kisses.

Kiss Shot

And then he put his mouth between her legs. She cried out the instant his tongue met her clit, but he ignored her, continuing to dance his tongue around her clit until he finally sucked it. She moaned with pleasure. Nothing she'd ever done to herself had felt this good. But half the excitement wasn't what he was doing to her, but who he was. She'd been hot for Shane for so long, had imagined him making love to her a thousand times. No man she'd met on her travels had come close to eclipsing Shane's place in her heart. Loving a man who was a virtual stranger was crazy. Loving a guy she was paid to spy on was even crazier.

Shane sucked and teased her nub and tickled her until she was close to losing control. He seemed to know when to increase and decrease the pressure without her telling him. Which was just as well, because she hadn't a clue what she was doing. Oral sex was new territory for her. The mere act of letting go and allowing someone such an intimacy was an enormous step for her, but Shane made it seem natural.

He eased the pressure and teased her with his tongue, making her ache with need.

Pleasure surged through her chest, and her breasts tingled with awareness. "Please don't stop what you're doing," she begged. "I'm so close..."

Shane brushed his lips over her inner thighs and reclaimed her clit. He applied more pressure this time, sending the spiral of need ever higher. When she came, she clenched her fists and cried out. A wave of pure bliss engulfed her, followed by another and another.

Ruthie sagged against his chest and felt his heartbeat against her cheek. "Wow," she said between breaths. "Just...wow."

He drew her close and kissed her on the mouth—hard, long, intensely. In the background, muffled laughter drifted into the shower room.

"Shit," Shane said, breaking the embrace. He grabbed their towels from their pegs and threw one at her. Ruthie caught it one-handed. "Get dry while I keep the guys out of the locker room." He wrapped his towel around his hips, blocking the exquisite view of his bare arse, and strode out of the room.

Ruthie pulled her towel around her body and went into the changing area. Shane's phone lay on the bench beside his sports bag. Her heart lurched in her chest. In her own bag, she had the equipment necessary to clone a phone. Remote hacking had proved fruitless—the Triskelion Team's security was rock solid—but she might manage it with a live phone. Pulse pounding, Ruthie took a step toward the bench. Shane's phone was mere centimeters away. She reached out a hand.

The door swung open and she leaped back.

"Sorry. Did I give you a fright?" Shane appeared before her, clad in clean underpants and T-shirt and carrying Flash in his cage. "I told the guys Flash and I were standing guard while you showered."

Kiss Shot

She gave a shaky laugh. "Did they believe you?"

"No," he said cheerfully. "I'm guessing the grin on my face was a dead giveaway."

Ruthie pulled on her usual uniform of functional underwear, combat pants, lace-up boots, and T-shirt. During training, she'd hacked phones, bugged premises, and eavesdropped on private conversations. But she hadn't known any of the people she was spying on, and had the advantage of knowing that everyone she tracked deserved to be behind bars.

Shane was different. Shane was...a mad idea leaped into her mind, danced around, and formed the basis of a plan. Maybe there was another way to get information on Shane and his family. A way that didn't involve betraying Shane. Her heart rate kicked up a notch. If she fessed up during their dinner date, perhaps she could make him understand why she'd agreed to spy on him and his family. With his help, maybe she could glean enough info to feed to the Jarvis Agency, yet not violate the Delaney family's privacy. It was a crazy scheme, but it might just work.

Still lost in thought, she twisted her damp hair into a bun and held it in place with a large clip. "I'm ready when you are."

Shane quickly pulled on his clothes and reached down to pick up Flash's travel cage. The puppy shifted position but didn't wake. "We'll go out the back entrance, aka the fire exit." Shane slid a card from his pocket and held it aloft. "The door is hooked up to an alarm, but I have a key card to disable it temporarily."

Ruthie slung her sports bag over her shoulder and followed him through the changing area to the fire exit. He slid the key card into the lock and punched in a code. Seconds later, they were outside in the lane. The morning was shaping up to be a warm one.

Shane leaned against the wall, and his cheeky smile made her heart skip a beat. "Same time tomorrow morning?" he asked.

Ruthie shoved a stray strand of hair behind her ear and shifted her weight from one leg to the other. Guilt pressed down on her shoulders. Tomorrow would offer her a fresh opportunity to access Shane's phone and perhaps his cousins' phones as well. She had to get him on side and put an end to the subterfuge. "Sure. As long as the early start is okay for you."

Shane's phone beeped. He drew it out of his back pocket, and a frown line appeared between his brows when he glanced at the display. "Shit. Something's come up. I might need to take a rain check on takeout."

"Oh, okay. Maybe another time." Ruthie's heart sank. So much for her cunning plan. She forced a smile to disguise her disappointment.

Shane blew out his cheeks. "The text is from my sister. Something's up. I suspect that something is Reuben."

Ruthie screwed her nose up. "Ouch."

Kiss Shot

"Yeah. It's not like Kaylee to be awake this early. She hasn't contacted me in months." A frown line appeared between his brows. "If Reuben's done something to hurt her, I swear I'll kick that fucker's arse. No one screws with my family."

Ruthie's drew in a sharp breath at the venom in his voice. The Delaneys were a tight-knit bunch and placed a high value on family loyalty. Who had she been kidding when she'd considered telling Shane she'd been sent to spy on them? He'd be furious. "Does Kaylee want you to go around to her place straight away?" she asked faintly.

"She says nine o'clock, but she's probably assuming I'm still asleep." Shane rubbed his neck and appeared distracted. "Listen, before I forget, Siobhan's birthday party is next weekend. That was what Gen was referring to earlier. Do you want to come?" A pink flush stained his cheeks, lending an adorable vulnerability to his bad guy image.

Ruthie's stomach lurched. Here was the chance she'd been waiting for to observe the Delaneys en masse, so why was she struggling to respond? Guilt? Desire? A mixture of both? "Which day is the party on?"

"Saturday evening. I can text you the time. Big Mike will also be there."

Her jaw dropped. "Seriously? When did Dad start hanging out with her?"

Shane shrugged. "A few weeks. Word on the street is that they're seeing each other, but I don't know if that's true."

Her face stretched into a grin. Dad needed a woman in his life, and he and Siobhan would be a good fit. "Maybe I can try my hand at a spot of matchmaking. Do I need to dress up?"

"I'm afraid so. I'll be in a suit and tie. Gen and her sister mentioned going shopping for evening dresses, so I guess that's what the women will be wearing."

Ruthie shuddered. The last time she'd worn a dress was to her First Holy Communion.

Shane shoved his phone back into his pocket. "I need to get moving. If Kaylee wants me at hers by nine, I need to get some work done first."

"Go. I'll see you tomorrow morning if you can't make it tonight."

"I'll let you know either way."

"And Shane?" She hesitated, her attention riveted by the intensity of his blue eyes. "Thanks for helping me out with the money yesterday."

He dropped a kiss onto her forehead. "Not a problem. Have a good day, Ruthie."

Then he disappeared out of sight, leaving her with a racing heart and conflicting emotions. *Dammit.* There was no use in denying the truth. She was in love with Shane Delaney. Of all the men in the world, she had to fall for the one guy she could never have a future with. How could a connection based on lies flourish into a lasting relationship? The quicker she left Dublin, the better.

One way to ensure her exit from Shane's life was sooner rather than later was to gather whatever info she could find on the Delaneys. If confiding in him was out of the question, she'd press on and aim to get results fast. And she'd figured out a way to make a start: the shopping trip Shane had mentioned. All she needed to do was arrange to bump into Gen and her sister, Emma Reilly. The Triskelion Team's security was tight, but could the same be said of Emma Reilly's? As her firm's lone private investigator, Emma was unlikely to have the resources to prevent Ruthie finding an easy backdoor into her system.

Ruthie checked her watch. Five-fifteen. It was time to do some early morning sleuthing.

FIFTEEN

Shane hit the accelerator and drove toward his sister's house. He tugged at his shirt collar. Man, he needed to pull himself together before he arrived. Between the memory of Ruthie in the showers and Kaylee's text, his mind was all over the place. Ruthie's sweet taste was still on his lips. She was fucking gorgeous—all toned muscle and feminine curves. On their ill-fated night of passion five years ago, they hadn't gotten far enough for him to see her fully naked.

The memory of that night weighed on his conscience. Ruthie was right to be pissed that he hadn't contacted her before he left for Australia. He'd driven by her house countless times and deleted several unsent text messages. Problem was, Ruthie stirred up emotions he'd rather not feel. While he was no player—he left that to Lar and Dan—Shane had hooked up with plenty of women over the years. None of these liaisons had developed beyond the casual booty call stage. That suited

Shane just fine. He didn't do relationships. Wasn't cut out for them. As soon as a woman showed signs of getting clingy, he ended it, politely but firmly.

And then Ruthie Reynolds burst back into his life, reigniting the feelings he'd convinced himself he'd imagined five years ago. In the two days since he'd bumped into her at the pub, he hadn't been able to stop thinking about her. Perhaps he was crazy, but a big part of him wanted to do right by her, maybe try out the boyfriend-girlfriend thing.

His phone beeped with an incoming email, drawing his attention back to his destination. His sister's text message had inflamed the sense of unease he'd harbored for months about her situation. Shane slowed to a halt at a stoplight and read the text again while waiting for the traffic lights to change.

Hey, Shane. Sorry I haven't been in touch for a while, but I need your help. Can you come over to my place today? Maybe nine o'clock? Thanks. Kaylee xx P.S.: If you hear from Reuben, please don't tell him I contacted you.

Why didn't she want her husband to know she'd sent Shane a message? And why would she think he'd want to communicate with his arsehole of a brother-in-law unless he had no choice?

He'd never seen eye-to-eye with Reuben Kowalski. After Frank had discovered his only daughter had starred in a couple of porn films to support her drug addiction, he'd lost his temper and thrown Kaylee out of the house.

In Shane's opinion, the more sensible course of action would have been to get her into rehab, but Frank was big on image and even bigger on hypocrisy. In Frank's world, owning a lap dancing club with a not-so-secret brothel in the basement was perfectly acceptable, whereas having a daughter who'd screwed on camera was not.

Within a few months of being turfed out of her home, Kaylee was pregnant by Reuben Kowalski. Rueben had made damn sure Frank knew he was expected to feel grateful that someone was willing to marry his daughter after her checkered past. Shane's nostrils flared. What a load of sexist nonsense.

When he pulled up outside his sister's house, the curtains were drawn and the garden was empty of playing kids, despite the lovely weather. The hairs on the nape of Shane's neck stood on end. Something was very wrong. He locked the car and jogged up the path to the door.

He rang the bell twice, but no one answered. His pulse kicked up in pace. What now? Kaylee wouldn't have gone out, not after she'd asked him to come over immediately. The request was out of character—she'd never have contacted him unless she was desperate.

Shane ran to the back of the house and banged on the back door.

No response. *Shit.*

He peered through the kitchen window and rapped on the glass. "Kaylee," he called. "Are you in there?"

Kiss Shot

After a moment, the back door opened a crack. "Shane?" Her voice was tentative and laced with fear.

"Yeah, it's me. Will you let me in?"

His sister stood back, and Shane stepped inside.

"Holy fuck," he said, his gaze riveted by the scene before him. "What the hell happened?"

Someone had trashed the kitchen. The table lay on its side, and the remains of two chairs were scattered across the floor. The food processor had been hurled against the wall, leaving a sizeable dent in the plaster.

"If you think this is bad," Kaylee said in a weary voice, "you should see the state of the living room."

Shane whirled around and took in his sister's appearance for the first time since he'd entered the house. "My God," he breathed. "What did he do to you, Kaylee?"

One of Kaylee's eyes was swollen shut, and an angry red welt showed on her cheekbone.

"Are those ring marks?" he asked in horror, reaching out to touch her.

She flinched as though he'd strike her, and shuffled into the shadows. "I'll be fine."

"Where is he?" he demanded, his fingers curling into fists.

"He's not due back until tonight. And I don't intend to be here when he arrives." Her eyes met his. "Will you help me, Shane? I can't ask Dad, and Greg and Tom are useless."

"Of course I'll help you." And if helping her included beating Reuben to a pulp, all the better. Shane had never warmed to Kaylee's husband, even though the guy had made efforts to be friendly to his brothers-in-law. Now all he wanted to do to the man was kill him.

Beneath her bruises, his sister looked pale and drawn. Her face was devoid of the heavy makeup she usually wore, and her long blond hair hung lank around her shoulders. Bruises or not, his sister looked as though self-care hadn't been high on her list of priorities for some time.

"Where are the kids?" he asked, moving toward the living room.

"They're upstairs watching a Disney movie."

Thank goodness for that. As Kaylee had said, the living room was a wreck. The luxury flat-screen TV Rueben had boasted about last Christmas was smashed. A bookcase had been pulled from the wall, and its contents spilled onto the carpet. Picture frames were strewn all over the floor in a mad mess of broken glass, ripped paper, and shards of metal.

Shane turned to his sister, and his hands balled into fists at the sight of her bruised and battered face. "Where else did he hurt you?"

"My ribs and stomach," she said dully. "He kicked me."

Shane tasted bile. "My God, Kaylee. How long has this been going on?"

His sister dropped her gaze to the floor. "A while."

"Why didn't you tell me?"

"I've told you now that it's relevant. I'm sorry to drag you into it at all, but the whole family will be affected." She squinted at him through her one good eye. "I want to file for divorce."

Shane's stomach clenched. Reuben wasn't going to like being dumped. "Good for you."

"I'd like you to change the locks for me." Kaylee pulled her dressing gown tight around her thin body. "This isn't our home anymore. Not as far as I'm concerned. But I need to be careful, Shane. Reuben's an animal. Even Adam can't control him."

His fingers dug into his palms. His blood boiled at the thought of that big lummox laying hands on his sister. "Is Adam aware Reuben beats you?"

Kaylee shoved a lank strand of hair out of her face. "I'm not sure. Adam knows things have been tense between Reuben and me, and I doubt it'll be a surprise when I leave his brother."

Shane's lip curled. Little occurred in Adam Kowalski's business that Adam wasn't aware of, and that included his younger brother's dubious shenanigans. People in Kilpatrick referred to the Kowalski brothers, but despite Reuben's strutting about like a peacock, everyone knew that Adam was the man in charge. "I'll keep you safe, Kaylee. You and the kids. I can handle Reuben."

His sister's eyes filled with tears. "I don't know if anyone can. He's been spoiling for a fight for months."

And using her as his punching bag to vent his frustration. Shane put a tentative hand on his sister's arm. "I won't let him hurt you again."

"It's you I'm concerned about now that I've dragged you into this mess."

"I can look after myself." He paused for a moment, weighing his next words. "I know this isn't what you want to hear, but we'll have to tell Dad. If anyone can keep you out of Reuben's way, he can."

His sister stared at him through tired eyes that had seen too much. "I told Dad about the abuse a couple of weeks ago. He didn't want to know. He just slammed the door of his shithole club in my face."

Shane's spine stiffened. So much for his father's talk of family loyalty. How could Frank turn his back on his daughter when she was in obvious distress? Everyone knew Reuben Kowalski was a mean son of a prick. "Let me get this straight—our father knew what Reuben was doing to you and refused to help?"

Kaylee blew out a breath and nodded. "He doesn't want a fight with the Kowalskis, especially now that Jimmy Connolly is dead."

"What does Connolly's death have to do with anything?" Shane asked, frowning. "Does he suspect the Kowalskis of being behind the hit?"

"That was the impression I got."

Kiss Shot

And yet Frank had told Shane that Lar was behind the killing. His hands balled into fists. The conniving bastard. "Fuck Frank. You can always rely on me, Kaylee."

"I know. And I appreciate it. I didn't know who else to call. Since I married Reuben, I rarely see anyone apart from my neighbors, and that's only when he lets me."

He uttered the question that had been on his lips since she opened the door. "Has he ever hurt the kids?"

She hesitated a moment too long and then shook her head. "No. He's never hit them. But he is hard on them, particularly on Robbie."

Shane could picture it well. Reuben and Kaylee had two sons: Reuben Junior, known as RJ, and Robbie. RJ took after his father. He was a rough-and-tumble boy who was spoiled by his father. Robbie was a different build and more sensitive child than his brother. He reminded Shane of himself at that age. He always made a point of chatting with the kid when he saw him because the child was often overshadowed by his more confident brother.

He pulled his phone out of his pocket. "We need to get you to a doctor. And then we're calling the cops."

"No." Kaylee grabbed his wrist before he could dial the number for the local hospital. "Please, Shane. No doctors. No cops. Until I find another place to stay, I have to be careful."

"You have a place to stay. My apartment's not big, but we'll manage until we find an alternative."

His sister hunched her narrow shoulders. "I can't ask that of you. There's not enough space for all of us. I've managed to hide a bit of cash. I was going to stay at a hotel for a few days, just until I find an alternative."

"Hotels and hostels are the first places Reuben will look."

She raised an eyebrow. "You don't think he'll check out your place?"

"Of course he will." Shane's jaw tightened. "And I'll be waiting for him. Look, you and the kids can have my bedroom. I don't mind sleeping on the sofa until we find a new place for you to live. I just got a puppy. The boys will be delighted. And if we find a more secure place for you to stay, all the better."

She bit her lip, clearly torn. "I don't want you to get into trouble."

"I'm already on Reuben's shit list over a different situation," Shane said with a grimace. "Right now, my priority is getting you and the children away from here."

His sister displayed the first hint of a smile since he'd arrived. "What did you do to piss off Rueben?"

Shane noticed how careful she was to name the man instead of referring to him as her husband. He rolled with it. The sooner the rat was no longer related to them, the better. "Long story short, he kidnapped my friend's brother over an unpaid debt. I helped her negotiate his release. If 'negotiate' is the correct term to use where Reuben is concerned."

Kiss Shot

Kaylee's face displayed no flicker of surprise at the news that her husband had kidnapped a guy. "Reuben likes screwing with people. Your friend and her brother should stay away from him."

"They'd like nothing better, but there's the not-so-small matter of the unpaid debts." He moved past his sister and headed toward the stairs. "Come on. I'll help you pack. I'll respect your request not to see a doctor as long as you let Dan have a look at your wounds. He can put his paramedic training to good use. I need to swing by the Triskelion Team offices in any case."

His sister glanced at her watch. "We'll need to hurry with the packing. Rueben isn't due back for another few hours, but I wouldn't put it past him to show up early, just to mess with my head."

Shane didn't ask where the man was. He didn't want to know. Reuben was either screwing one of his many other women, or breaking some poor fucker's face. He'd tried to talk to his sister on numerous occasions about her husband's infidelity and bad treatment of her, but Kaylee had shut him down as soon as he started. He'd reached the conclusion that it was better not to push her on the issue, in case she shut him out of her life and he wasn't around to help her if and when she asked for help.

It seemed today was that day.

***

The moment Ruthie got back to her dad's house, she put her plan into action. Armed with an accouterment of electronic equipment and a pot of coffee strong enough to wake the dead, she set up camp in her dad's office. Big Mike and Kevin were still asleep upstairs, but her father would be up soon to walk the dogs.

While her fingers flew over her laptop keyboard, she sifted through the information she had on Emma Reilly. Born Gemma McEllroy in Northern Ireland, she'd been orphaned after an I.R.A. explosion had claimed the lives of her entire family. She'd been initially taken into the witness protection program and later placed with a foster family. A few years later, this family had adopted her, thus completing Gemma McEllroy's transformation into Emma Reilly. It must have been quite a shock when her dead sister had strolled into her office a few weeks ago...

Ruthie scrolled through Emma's curriculum vitae. After a number of short-lived careers including actress, street performer, yoga teacher, and barista, she'd set up shop as a private detective. Despite her unconventional background experience, she'd proven to be good at her job, if chronically underpaid. Emma's tendency to take pro bono clients didn't lead to a healthy bank balance and might have prompted her decision to accept private investigation work for the Triskelion Team on a freelance basis.

Kiss Shot

Ruthie leaned back in her chair. The internet search on Emma had shed no new light on her character and certainly didn't provide magical access to her computer files. That would require a little more work on Ruthie's part. A solid hour later, she'd hacked into Emma's phone.

Unfortunately for the Jarvis Agency, Emma Reilly wasn't stupid. No text messages of interest leaped out and pointed a trail to the Delaney family. While Emma recorded client appointments on her digital calendar, she used code names to hide their identities. Luckily for Ruthie, Emma didn't afford her sister the same caution. Next Wednesday afternoon had been blocked off with a single entry: Gen—Dundrum Shopping Centre—2 PM.

Bingo.

With a smile of satisfaction, Ruthie refilled her coffee cup and sat back in the chair to plot her next move.

SIXTEEN

Shane punched in the code for the Triskelion Team's headquarters, and the elevator doors slid shut. Tension oozed from his sister and nephews. Robbie clutched Shane's hand. The worried expression on his little face tugged at Shane's heartstrings. RJ clung to his mother, his lips set in a grim line. Kaylee's haggard appearance was a far cry from the vivacious young woman she'd been before she'd hooked up with Reuben Kowalski. A muscle in his jaw twitched. How could the man inflict such damage on the very people he was supposed to love and protect?

He gave the boys a reassuring smile. "You're going to love Flash, my new puppy." That, of course, was assuming the dog didn't destroy the apartment before the kids got there.

A flicker of a smile appeared on Robbie's face, but RJ's scowl deepened. "I like dogs," Robbie said. "Does Flash play catch?"

Kiss Shot

"I haven't had a chance to teach him yet." He swallowed the words, *Maybe you can help me,* and met his sister's eye. They both knew that taking the boys to the park to play with the dog was out of the question. Too many people in Kilpatrick would recognize them by sight.

"You sure about this?" Kaylee punctuated her question with a frown that drew Shane's attention back to the bruise on her forehead and her swollen eye. His nails dug into his palms. When he got his hands on Kowalski, he'd make the fucker pay.

"I'm positive," he said as the elevator shuddered to a halt. "We need help, and Lar and Dan are the guys to provide it."

The metal doors slid open. Shane ushered Kaylee and the boys out of the elevator and through the bulletproof glass doors that separated the hallway from the Triskelion Team's offices.

"This is posh," Kaylee murmured, taking in the plush leather sofa and the sleek glass-and-chrome reception desk. "Where did Lar get the cash for all this?"

Shane's jaw tightened. *From selling us out to Irish intelligence.* "Lar was always good with money."

Imelda, one of their many cousins, sat behind the reception desk, filing her nails. Her eyes widened when she clocked Kaylee's face. "Jaysus, look at the state of you, girl. What happened?"

Kaylee grimaced. "Reuben happened."

"Please tell me you've left him." Imelda wielded her nail file as one would a weapon. "Did you knee him in the balls?"

Kaylee's nostrils flared. "Not yet, but I intend to."

"Mummy, I need to pee." Robbie did a little dance to emphasize the point.

"So do I." RJ imitated his brother's back-and-forth movements.

"Bathroom is down the corridor," Shane said. "Second door on the left."

"I'll go with them." Kaylee gave a wan smile. "Just in case they try to flood the place."

When Kaylee and her sons had left in search of the toilets, Shane turned to Imelda and jerked a thumb at Lar's closed office door. "Are the lads in?"

Imelda shrugged. "I guess so. I didn't see them leave, but I wouldn't put climbing down walls past Dan. Do you remember the time he scared the shite out of Siobhan by scaling the wall up to our flat?"

Given that Imelda and her family had been living in a tenth-floor apartment at the time, that was no mean feat. Shane grinned. "I'll take that as a yes. Can you bring us in coffee? And maybe entertain the boys for a while?"

Imelda rolled her heavily kohled eyes in an exaggerated fashion. "I go out to work to get away from the twins and now you're saddling me with more kids?"

Orlando and Mickey, Imelda's demonic offspring, were notorious in the Delaney family for their ability to create havoc wherever they went. The last time the twins had visited Shane's apartment, they'd locked him and Imelda out on the balcony and proceeded to ransack his collection of vintage porn magazines. He hadn't invited them back.

Shane sighed and reached for his wallet. "I'll pay you extra."

"Deal," Imelda said, pocketing the proffered fifty-euro note. "I'll find shite on YouTube for them to watch. The twins love that."

When Kaylee and the boys reappeared, Imelda supplied the youngsters with glasses of milk and an iPad.

"Behave yourselves," Kaylee said, and kissed each boy on the cheek.

"Ah, we'll be grand," Imelda said, waving her freshly lacquered nails. "They can't be any worse than the twins. Sure, how much mischief can they get into in thirty minutes?"

Shane winked at Kaylee and steered her toward Lar's office. "If Orlando and Mickey are anything to go by," he whispered when Imelda was out of earshot, "two boys can cause mass destruction in thirty seconds, never mind thirty minutes."

For the first time that day, Kaylee's laugh was heartfelt. "Thankfully, Robbie and RJ are better behaved than the twins. Most of the time."

Shane knocked on Lar's office door. A moment later, it swung open to reveal a grinning Lar and Dan. Their smiles faded the instant they registered Kaylee's injuries.

"What the hell?" Lar demanded, then his jaw set in a hard line. "The bastard."

Dan's fingers curled into fists. "I'll fucking kill him."

"No one's killing anyone," Shane said firmly. "At least, not yet. Can you take a look at Kaylee's wounds, Dan? The one over her eye needs stitches."

"Sure." Dan took Kaylee's arm. "Come on. I have a first aid kit in my office. We'll leave these two to plot."

Dan and Kaylee left just as Imelda arrived with their coffees. Shane's was a frothy latte, liberally doused with caramel sauce. His cousin might lack the tact preferable in a receptionist, but she made a damn fine coffee. "Thanks," he said, taking a grateful sip of the sweet beverage.

"No bother." Imelda narrowed her eyes. "Please tell me you're going to beat the shite out of Kowalski."

"I'd like nothing better than to kneecap the fucker," Shane said, "but we need to push our anger aside and look at the big picture. We have to do whatever will keep Kaylee and the boys safe."

"Ever the philosopher," Lar said dryly. "You were always the sensible one. I envy your ability to keep your emotions in check."

Shane bit back an acid retort. Lar was correct. Concealing his feelings and controlling his emotions were skills he'd honed over the years. Growing up with Frank as a father, they were essential.

After Imelda had closed the door behind her, Lar slid behind his desk, and Shane dropped into the seat opposite. It was the first time they'd been alone in a room for weeks. The resentment that had been burning inside of Shane rose to the surface. His grip on the coffee cup tightened. Time to put his lauded skill set to use.

Lar leaned back in his chair and cradled his coffee cup between his palms. "So, spill. What's the story with Kaylee?"

"As you've probably guessed, she wants to file for divorce. Until things are settled, she needs a safe place to stay. Somewhere Reuben won't find them. We run a private security firm. Who better to protect them than us?"

"Of course. Kaylee and the boys are family. Delaneys look after their own."

Except when we don't. An image of seventeen-year-old Lar loomed in Shane's memory. Dad and Uncle Patrick should have looked after him. Instead, they'd manipulated an impressionable boy into taking the fall for a crime he didn't commit. Shane's rational side understood Lar's decision to trade family loyalty for freedom, but his emotional side wasn't ready to let go of the hurt.

Lar took a sip of espresso, his brows drawn together in contemplation. "Do you have a place in mind for them to stay? If not, I might have a solution."

"If you have a suggestion, I'm all ears. I thought of my apartment, but that's not going to work for more than a few hours. As soon as Reuben realizes Kaylee's left him, he'll be on the war path."

"And the first place he'll look for her is your apartment," Lar finished for him.

"Exactly." Shane's lips formed a grim line. "He'll know Kaylee won't go to our father for help, and our brothers are useless. Greg's too busy beating up his own women to care about Reuben hitting Kaylee, and Tom hates confrontation."

"I have a holiday cottage in Wicklow that I rent out to tourists," Lar said carefully. "It's a five-minute walk from Brittas Bay."

Lar owning a rental cottage was news to Shane, but he rolled with it. No doubt his cousin was involved in plenty of schemes whereby he could invest the money he wasn't supposed to have. "Is it vacant at the moment?" he asked. "Like, could they move in today?"

"Yeah. I've had it renovated. If Kaylee and the boys don't mind the smell of paint, it's theirs. The next group of holidaymakers won't arrive until August."

"I'm sure the boys would love spending the summer at the beach." The words weighed heavily on Shane's tongue. Seeking Lar's help was the smart move, even if it chafed at the raw wound left by his cousin's betrayal. If Shane could have guaranteed Kaylee and the boys' safety, he'd have kept their cousins out of the loop, but only a fool would underestimate Reuben Kowalski. The man was a dangerous motherfucker. In contrast to Shane playing the lone wolf, the Triskelion Team had access to resources such as weapons, surveillance equipment, and highly trained bodyguards, all of which would come in handy in the weeks to come.

He sighed. He'd made his decision before he'd walked into Lar's office and asked for help. "If we send them to Wicklow, I want them to have round-the-clock protection."

Lar nodded. "That's Dan's department, but I'm sure he can arrange it, even if it means us taking turns until we have a team in place."

"Whatever's needed, I'm game."

"I'll discuss the details with Dan. In the meantime, Kaylee and the boys can stay here."

"I promised them I'd introduce them to Flash."

The corners of Lar's mouth quirked. "Are you planning to train him as a guard dog?"

"Given his behavior, that would take a miracle."

Now that they'd discussed Kaylee's situation, an awkward silence descended.

Shane broke it by extracting two folders from his backpack and sliding them across the desk. "Here's the

Donnelly file, plus an update on my investigation into attack on The Lucky Leprechaun."

Lar picked up the file on The Lucky Leprechaun and opened it. "Anything significant to report?"

"My progress has been frustratingly slow. I keep hitting brick walls." Not to mention the fact that digging into Lar's shady past was taking up far too much of his time. "The only potentially interesting discovery is that two members of staff died in the months after the attack."

Lar's head jerked up from his perusal of the folder. "Anything mysterious about their deaths?"

"On the surface, no. A doorman named Jared Klune was killed in a car accident two months after the shootings. The official cause of death was a head injury. The pathologist expressed some doubt as to whether Klune could have sustained this particular injury by hitting his head against the steering wheel of the car, but the police found no reason to investigate further."

"Hmm." Lar flicked through the file. "What about the stripper, Marlene Thomas?"

"She died of a heroin overdose," Shane said. "Unlike Klune, she'd been present on the day of the attack and survived by barricading herself in a storeroom."

"Anything odd about the overdose?"

"According to the police, no. However, Marlene's friends insisted she didn't take drugs and would never have injected herself with heroin. For what it's worth, the pathologist found no track marks and concluded she'd relapsed after a period of being clean."

"Let me guess—the police didn't follow up on the friends' claims because Marlene stripped for a living?"

"That's my conclusion." Shane sighed. "Like I said, the two deaths might not be connected to the shootings, but Marlene's, in particular, bothers me."

"What's the plan?" Lar asked. "You going to dig deeper?"

"Yeah. I'd like to follow it up. Try to track down two of Marlene's friends who gave statements."

Lar blew out his cheeks. "Frank's been breathing down my neck about this case. He wants results."

"Patience was never one of my father's strong suits. We told him we'd do our best and in our own time."

His cousin drained his espresso and eyed Shane. "Might be smart to have someone trail Kowalski for a while. Make sure he remains clueless."

"Yeah. Let's put the new guy, John Molloy, on the case. He's had army training in surveillance. As long as I can bring Flash with me, I can take tonight's shift watching over Kaylee and the boys."

Lar frowned. "Okay, but I'm thinking it's smarter to do rotations in pairs. If Kowalski does show up, he won't come alone. Why don't we see if Dan and one of the other guys can cover the afternoon and early evening? Then you and I can stay overnight. We can even bring your dog down with us to amuse the boys."

Shane swallowed hard. He didn't exactly relish the prospect of a night shift with Lar, even if they'd be taking turns sleeping. On the other hand, Lar was a tough customer and an excellent shot. If Reuben and his Rottweilers appeared, Shane was going to need all the help he could get.

"But there's a catch to the plan," Lar said, "and I'm pretty sure you're not going to like it."

Shane eyed his cousin warily. "Sounds ominous."

Lar's pained expression didn't alleviate his fears. "I promised Big Mike I'd track down a some guys who owe him money, and he wants me to take care of it personally. I could do with help, especially if we're using our limited manpower to look after Kaylee."

Despite himself, Shane chuckled. "Setting up the Triskelion Team was supposed to free you from the need to do shitty enforcing jobs."

"That was the idea." Lar screwed up his nose and sighed. "Problem is, I need to keep on Big Mike's good side. He's got two lucrative assignments coming up for us over the next few months."

Shane leaned back in his chair and folded his arms across his chest. "So you've agreed to take this on to keep him sweet?"

"Exactly."

Shane grinned. "Let me guess. Does this involve your old pal, Spoons Maginty?"

Kiss Shot

"Yeah. And it gets better. Remember Murph and Dec from school?"

"Jaysus, yes. I ran across those eejits just the other day. Ruthie was beating the crap out of them in Power's Pub."

"I'd love to have seen that." Lar's smile widened. "And 'eejits' is the perfect description for them. Murph, Dec, and Spoons robbed a Chinese takeaway on Capel Street last night and made off with a few thousand euros. They tried to break the surveillance camera, but did a piss-poor job of it."

"Why doesn't that surprise me?" Shane asked dryly.

Lar laughed. "Yeah. Typical Spoons shenanigans. Anyway, the owner of the takeaway is in debt to Big Mike, and his next payment was part of the stolen money. Once he watched the surveillance footage and recognized the culprits, he opted to call Big Mike instead of the police."

"Smart man. Big Mike will get results and ask no awkward questions about dodgy bookkeeping." Shane cracked his knuckles. "When do you need me to come with you?"

"That's the other catch: I don't know. I've got a couple of guys trailing Spoons and company to find out where they've stashed the loot. Once we have an idea where it is, we'll make our move."

"Let me know." Shane got to his feet and stretched. "Dan should have finished patching up Kaylee by now.

I'm going to ask him to get on scheduling bodyguard rotations for Kaylee and the boys."

"Okay. And Shane?"

He met his cousin's gaze. The bemused look of a moment ago had vanished, replaced by an intense stare. "Yeah?"

"We're not going to let Kowalski get away with this. One way or another, he's going down."

Shane's chest tightened. "Amen to that."

SEVENTEEN

Ruthie scanned the clothing racks with distaste. Fancy department stores were her personal nemesis. They overwhelmed her with their arrays of fashionable clothes, bright makeup counters, and snobby assistants. The perfume section alone had her gagging. She glanced at her watch. Two-thirty. *Jaysus.* How long did it take to pick a fucking bra?

Emma and Gen had been punctual for their shopping appointment, meeting at the entrance of the shopping center as the church bells chimed the hour. In real life, they were even more alike than in their file photographs. Both had curly blond hair, bright blue eyes, and porcelain complexions. Although Gen was a few centimeters taller than her sister, their builds were similar—slim but curvaceous.

After greeting one another with a brief hug, the sisters made a beeline for House of Fraser. Her baseball cap pulled low, Ruthie followed them to the women's department, but the opportunity to engineer a chance encounter was temporarily thwarted when the sisters disappeared into the changing rooms with a pile of underwear and a professional bra fitter.

Half an hour and countless bras later, Ruthie was bored senseless. Blowing out a sigh, she rifled through a selection of tops in garish colors. She'd half hoped Shane would uninvite her to the party, just so she could wriggle out of this shopping trip, but he was determined to make up for the postponed takeout, and she needed to avail of the chance to "bump into" Gen and her sister.

The thought of Shane brought the butterflies in her stomach to life. She'd only seen him once since what she mentally referred to as the Shower Incident. With his sister's crisis, he'd squeezed in a short training session on Tuesday morning, and they weren't due to meet again until tomorrow. Ruthie was counting the minutes.

In the pocket of her cargo pants, her phone vibrated. Unknown caller. *Fuck.* She pressed the phone to her ear. "Hello?"

"This is Travers."

Ruthie blew out a sigh. She'd been afraid of that. "Did you get my report?"

Travers' cold voice dripped disdain. "If you're referring to the email you sent me last night, yes, although calling it a report is a stretch."

Her grip on the phone tightened and she counted to five before responding. "You asked for a report within seventy-two hours, and I obliged. What's wrong with what I wrote?"

"Your progress is lamentably slow. With your insider knowledge of the area and the people, I expected you to produce results faster."

She rolled her eyes. "Seriously? I've been back in Dublin a couple of weeks, and the people in question aren't exactly my besties." Ruthie glanced around, but no one was paying any attention. She lowered her voice. "Now's not a good time. I'm shopping for the party I mentioned."

"Which isn't until Saturday. What are you doing between now and then?"

Jeez. What was the guy's problem? On all her previous assignments, Travers had been a pain in the arse, but his current behavior was well into crazy territory. "Why the urgency? Has something happened?"

He hesitated a moment too long before replying. "Just get the job done, Reynolds. You'd better produce pure fucking gold after Saturday's party, or you're off this assignment."

"You said I had until the end of the month." Her voice rose a notch. "What's changed?"

"If you want us to pony up the rest of your obscene bonus, do the job we're paying you to do."

She opened her mouth to respond, but he'd disconnected.

Arsehole. He pulled that stunt every phone call. If she weren't reliant on the money, she'd tell him and the agency to take a flying leap. Unfortunately, she needed the cash, especially since she now owed Shane two thousand euros in addition to the sum the Kowalski brothers were expecting.

She scrunched her nose. What shades looked good on her? She hadn't a clue. Black, white, and khaki were her faves, with the odd beige item thrown in for variety. She cast her mind back to previous neighborhood gatherings that had included Siobhan Schneider-Delaney. Siobhan was a good-looking woman with a natural sense of style that her lack of funds couldn't dampen. She'd be dressed to the nines and expect her guests to make an effort with their appearance.

Ruthie yanked a maroon top from a rack and held it against her chest. She pulled a face at her reflection in the floor-to-ceiling mirror. Not maroon, then. She was in the process of returning the top to its place when a familiar voice floated toward her. Ruthie froze in place. Gen and Emma exited the changing rooms and began browsing a selection of evening dresses. Her heart rate kicked up a notch. Her brief introduction to Gen at the gym the other day had given her a fleeting impression of an outwardly friendly woman with wary eyes. Gen McEllroy was no fool.

Time to make her move. Ruthie breathed past her fears and forced her legs into motion. What better way for some girly bonding than bumping into one another while shopping for clothes? Not that Ruthie knew the first thing about fashion, but that was going to be part of her cover story.

She grabbed a dress from a rack without checking the size and headed in the direction of the changing rooms. She charged past Emma, bumping into her and causing her to let go of the bundle of dresses she was carrying.

Score.

Ruthie dropped to her knees and gathered up the fallen garments. "I'm sorry. I was in another world. Here you go." She handed the pile of clothes to Emma with a winning smile.

The annoyance on the other woman's face vanished. "Don't worry about it. I'll take it as a sign that I should put a few of these dresses back. It takes me forever to decide."

You don't say.

"Hello, Ruthie." Gen raised an inquiring eyebrow. "Fancy meeting you here."

"Hey, Gen." Ruthie itched to shove her hands into her pockets to hide their shaking. On the couple of occasions she'd run into Gen McEllroy at the gym, she'd felt the force of the woman's appraising stare. Maybe she was being paranoid, but she couldn't shake the sensation that Gen didn't trust her.

Gen's gaze dropped to the dress Ruthie was holding. "Special occasion?"

"Ah, yeah. Shane asked me to go to Siobhan's party." Ruthie didn't need to fake the flush on her cheeks. "Problem is, I have nothing to wear."

Gen turned to her sister. "This is Ruthie, Shane's new girlfriend."

Emma whirled around to examine Ruthie. "Shane has a girlfriend? Seriously?"

Ruthie's throat constricted. Once upon a time, being Shane's girlfriend had been all she'd wanted. "I wouldn't call myself his girlfriend, exactly, but we're...seeing each other."

"Ah." Emma's face lit up. "You're a much better choice than the one he brought to Dan's birthday party."

"This is my sister, Emma," Gen said, giving her sibling a warning look.

"Nice to meet you." Ruthie schooled her expression into a friendly smile and examined Emma Reilly up close. So this was the Triskelion Team's go-to private eye with a penchant for disguises—the agency's files had been thorough.

"We're shopping for something to wear to Siobhan's party as well," Emma volunteered, "and then for her present."

"Any idea what she's into?" Gen asked Ruthie. "I like Siobhan but I haven't known her long."

"Bling," Ruthie replied with a grin, "but tasteful stuff. Want to pool our resources and get her something nice?"

"Sure. We can check out the jewelry section after we pick our dresses." Gen regarded the dress in Ruthie's hand with frank appraisal. "No offense, but that shade of pink isn't for you."

She decided honesty was her best course of action. "I'm not a clothes person. As you can probably tell." She gestured to her khaki combat pants and biker boots. "I'm totally out of my depth here. How formal is this shindig likely to be?"

"Semiformal. Siobhan likes people to make an effort. The guys will show up in shirts and ties, and the women will wear dresses, skirts, or a nice pants suit." Gen's smile widened. "I have an idea. Emma is brilliant at picking out makeup, and I have a good eye for clothes. Do you want us to help you find the perfect dress?"

"I, uh, probably could do with a bit of guidance." "A bit" was an understatement.

Emma gave her a once-over. "How do you feel about getting a makeover? Clothes, makeup, the works?"

"Emma..." Gen said in a warning voice.

"Sorry." Emma screwed up her nose. "Am I being too direct?"

Ruthie laughed. "Don't worry about it. As for the makeover, my feminist side rebels, but I know I need help if I want to look the part for Siobhan's party." And a makeover would take a while, giving her plenty of time to get to know them. With Travers threatening to fire her, the second installment of Kevin's debt repayment depended on the quality of her information. Thus, latching on to Gen and Emma was a smart move. They weren't Delaneys, but Gen was directly involved in the investigation into The Lucky Leprechaun attack and a person of interest for the Jarvis Agency.

Gen eyed her thoughtfully, making Ruthie squirm. "And what about your feminine side? Does that secretly crave pretty makeup and clothes? Even for one evening?"

Hell, no. "All right," she said, "do your worst. I want to look fab for Siobhan's party."

"And wow Shane?" Gen raised an eyebrow and smiled. "I suspect you've already done that."

Ruthie's cheeks grew hot. "I'm not sure."

Gen threw back her head and laughed. "I haven't known Shane long, but I'm pretty good at reading people. He's smitten with you."

Her stomach churned with guilt. Why hadn't Shane been smitten with her five years ago? Why hadn't he chased her down and asked her to run away to Australia with him? Why hadn't she taken a leap of faith and run after him? She took a steadying breath and focused on the end goals: Kevin's debt paid in full, and freedom for her. "Where do we start?" she asked. "Clothes or makeup?"

"Seeing as we're surrounded by potential outfits here," Gen said, "let's start with the clothes."

Ruthie fingered the bulge in her pocket where she'd shoved her wallet. The agency had given her a credit card to use for assignment expenses. She could afford to buy some makeup and new clothes, but she couldn't go overboard. She smiled at the thought of the report she'd have to write in which she explained her need for lingerie and cosmetics. But that was the agency's problem. They'd given her a job to do, and she intended to do it. If this involved kitting herself out like a cast member on a reality show, so be it. Served Travers right for being an arse to her on the phone.

"Oh, this would look perfect on you." Emma pulled a dress from a rack and held it up against Ruthie. The dress was a shade of dark purple with a plunging neckline and a tight skirt that ended with a playful flair.

"I don't think—" she began, but Emma cut short her protestations.

"What size are you?" Emma scrutinized her figure. "We're around the same height, but you're skinnier than I am. A size ten, maybe?"

"I don't know. I haven't shopped in Ireland for years. I'm a size thirty-six in Switzerland."

"That's a size ten here," Emma said, checking the label of the purple dress. "My guess was correct."

Gen winked at Ruthie. "It usually is."

"I'm good with clothes," Emma said with no trace of modesty. "It's a handy trait to have in my line of work."

"For tracking people, you mean?" Ruthie asked, seizing on the opportunity to discuss Emma's job. "Shane mentioned you were a private investigator."

"That's right," Emma replied cheerfully. "Creating effective disguises is part of the job. I buy clothes in various sizes in case I need to make myself heavier." She pinched her waist. "Making myself skinnier is a no-go, unfortunately."

Gen snorted. "If it were that easy, Dan would be out of a job."

At the mention of Dan's name, Emma turned beetroot. "I don't think Dan's clientele are there to lose weight."

"Some are," Ruthie said. "You'd be surprised. Yeah, there's plenty of guys who train at a boxing gym to act tough and beat the crap out of each other without the risk of sustaining a serious injury, but some guys take up boxing as part of a weight loss regime. Our area of the city is alpha male central. Many haven't evolved enough to want to be seen dead at a fitness studio."

Gen nodded. "That's true. Lar's more evolved than most, but he prefers Dan's place to my gym. We compromise. We go for a run together every second day, and I go with him to Schneider's for an early morning workout a couple of times a week."

"I'd love to see some of your disguises some time, Emma." The request was genuine, but Ruthie was well aware that getting friendly with Emma was a way to get friendly with Emma's sister. For some reason, the agency was particularly interested in knowing more about Gen.

"Sure. We'll make that happen." Emma grinned. "Now get into that dress."

Without waiting for Ruthie to raise another objection, Emma took her by the arm and frogmarched her into a changing cabin. After Emma had left, Ruthie wriggled out of her cargo pants and pulled off her T-shirt. On its hanger, the purple dress shimmered under the soothing lights. She fingered the silky material and slipped it free from the hanger.

As Emma had predicted, the dress fit her like a glove. A cleverly concealed side zip meant she didn't require assistance doing the dress up. Ruthie turned around to get a look at the dress from all angles. Her breath caught. It was like looking at a stranger in the mirror.

"Are you decent?" Emma called through the door. "Gen's found more dresses for you to try on."

"Okay, but I think you might have hit the jackpot on the first go." Ruthie opened the door.

Emma and Gen gasped when they saw the dress. "You look gorgeous," Emma said.

"Ravishing." Gen's smile was sly. "Shane won't be able to keep his paws off you."

For the umpteenth time that day, Ruthie's cheeks grew warm at the mention of Shane. "I'm not dressing to impress a man."

"Of course not," Gen said smoothly. "But it's an added benefit. Shane already fancies you. Seeing you in this dress will merely seal the deal."

"Watch out," Emma said. "Gen was single for years before she and Lar became an item. She's now determined to matchmake everyone else."

"Hey, I've never tried to matchmake you." Gen regarded her little sister and laughed. "Although you could do with some help."

Now it was Emma's turn to flush. "I never should have mentioned him being hot. It was a mistake."

"Who's hot?" Ruthie asked, slipping out of the purple dress and trying on a black skirt and blouse combo Gen had chosen.

Gen laughed at her sister's red cheeks. "Dan Schneider. Emma has a crush on him."

"I do not," Emma said indignantly. "What is this? Secondary school? All I said was that the man had muscles."

"And tattoos," Gen added with a mischievous smile. "You mentioned those as well."

"I just happened to see him training with his shirt off when I collected you from his gym the other day," Emma said. "If I stopped to admire the view, who can blame me?"

"Not I," Ruthie said. "He's hot."

"And interested in Emma." Gen laughed at her sister's spluttered protests. "I've seen the way he looks at you."

"He *glares* at me," Emma said. "He's sexy, but he terrifies me. There's no way he's interested in me."

"He *broods*. He's definitely not glaring at you." Gen grinned at her sister. "Dan likes to get his grump on, but I'm sure you can persuade him to smile."

"Dan is a decent guy," Ruthie admitted. "A definite plus with all the scumbags strutting around Dublin."

"And many of those scumbags frequent Dan's gym, unfortunately," Emma said dryly. "I don't know how you two tolerate them."

"We rarely see them," Gen said. "I train with Lar early in the morning before anyone comes in, and Ruthie has started to do the same."

"Dan is reluctant to let us use the gym while the regulars are there until he builds a separate changing area for women," Ruthie explained. "As long as I get my training in, I don't mind. I'm not keen on showering with those Neanderthals."

"They're not all idiots," Gen mused, "but some are best avoided. I'm not fond of the Connolly boys, for example, even if they are Dan's pals."

Ruthie snorted. "Those fuckers? They were sexist arseholes back when I knew them. I doubt the intervening years have changed them for the better."

"They're now sexist arseholes with a major grudge," Emma added. "Did you hear someone gunned down their father?"

"I heard." According to the agency's files, the culprit was still at large, and the police were baffled. With gangland killings on the rise, the police had attributed

Jimmy Connolly's murder to an unknown rival. "Do you have any idea who did it?"

Gen's expression remained impassive, but Emma shook her head. "None. I guess Connolly pissed off the wrong person."

"Now that we have your dress picked out for Siobhan's party," Gen said, drawing the conversation back to the task at hand, "it's time to add shoes and underwear."

The next half hour passed in a blur of heels and frills. Ruthie asked questions about the Triskelion Team, careful to keep them casual. Gen was all smiles and happy to talk about her boyfriend's new private security firm, yet Ruthie wasn't fooled. The woman was a pro. She gave the minimum of information in answer to Ruthie's questions and became vague and distracted when Ruthie asked if they had any interesting assignments at the moment.

"Oh, you know," Gen waved a hand airily. "Nothing terribly exciting. Of course, they all have confidentiality agreements, so I can't give details."

"It sounds intriguing."

"Your life interests me." Gen's gaze sharpened, yet her lips retained the friendly smile. "What's it like moving from place to place? Shane said you've lived all over Europe."

"Pretty dull, to be honest. I did the mixed martial arts circuit for a couple of years, but I had to give it up due to a knee injury. Most of the travel involved swapping one hotel room for another. I didn't get a chance to see much of the countries I visited."

Gen nodded, apparently satisfied with her answer. "Are you back in Dublin permanently?"

"No. Just staying with my dad for a while." Ruthie fingered the sheer material of the underwear set she'd chosen. "What brought you to Dublin? Was it Lar?"

Gen's eyes narrowed a fraction. "In a manner of speaking."

"Dad said you used to go out with Lar years ago," she said breezily. "I love second chance romance stories." Ruthie's father had said fuck-all about Lar Delaney's love life, but Gen wouldn't know that. Unless they impacted on him or his, Big Mike's interest in other people's affairs was precisely zero.

"Word travels," Gen said, checking that Ruthie had all the items of clothing necessary for the party.

"Ah, you know. People love to gossip, especially around here. Lar's considered quite a catch."

Gen laughed. "People don't gossip with me. I'm an outsider with the wrong accent."

"I get it. I've been gone too long to be considered a local." And even before she'd left, she'd never fit in. She was too different to slot into any particular group. She wasn't pretty enough or sporty enough to belong to the popular crowd. She wasn't smart enough or nerdy enough to hang with the geeks. Sometimes, teenage

Ruthie had felt she wasn't enough. The irony was that her sporting prowess hadn't come into its own until she'd been in her late teens and had taken up kickboxing and mixed martial arts. And even then, her talent had been considered freakish and unfeminine.

"You've made a conquest of your own in Shane," Emma added, interrupting her trip down memory lane. "Is that another second chance romance?"

Ruthie shifted her weight from one leg to the other. "Not exactly. Well...maybe." Like, in her dreams.

"Hmm..." Emma teased. "Sounds intriguing."

Gen picked up Ruthie's clothes. "I think my work here is done. Over to you, sis."

"Excellent. Now it's my turn to work my magic on you." Emma gave Ruthie an impish smile. "Let's hit up the makeup counters."

Emma carved a path through the crowds to the makeup department. With a sinking stomach, Ruthie scanned the sleek displays with their colorful array of cosmetics. She had no clue where to start. The names of the various cosmetic companies meant nothing to her.

Emma, thankfully, knew what she was doing. She made straight for the Bobbi Brown counter. "Her colors will suit you, and she has plenty of neutral options. If you're not used to wearing makeup, we'll go for a subtle look."

Kiss Shot

"See any shades you like?" Gen asked and picked up a lipstick. "This mauve lip tint would go well with the dress."

"I have no idea what I'm looking at," Ruthie confessed. "I don't wear makeup."

Gen eyed her thoughtfully. "Are you sure you want to buy cosmetics? We can skip them if you prefer. You have gorgeous skin. You can easily get away with not wearing foundation."

Ruthie stared at her short nails. "Thanks, but if I'm going to the trouble of dressing up, I might as well go the whole hog."

Gen stared at her curiously. "Haven't you experimented with makeup before?"

"Yeah, and it ended in disaster. When I was a teenager, I managed to stick a mascara wand in my eye."

Gen and Emma roared laughing.

"It took me a while to get the hang of it," Gen said. "My mother—my adoptive mother—didn't believe in makeup. Her disapproval made me all the more determined to master the craft."

Ruthie averted her gaze. "My mother was very glamorous, but she died before I was old enough to care about makeup."

"I'd be happy to show you the basics," Emma said. "We could even help you get ready for the party. Right, Gen?"

Gen nodded. "Sure."

Guilt gnawed at Ruthie's stomach. She hated subterfuge, especially lying to people who might have been her friends under other circumstances. "I can't ask you to do that. It would take you ages and probably be an exercise in frustration."

"I'm sure it wouldn't be that bad," Emma assured her. "I love messing around with makeup. We can choose a few basic colors today, seeing as your coloring is so different to mine and Gen's. And then we can meet up at my place on the evening of the party, and I'll show you how to put it on. How does that sound?"

It sounded like Ruthie's idea of torture, but she plastered a smile on her face. "Sounds great. Thank you so much."

Knowing her luck, Gen and Emma would give her up as a lost cause after a few minutes, and she still wouldn't have had a chance to pump them for information. But this sort of opportunity was what she'd been angling for, and she had to make the best of it, however crappy the deception made her feel. One way or another, she'd convinced them to trust her, Emma more than Gen. With a bit of luck, that trust would lead to useful information.

Gen's cool blue eyes met her brown ones, and a prickle of fear crept down Ruthie's back. If she didn't know better, she'd say the woman could read her thoughts.

"Well," Gen said with a bright smile that didn't meet her eyes, "let's get shopping."

EIGHTEEN

When Ruthie got back to the house, the lights were on. "I'm home," she called, dropping her shopping bags onto the hallway floor and shrugging out of her jacket.

Her father stuck his bald head out of the kitchen, and his bulldog face creased into a smile. "Hello, love. Fancy a cup of hot chocolate?"

"I'd love one." She indicated the bags at her feet. "I'll just put these upstairs."

Her dad chuckled at the sight of the labels. "Siobhan mentioned that Shane had invited you to her party. Did you find something nice to wear?"

"I hope so." Ruthie scrunched up her nose. "You know me and clothes. Shopping isn't my favorite pursuit. Why didn't you tell me you were seeing Siobhan?"

Her father turned beetroot. "We're not seeing each other. We're just...getting to know one another."

Ruthie grinned. "Is that what they're calling it these days?"

Kiss Shot

"Get your mind out of the gutter. We're nowhere near that stage."

"Yet," Ruthie added, enjoying seeing her father go even redder. "Play your cards right, Dad. I like Siobhan."

"So do I." Her father cleared his throat. "I'd better make sure I don't burn the hot chocolate."

"I'll join you in a minute." Ruthie jogged up to her room and deposited the bags on her bed. As Emma and Gen had instructed, she unpacked the dress with care and hung it in her wardrobe. The makeup and other stuff could wait until later.

Back on the landing, she glanced at Kevin's bedroom. The door was closed, but the strains of punk rock seeped into the hallway. She knocked on the door. "Kev? Dad's making hot chocolate. Do you want to join us?"

"I'm going out in a minute," he called through the closed door. "Maybe another time."

A wave of disappointment washed over her. For once, she'd like them to do something as a family, not just sit across from one another to eat a meal they'd have consumed anyway. "Suit yourself. If you change your mind, you know where we are."

Down in the kitchen, her father had set two steaming mugs of hot chocolate on the table.

Ruthie took a seat and cradled her mug in her hands. "Thanks, Dad. This smells divine."

"Looks like the summer came and went. I was freezing when I got home. I thought this would warm me up."

"It's the damp. It gets into your bones." Surely small talk about the weather wasn't going to be the sum total of their conversation?

The grooves on her father's forehead deepened. "Listen, Ruthie..."

Ah, here it comes. He wants to talk about Kevin.

"I'm sorry I snapped at you the other day," he said. "I shouldn't have walked out on you like that."

"Don't worry about it. If I hadn't needed to go out straight after, I'd have come out to the yard and talked to you then."

Her father brooded into his mug, cradling the ugly pottery as though it were porcelain. "I feel like we've fallen into a pattern of tiptoeing around one another, and I don't want it to be like that. I'm sorry I shut you down the other day. I want us to be able to talk, even when we don't like what the other has to say."

"Fair enough. I want that too. What I want more is for us to be able to talk to each other even when I'm not here." She took a deep breath and plunged into the conversation she'd wanted to have with her father for years. "Why don't you call me more often, Dad? If I don't make the effort, it takes you a couple of months to get in touch."

Her father shifted in his seat, exuding discomfort. "I'm not good on the phone, love."

"Then email me."

Kiss Shot

A hint of a smile played at the corners of his mouth. "You know me and computers. I can barely type."

"See, you always have an excuse." Ruthie placed her mug on the table and looked her father straight in the eye. "You don't visit me because you don't like to fly. You don't call because you don't like talking on the phones. It hurts to be made to feel unwanted."

Her father jerked back in his seat. "Of course you're wanted. I love you to bits. You, Brian, and Kevin mean the world to me."

"Then why don't you keep me in the loop?" she demanded. "This family has too many damned secrets."

"You heard about my heart attack." It was a statement, not a question. "Did Kevin tell you?"

"Yeah. If he hadn't, someone else would have mentioned it eventually. Why the hell didn't you tell me?"

Her father spread his palms wide and dropped his eyes to his hot chocolate. "I didn't want you rushing back to Ireland, thinking you needed to look after me. I didn't want you to feel obligated."

"Of course I'd have come home," she said in exasperation. "You're my father. I'd have wanted to be with you while you were sick."

"When my mother was dying, she expected my sister to look after her, simply because Jackie was the only girl. I don't hold with that bollocks. You've got to live your own life."

"Don't be daft, Dad. I know you wouldn't expect me to drop everything to play nurse." She reached across the table and took one of his meaty hands. "You still should have told me you were sick."

"You're right. I should have called, or asked Kevin to contact you." His eyes met hers. To her surprise, they were moist with unshed tears. "Your mother wouldn't have made such a stupid decision."

No, she wouldn't have, but dwelling on Mum's absence was a huge part of this family's problem. "Promise me you'll tell me if something important happens in the future."

"Okay, love." He took a deep breath. "I've thought about what you said. About Kevin."

Ruthie stiffened. "You have?"

"I'm not going to put Kevin in a hospital, but I am prepared to make seeing a psychiatrist part of the deal if he wants to keep living at home."

Ouch. An ultimatum could backfire dramatically. "You're going to have to be careful how you phrase that, Dad. You don't want Kev to leave in a huff."

Her father stiffened. "I have no intention of blurting it out. I'll bring it up gradually. Warm him up to the idea."

"Whatever you think, just…be careful, okay?"

"I will, love." Her father drained his mug and heaved himself out of his chair. "Time to take the dogs for a walk. Do you want to join me?"

Kiss Shot

It was on the tip of her tongue to say yes when her phone vibrated with an incoming call. One glance at the display turned her blood to ice. "Sorry, Dad. Another time. I need to take this call." She waved goodbye to her father and raced upstairs to her room, taking the steps two at a time. "Travers," she said the instant she closed her bedroom door. "What do you want?"

"We have a problem." The man's detached calm didn't match his words.

"What sort of problem?" she demanded. "I told you I'd send you my next report after Saturday's party."

"You can hand in your last report when you get back to Geneva. Your flight leaves on Monday evening. I'll email you the details."

Ruthie dropped onto the bed, and her fingers around the phone turned numb. "You're pulling me out?"

"We have no choice."

She stared at the phone, stunned. "But why? You told me I had all month."

"A situation has arisen that makes your extraction expedient."

Could the guy sound any stuffier? "What situation?"

"I'm not at liberty to tell you," he said with a haughty sniff. "Suffice it to say, you're off the case as of Monday evening."

"What about the bonus I negotiated?"

"The bonus is payable if you provide us with information that leads to a significant breakthrough. So far, you've given us diddly-squat."

Diddly-quat? Did anyone over the age of five use that phrase? "If you think I've given you fuck-all, it might have to do with the fact that I just arrived. You've done undercover work. You know these things take time."

"Time is what we don't have, Ms. Reynolds," Travers snapped, his smooth veneer showing chips. "We thought we could wait until the end of June, but that's become impossible."

Ruthie sucked air through her teeth. "Let's not fuck around, Travers. I need that money. I didn't get specific, but I have no doubt that you know all about my brother's debts. What do I need to do to get that bonus?"

"We need specifics on what the Triskelion Team knows about the shootings at The Lucky Leprechaun. We need to know why they're digging for information after all this time." A pause. "I've been given permission to send you Shane and Laurence Delaney's complete files."

"What the hell? Are you saying the files you gave me in Geneva were edited? How did you expect me to do my job without knowing all the facts?" The rat. He'd set her up to fail.

"You saw what we needed you to see at the time and no more. With the situation escalating faster than any of us had anticipated, we're prepared to share the full files with you." Travers sniffed. "Not that I think they'll do you any good. Shane Delaney is only of interest to us because he's the Triskelion Team's internet research person. However, the extra information in his file might help you identify his weak points."

Ruthie stomach flipped. The last thing she wanted was to pry into Shane's private life. Going after information he'd dug up for the Triskelion Team was one thing, but if his uncensored file contained personal details she'd rather not know, she was happy to live in ignorance.

"Now is not the moment for doubts," Travers said, as though reading her thoughts. "I realize that Shane Delaney is your friend, but you're not in Dublin to reconnect with him for old times' sake. You have an assignment—an assignment for which you're being well compensated to perform."

Damn the man for his perceptiveness. Of course it was the idea of straying too far into the personal that had activated her mental brakes.

"The practice of limiting the information shared with agents is ridiculous. How am I supposed to do my job if the agency isn't prepared to let me decide what is relevant and what isn't?"

"As I said, we provided you with the details we felt were relevant at the time. Given the change in our timeline, we decided it was necessary to give you more details on two members of the Delaney family. Perhaps you'll find the added information useful, especially if you're willing to play dirty."

Ruthie's limbs turned numb and her grip on the phone tightened. Playing dirty was the last thing she wanted to do, especially with people she knew and cared about. "If I come up with the goods before I leave, will you pay the bonus? No dicking me around, Travers. I want the full amount."

"If...and only if...you return with solid gold intel, the bonus is yours. Otherwise, you'll be paid your regular salary plus expenses."

Ruthie gut twisted. The memory of Kevin in Reuben Kowalski's warehouse played back like an old film reel. "I can do it," she said with a conviction she didn't feel. "I'll see you on Tuesday."

NINETEEN

Flash leaned his head to the side and howled.

"Jaysus." Shane winced from the high-pitched sound. "Stop making that racket. You'll have the neighbors banging on the door and complaining to the landlord. I can't afford to get kicked out until I've got a house lined up for us."

He'd made an unsuccessful attempt to foist the dog onto Kaylee, but she'd been adamant that she had enough on her plate without adding a wild puppy to the mix. Shane couldn't blame her. He'd taken Flash down to the house in Wicklow the day Kaylee and the boys had moved in. Flash had wasted no time in leaving his imprint on the house. Literally. In addition to eating Kaylee's best knickers, the puppy had chewed through the TV cable, pissed on the kitchen floor, and identified Lar's boots as weapons of mass destruction.

Despite the chaos he brought in his wake, Shane had been relieved when Kaylee had turned his offer down.

He'd grown fond of the puppy. As well as the basics he'd purchased on the day he'd first brought Flash home, Shane had added a selection of toys, prompting Lar to accuse him of spoiling the dog. *Speaking of which...*he reached into the toy basket and selected a yellow duck. Maybe a plaything would help the puppy forget his grievance. "Here you go."

Flash gave the toy a baleful stare but made no move to take it. Instead, he pawed Shane's leg plaintively and resumed his howling.

With a sigh, Shane sat on the floor and gathered the puppy into his arms. Flash whimpered, and snuggled in for a cuddle. "I know you don't like being cooped up in here alone, mate, but I can't take you with me. Not tonight. I've got to go out with Lar."

His cousin had texted earlier to say the job for Big Mike was on that evening. Now that none of them needed to do bodyguard duty for Kaylee, they were making a conscious effort to go about their business as usual, especially with Reuben's guys tailing their every move.

Dan had worked fast. Within hours of Shane and Kaylee's visit to the Triskelion Team offices, he'd set up a team of bodyguards to watch over Kaylee and the boys, thus eliminating the need for Shane and his cousins to go back and forth to Wicklow. Once the bodyguards took over, Shane, Lar, and Dan had agreed to stay away from the cottage unless there was an urgent reason for them to visit. No point in going to all the trouble of getting Kaylee and the kids bodyguards if they were going to lead Reuben directly to the safe house.

Shane's phone vibrated in his pocket. He slipped it free and groaned when he glanced at the display. He hit Connect. "Hey, Greg. What's up?"

His older brother didn't waste time on small talk. "Did you know Kaylee's done a runner with the boys? Reuben's calling by the club every day, throwing his weight around and breathing down our necks."

"One of his goons barged into the Triskelion Team's offices yesterday demanding to know where Kaylee and the boys were, and I'm pretty sure they broke into my apartment." Shane had expected nothing less and had prepared accordingly. Apart from conducting a thorough search that yielded no information on Kaylee's whereabouts, Reuben's guys had left both the apartment and Shane's belongings unscathed.

"Do you know where Kaylee is?" Greg demanded. "Dad's losing his shit."

Shane clenched his jaw. He'd a fair idea of what was upsetting Frank, and it wasn't likely to be his estranged daughter leaving her brute of a husband. Their father liked to be left in peace to conduct his dirty wheelings and dealings. Reuben Kowalski barging into the club and scaring off the customers wouldn't suit Frank. "I don't know where she is," he lied, "but I don't blame her for leaving Kowalski."

Greg grunted. "Even if you did know where she was, you wouldn't tell me. I'm just calling you because Dad told me to. If you do talk to Kaylee, tell her to stay the fuck away from Dublin. Better yet, tell her to get out of Ireland."

So the man wasn't as stupid as he looked. Getting Kaylee and the boys out of the country was the first thing they'd considered, but Kaylee had refused. She wanted Reuben off her back, but she had no desire to live the life of a fugitive.

"How's tricks?" Shane asked, keen to change the subject. "Olga said you were moving in together."

"Yeah, right." His brother gave a snort. "Stupid bitch is deluding herself."

In other words, Greg's short attention span had moved on to another woman before he'd gotten as far as sealing the deal with Olga. Poor kid had bleached her arse for nothing. On the plus side, she'd had a lucky escape, even if she didn't realize it now.

"If you hear from Kaylee, let us know," Greg said. "I mean it, Shane. No fucking us around. Kowalski's spoiling for a fight, and we don't want his stench in the club. Maybe Dad can fix her and the kids up with fake passports or something."

It was the "or something" part that worried Shane. Frank looked out for Frank. If Kowalski exerted enough pressure on him, Shane wouldn't put it past their father to grass on his own daughter. "Sure," he lied. "I'll give you a bell if I hear anything."

He disconnected and slipped the phone back into his pocket. Flash's large eyes stared up at him, the dog begging not to be left alone. Shane rubbed the back of his neck. If the dog howled down the building, his landlord would be on the doorstep pronto. With all the shit going down with Kaylee and Lar, he hadn't had a chance to look at houses. Unless he fancied kipping on a camp bed at the office, he needed to keep this place for a while longer. "All right, mate, you can come. You'll have to stay in the car and no howling."

Flash barked and licked Shane's nose, making him laugh. "Steady on. Let's get you into your cage and we'll get going."

In the hallway, Shane shrugged into his leather jacket. He caught sight of his reflection in the hall mirror. Man, he looked like hell. Had the shadows under his eyes reproduced since yesterday? He rubbed his jaw and read weariness in his eyes. Working two jobs was taking its toll, sure, and the stress over Lar and Kaylee wasn't helping. He flexed his stiff neck from side to side, then checked his pistol and ammo. Where he and Lar were headed, going in armed was smart, but he hated carrying. Always had. He grinned at his reflection. Given the Delaney penchant for weapons, he must have rogue genes somewhere in the mix.

When Shane left his building, the bells of St. Patrick's Church chimed in the distance. Ten o'clock. The night was cool with the barest hint of rain. Shane walked the short distance to the Triskelion Team's offices, carrying Flash's cage.

Lar stood at the entrance, his car key in his hand. His jaw dropped when he saw the dog. "You have got to be kidding. No fucking way are we bringing that mongrel."

"Speak for yourself," Shane said cheerfully. "Besides, Flash might come in useful."

Lar's eyebrows shot up. "How? By pissing on the cash we're supposed to retrieve? Yeah, Big Mike would love that."

"It'll be grand," Shane said, putting Flash's cage in the back of the car. "I can't leave him at home. He howls the place down."

"I'll howl *him* down," Lar muttered and slid behind the wheel. "I swear, Shane, if he fucks up this job—"

"He won't," Shane said, an edge of steel to his voice. "If you want my help, Flash is part of the deal."

"Jaysus, man." Lar flexed his shoulders. "We'll be a laughing stock. We've got a reputation to live down to."

Shane rolled his eyes. "We're going after Spoons, Murph, and Dec. They're not exactly master criminals. I don't see how Flash can mess that up."

Lar cast a dark look over his shoulder in the direction of the backseat. "That beast wrecked a pair of steel-toed boots. I wouldn't put anything past him."

"I'll buy you new ones. Don't get your knickers in a twist."

Muttering about demon dogs under his breath, Lar drove to a back alley in one of the seediest parts of the city. A group of cut-rate prostitutes huddled on a street corner, sharing a spliff. One raised an eyebrow when the car cruised past, but they shook their heads.

"Fucking hell." Lar gestured to the half-hearted graffiti on a boarded-up shop. "Even the graffiti artists have given up on this part of town."

"Whose genius idea was it to stash the cash here?" Shane asked.

"Who knows? Between them, Spoons, Murph, and Dec might figure out how to change a light bulb. Pity we can't say the same for their common sense."

Lar pulled up at the end of a lane and killed the engine. "This is the place."

It was dark and deserted with only one functioning light to illuminate the entire lane.

"Lovely location," Shane said. "It's the sort of hovel I'd expect to find Spoons wanking in."

Lar shuddered. "Don't start. I've seen more of that man than I ever wanted to."

The instant Shane opened the passenger side door, Flash began to bark. Shane leaned into the back of the car and loosened the lid of the puppy's cage. He offered him a doggie treat, but the puppy only ceased barking long enough to swallow it in one. "Fuck. I guess we'll have to bring him with us."

Lar stared at him, open-mouthed. "Are you mad? We are not bringing that hairball anywhere."

"Cheer up, cuz. Maybe he can sniff out our prey." It was childish, but seeing his cool-as-a-cucumber cousin irritated was amusing the hell out of him.

"He's not a fucking bloodhound," Lar snapped. "Besides, anyone can smell Spoons from a mile off. We don't need help."

"If we leave him in the car, his barking will alert them that they have company."

"There's got to be other dogs in the neighborhood," Lar muttered. "For all Spoons and his pals know, it's just a random dog freaking out."

"Ah, well," Shane said, stepping out of the car. "If you want to take the risk, it's on your head." Yeah, he was enjoying watching Lar squirm. If he wasn't in a position to confront his cousin, he'd take his pleasures where he could.

The instant Shane shut the car door, Flash's howls increased to an ear-splitting volume.

"Fuck," Lar muttered. "How do we shut him up? A doggie treat?"

Shane rocked back on the balls of his feet and grinned at his cousin. "I tried that trick. It worked...for about five seconds."

Kiss Shot

Lar rubbed his jaw and scanned the lane. "Spoons and the boys are holed in one of these garages. Last my man saw, they were counting the money."

"Spoons can count?"

This elicited a small smile from his cousin. "When he's sober. Which is never."

Flash added an ear-splitting whine to his repertoire.

Lar sighed. "All right. We'd better take your daft dog with us before he rouses the neighborhood nuts and their shotguns."

Shane opened the back door for Flash. The dog leaped out of the car and performed a mad dance around Shane's ankles. When he clipped on the puppy's lead, Flash took off into the lane.

"Where does he think he's going?" Lar asked, shaking his head. "Puppy all-you-can-eat?"

"I dunno," Shane said. "He acts like this when he smells food."

"What's he going to find in a dingy lane? Roadkill?"

"Come on, you. Stop bellyaching. We have three eejits to apprehend."

Grumbling, Lar followed him into the lane. "I don't know what your problem is, You've been a grouch these last couple of weeks."

"I'm a grouch? You've just spent the last ten minutes bitching about my dog."

"Ah, come on, Shane. You've got an edge to your tone that didn't use to be there. What the hell is going on?"

"You want to have this conversation now?" Shane asked. "Seriously? We're in the middle of a fucking raid, man."

Lar hunched his shoulders to ward off the chill night air. "With that damn dog along, the raid's going to go tits up. I've got nothing to lose by bringing this up now. When else have I seen you on your own recently? The night at the cottage, you acted like I had Ebola."

"I've got stuff on my mind." This, at least, was true.

"What's up with you these days?" Lar demanded. "You've been narky for weeks, but never with Dan. Is it because of Gen?"

"Don't be daft. I told you I don't have a problem with Gen. I don't know her very well, but she seems grand."

Lar frowned, skepticism rolling off him in waves. "We used to hang out a lot more than we do at the moment, and it started around the time Gen moved in with me."

"There you go. You're the one who's been busy."

"Yeah, but every time I suggest we go out for a drink, you shoot me down."

"Just drop it, Lar. Which one of these garages is Spoons in?"

"Fuck Spoons. Fuck Big Mike and his money. I'm not going to drop it. You've had a bug up your arse for weeks, and I want to know what it's about."

They both stopped and glared at one another for a long moment.

Kiss Shot

Lar softened his tone. "Come on, Shane. I've known you my whole life. Why won't you tell me what's going on?"

Shane made to move past him, but Lar blocked his path. Shane knocked his hand away. "You really don't want to do that."

"Talk to me. What's going on? Is it this Ruthie person?"

"'This Ruthie person' happens to be Big Mike's daughter."

"I don't give a crap who she is if she's upsetting you. But here's the thing—you've had a shitty attitude for weeks, so this can't just be about her. Look, I know you're a private person and don't like to talk about your feelings—"

This made Shane laugh. "Do any of the men in our family talk about our feelings?"

"With great difficulty," Lar said with a grin. "But I'm talking about you. Look, I have vouchers for a weekend at a spa hotel. Why don't you join me and Gen and invite Ruthie?"

"You want to go to a spa hotel?" Shane snorted. "This was Gen's idea, wasn't it?"

Lar reddened. "Well, yeah. She'd like to get to know you better, and she's noticed the tension between us. She thought—we both thought—a weekend away would be fun."

Under different circumstances, Shane would have jumped at the chance, but as things stood, the last thing he wanted to do was spend a weekend cooped up with Lar.

"Come on, Shane. I'm trying to do you a good turn, you eejit. With all the stress over Kaylee, I figure you could use a break. I know I could. We've been working flat out for months."

At that moment, standing under the shitty half-light of a streetlamp, all the anger that had accumulated over the last few weeks bubbled to the surface. Shane's fingers curled into fists and he struggled to breathe. He wanted to hit Lar and keep on swinging. He wanted to tell him what a prick he was for not confiding in Shane years ago. He wanted...

An insistent bark shattered the moment. Shane wrenched his attention away from his cousin and focused on Flash. The dog pawed at a garage door. Shane dragged oxygen into his lungs. "I'm guessing that's where we'll find Spoons."

In an instant, Lar was all business. He produced a Swiss army knife from his pocket and picked the garage lock. Then he nodded to Shane and swung it open.

Inside, the place stank of bad Chinese takeout, beer, and piss. Spoons was slumped on a mattress, a beer in one grubby hand and a wad of cash in the other. He peered at them from under a fringe of greasy hair. "What the devil are you doing here?"

Kiss Shot

Flash skidded over the floor, his barking fit loud enough to wake the dead.

"Get out," Spoons yowled before hurling the wad of cash at the dog. The man stared at his empty hand, then at the one clutching the beer can. "Well, feck."

"Wrong hand?" Lar asked, scooping up the fallen cash.

"I've a better throw with my right hand," Spoons whined. "Now look what you've made me do."

"From what Lar's told me, your right hand gets a regular workout," Shane said, deadpan.

Spoons squinted at him. "Who the feck are you? Wait...ah, hell. You're another Delaney. Plague of my life, you lot are. Can't you leave a man in peace?"

"Not when you owe Big Mike money." Lar opened a rickety chest of drawers and rifled through it. "Where's the rest of the loot?"

"I don't know what you're talking about," Spoons said with dignity. "There's nothing in them drawers. And Big Mike can feck off. I paid him off weeks ago." He shot Lar a dark look. "You saw to that."

"Then allow me to enlighten you, Spoons. You and two of your pals ripped off a Chinese takeaway on Capel Street a few nights back."

Spoons shifted in his seat and farted. "What of it?" he demanded. "I'm not saying I did. I'm not saying I didn't. Either way, it's got nothing to do with Big Mike."

Shane grinned. "See, that's where you're wrong. The guy who owns the shop owes Big Mike. And you stole the money he was going to use to pay his last installment."

The weedy man's eyes bulged. "How was I supposed to know that?" he spluttered. "A drinking pal of mine had a job planned and asked for my professional assistance."

"Your professional assistance being cracking a safe?"

Spoons shrugged. "Maybe."

Despite his appearance, Spoons had one talent. He was an excellent safecracker. Unfortunately for his criminal career, he was lousy at everything else. Unless he teamed up with a brainier partner, Spoons had a tendency to get caught.

"Since when do you hang out with Murph and Dec?" Shane asked. "Aren't they a bit young to be drinking pals of yours?"

Spoons's right shoulder twitched in what might have been a shrug, albeit a half-hearted one. "Ah, you know. Sitting at the bar, you get chatting to people."

In other words, Murph and Dec had needed a safecracker for their harebrained scheme and figured Spoons would be a cheap option.

"What's your cut of the deal?" Shane demanded.

Spoons sniffed as though this were a sore point. "Twenty percent. Thieving bastards. They promised me an even third and then they went and stiffed me." The man pointed to the cash strewn across the floor. "You can't blame me for helping myself to a bit extra. The two eejits even told me where they were stashing the cash. What did they expect?"

"Where is the money?" Lar asked, rifling through bags and boxes.

"Do I get to keep my share if I tell you?" Spoons asked. "And no hassle from Big Mike?"

"No," Shane and Lar said in unison. "But you will get to keep your kneecaps," Shane added. "Always a plus."

For a long moment, Spoons' belligerent stare didn't waver, but then he relented. "Ah sure, feck it. The money's in that there sports bag." He gestured to a ratty-looking sports bag in the corner of the room. Lar unzipped it. Sure enough, the bag was stuffed with cash.

Lar picked up the bag, and Shane added the notes from the floor.

"Ah, come on, lads. Show some pity. Can't I have a bit of cash? Even a fifty? How am I supposed to live?"

Shane pulled a fifty from his wallet and tossed it onto the mattress. "Don't spend it on drink," he said to Spoons. "Come on, Flash. Time to go."

Outside in the lane, the damp drizzle of earlier had given way to heavy rain, making the cobblestones slick and slippery. Shane turned up his collar and tugged on Flash's lead.

As they trudged toward the end of the lane where the car was parked, Lar turned to Shane and shook his head. "Of course Spoons will bloody well spend that money on drink. You're such a sap."

"Maybe. I'd rather be a sap than so hard-hearted I'd lost my humanity."

Lar scowled. "Is that comment directed at me?"

Before Shane could answer, Flash began to bark. Shane stopped dead. A prickle of unease settled on his shoulders. They weren't alone. Slowly, he turned around. Shadows moved toward them, but the lane was too dimly lit for him to see faces.

"Fuck," Lar's voice was a harsh whisper. "I'm guessing Murph and Dec have come looking for the money. And looks like they've brought a couple of friends."

But the faces that emerged from the shadows weren't Spoons' partners in crime. Reuben Kowalski stood before them, flanked by four large men. His lips drew back in a snarl. "I've been looking for you."

TWENTY

Ruthie glanced at her watch and drummed the steering wheel. What was taking them so long? Thanks to the lashing rain and the crap street lighting, she couldn't see much through her car windows. Shane and Lar sure knew how to pick a shitty night to hang out in an even shittier area of town.

After Travers' ultimatum, Ruthie had paid a couple of low-grade street hoodlums to tail Shane and Lar. She hated relying on paid informants, but she couldn't be everywhere at once. With a tight deadline, she needed results. If the Jarvis Agency was desperate for info, they wouldn't balk at her list of expenses.

At ten-thirty that night, a hash dealer named Rashers texted her to say that Shane and Lar were in a back lane in Cabra, up to goodness-knew-what. Despite not knowing if Lar and Shane's late-night trip was worth investigating, Ruthie decided to risk it. She'd borrowed her father's car and driven to the spot where Rashers had last seen the cousins. Sure enough, Lar's car was parked at the end of a deserted lane in a part of Cabra not even the drug addicts wanted to know. Ruthie parked across the road and hunkered down to wait. She looked at the time again. Fifteen minutes had passed since she'd arrived.

"Fuck this." Whatever the lads were up to, they were taking an age. If she wanted useful intel to report to Travers, she'd have to risk being seen. She pulled up the hood of her raincoat and stepped out of the car.

At that moment, a black SUV screeched to a halt, blocking her view of the lane. Five men tumbled out of the vehicle, all heavily armed. *What the hell?* Her pulse quickened, and the hairs on the nape of her neck stood on end. When one of the men turned and scanned the surroundings, Ruthie ducked behind her car, but not before she'd gotten a good look at the man's face.

Reuben Kowalski.

She swore beneath her breath. Shane had kept the details to a minimum, but she'd been with him when he'd received Kaylee's text message last Sunday. When she'd asked how Kaylee was doing, he'd said Kaylee and her sons had moved out of the family home. It didn't take a genius to connect the dots. Reuben didn't strike her as the kind of guy who'd treat his wife well, and he'd be livid at the idea of her leaving. Even if the weapons hadn't tipped Ruthie off, Reuben's menacing expression would have done the trick. He was here for Shane and Lar, and he didn't have a friendly conversation in mind.

Ruthie crept around to the passenger side of the car and opened the door. Unless her dad had changed the habits of a lifetime, there'd be a gun under the passenger seat. Unregistered, natch, but she wasn't in a position to split hairs. Sure enough, a pistol and a box of ammo were wedged under the seat. Ruthie checked the gun. It was loaded, thank goodness. She slipped the ammo into one pocket and the gun into the other, and drew her own pistol from its holster. If the fight got messy, having a second firearm could tip the balance in her favor. Courtesy of her agency training, holding her own in a gun fight was a newly acquired skill, and one that she hoped she wouldn't need to put into practice tonight. Still, it paid to be prepared.

Pistols at the ready, Ruthie jogged across the street. She paused at the entrance to the lane and scanned the terrain. No one was in sight. Then she slipped into the lane and inched her way along the side of the wall, moving in the direction of Reuben and his cohorts. With the poor lighting, it was hard to see what was right in front of her face, never mind twenty meters away, but she was in luck. They came to a halt under the lone streetlamp. Reuben gestured to the others, and they all retreated into the shadows.

They didn't have to wait long. A moment later, one of the garage doors swung open, and Lar and Shane stepped into the light.

Reuben was upon them in an instant, flanked by his flunkies.

A switchblade swished through the still air, its metal glinting under the streetlight. Reuben let out a roar of rage and stabbed at Shane.

Ruthie's feet were moving before her brain could register their action. She hurled herself at one of Reuben's flunkies and struck him in the kidneys. The man landed face-first in a puddle. The two guys on either side of him spun around to face Ruthie. In one fluid movement, she kicked the man brandishing a gun in the wrist while punching his pal in the heart with her left fist. Both men went down in a howling heap, dropping their weapons before they fell.

Ruthie pocketed the gun and the knife in the seconds before the fourth man went for her, his switchblade at the ready. She stuck her gun in his face. "Might want to rethink that move."

Before the man had a chance to react, Lar took him out with a kick to the back that propelled him forward. Ruthie leaped to the side before he fell, and then finished the job by knocking her opponent unconscious.

"Nice work," Lar said.

"We're not done yet."

Kiss Shot

Reuben was up in Shane's face, yelling and waving a revolver. "Where are they? What have you done with my family?"

Shane's impassive demeanor gave nothing away. She'd give him full marks for remaining calm in a crisis. Travers would love him. "Keep your hair on, Reuben," Shane said, deadpan. "Given the state of your hairline, you can't afford to lose any more."

"Smart arse," Reuben snarled. "Where's Kaylee and the boys? I know you hid them somewhere."

Shane raised an eyebrow. "Why would I do that? Oh, wait...your fist, Kaylee's face."

"She's my wife," Reuben bellowed, spittle flying. "I have a right to know where she is."

Shane's expression darkened. "You gave up all rights when you hit her."

One of the men on the ground groaned and made to push himself up. Ruthie kicked him in the ribs, and he collapsed back down. "We need to get out of here," she whispered to Lar. "When they come around, we're outnumbered. And for all we know, they have backup on the way."

"I agree," Lar said. "Come on, Shane. Time to move."

"Not before I have answers." Reuben pressed his revolver against Shane's forehead. "Where is my family?"

Sweat snaked a path down Ruthie's back. If she moved, Reuben would pull the trigger. But if she didn't do something, he might pull it anyway.

The next seconds occurred at lightning speed. Ruthie took a step forward at the same moment Shane punched Reuben in the solar plexus and grabbed his arm, twisting the man's wrist so the gun was pointed toward the sky. A shot rang out before Reuben released his grasp on the weapon. The revolver tumbled to the ground and landed on the cobblestones with a clatter. Shane was on top of Reuben, punching him in the face over and over.

"Hey," Lar yelled and tried to pull his cousin off the man. "You're going to kill him."

"No more than he deserves," Shane said darkly. "No one hurts my sister and gets away with it." He drew his elbow back to deliver another blow.

"Please, Shane," Ruthie said, her voice high and laced with panic. "Get up and walk away. This isn't the way to deal with Reuben."

Shane hesitated, indecision flickering over his handsome features. Then his stance relaxed and he hopped to his feet. "Let's get out of here," he growled, "before I change my mind."

They legged it to the end of the lane and onto the street where they'd parked.

When they reached Ruthie's car, Shane grabbed her arm. "What the hell are you doing here?" he demanded, fury etched across his face. "You could have been killed."

"If I hadn't shown up, you'd be dead. Reuben meant business."

"Maybe not dead, but seriously injured," Lar amended.

Kiss Shot

"Whatever," she said. "You could at least be grateful."

Shane's anger ebbed. "I am grateful for your help, but I still want to know what you're doing here. Did you follow Kowalski?"

No, but she'd roll with that story. Ironically, it was more plausible than the truth. "Yeah. I don't trust him not to pull another stunt on Kevin."

"Stay away from him, Ruthie. Pay him his money and leave it at that. Kowalski's not a man to fuck with."

"Bit late for that, don't you think?" Lar asked in a bone-dry tone.

Ruthie shivered inside her thin rain jacket. "I'm sorry you're mad at me, Shane, but can we take a raincheck on this conversation? Literally?" She indicated the puddles that were forming around their feet. "We'll have plenty of time to talk at the party on Saturday."

"She's right," Lar said. "We've gotta move before Reuben and the gang stagger our way."

Shane grunted, not entirely pacified. "Okay. We'll talk on Saturday. Just promise me you'll stay away from Kowalski between now and then."

"No promise needed." She flashed him a mischievous smile. "I have zero desire to hang with that motherfucker."

TWENTY-ONE

Ruthie tugged at the plunging neckline of her dress and faced the mirror. She sucked in a breath at the sight of her reflection. "Wow."

"Wow indeed." Emma stood beside her, a broad grin on her face. "You look gorgeous."

A stranger stared back at her. Emma had lined Ruthie's eyes with a smoky eyeliner and highlighted her brown eyes with subtly blended purple-and-gray eyeshadow. A light application of foundation was topped off with the mauve lip tint Gen had spotted at the store. Emma finished working her magic by coaxing Ruthie's straight hair into gentle waves, leaving it loose to skim her shoulders.

"Well done, sis." Gen nodded in approval. "The makeup is perfect and the dress is stunning. Shane won't know what hit him."

Ruthie slipped her stockinged feet into the strappy sandals she'd picked for the occasion. The heels were high enough to give her a boost, but not high enough for her to have trouble walking. "Thanks, ladies. I appreciate your help."

"See? That wasn't total torture, was it?" Emma's grin was infectious.

"No, even if I usually associate dressing up with weddings and funerals."

Gen refilled their wineglasses. "Get this down you while I call a taxi."

When Gen disappeared into the next room, Emma and Ruthie clinked glasses. "To a great night for all of us," Ruthie said. "I'm truly grateful for your help. I'd have made a hash of it on my own."

Emma's smile was infectious. "I enjoyed dressing you up. My sisters won't let me loose on them with my makeup kit."

"It doesn't look as though Gen needs help in that department," Ruthie said. "She's always impeccably turned out."

The other woman's smile faltered. "No, I meant my other sisters. I was adopted."

Shit. She'd put her foot in it. "Yeah," Ruthie said, choosing her next words with care. "I heard you and Gen had only recently gotten to know one another as adults."

The other woman cleaned a smudge of red lipstick from her glass and sighed. "Word travels fast. I suppose Shane told you."

He hadn't needed to. Ruthie had already gleaned the story of Gen and Emma's reunion from their respective agency files. "I'm sorry. I didn't mean to pry."

"No worries. It's still fresh, you know?" Emma smoothed the front of her forties-style red velvet dress and took a generous swig from her glass. Her gaze darted to the closed door that separated them from Gen. "To be honest," she said in a low voice, "I'm grateful for your company. I'm nervous about spending a whole evening with Gen and her friends."

"I thought you were one of the gang."

Emma shrugged and gave a wan smile. "If I am, I'm a brand-new member." She bit her lip. "I've only known Gen a few weeks. It's silly to be self-conscious, but I can feel people watching us when we're together, like they're wondering if there's awkwardness between us, or what it's like to be reunited with the sister you thought was dead."

"People are curious. Kilpatrick is officially part of Dublin now, but it's still got a village mentality, particularly among the older folk. Everyone knows everyone else's business."

Emma glanced up and met her gaze. "Is that why you left?"

"Yeah. Maybe. I don't know." Ruthie laughed. "Okay, it was a contributing factor."

"I've lived in Ireland my whole life. The farthest I've traveled is Holyhead on a school trip."

Kiss Shot

Ruthie's eyebrows shot up. "Are you serious? Do you not like traveling?"

Emma shrugged. "I haven't done enough of it to know. When I moved in with my adoptive family, I never wanted to leave. It took Mum twenty-four years to nudge me out of the nest, and even then I only got as far as Dublin. I guess I'm a homebody at heart. I get my kicks from my job, and then I'm happy to head to my family for Sunday lunch."

"You're close, then?" Ruthie asked.

"Yeah." Another glance at the closed door. "But that doesn't mean I don't want to get to know Gen. It's just... awkward. Sometimes I don't know how to act. Take this party for example. Siobhan added me to the guest list because I'm Gen's sister, and that automatically makes me one of her own. Only, I don't feel it, you know? It's a lovely gesture, but I don't know how to act around the Delaneys."

"Neither do I," Ruthie said, shifting uncomfortably in her seat. Emma would have been less inclined to confide in her were she not halfway through her third glass of wine. "I'm betting Gen feels equally unsure. The Delaneys are a big family, and she hasn't been with Lar all that long."

"True, but—"

Whatever Emma had been about to say was cut short by Gen's reappearance. "The taxi just pulled up outside. Grab your bags and let's go party."

By the time the taxi dropped them off at Dan's gym, Ruthie's alcohol-fueled courage had worn off. Her feet felt alien in her strappy sandals. Her stomach performing acrobatic twists, she tugged self-consciously at her dress.

"It'll be fine," Emma said, squeezing her hand. "You'll knock him dead."

"I think she'd prefer to keep him alive," Gen interjected with a wicked grin, leading the way to the door. "Dead men make lousy lovers."

A rush of warmth flooded Ruthie's face. Part of her yearned to have sex with Shane, and to hell with the consequences. The other part, the piece that contained her conscience, warned her to not succumb to temptation. She swallowed past the lump in her throat and pulled herself together. She'd worry about sex if and when the subject arose. In the meantime, she had sleuthing to do. "Let's go party. Do you have Siobhan's present?"

Gen held up the gift bag. "All wrapped up and tied with a bow."

Inside the gym, the place was packed with people. With the exception of the weights room downstairs, the training areas had been cleared and replaced with tables and chairs. Trays laden with food were arranged buffet-style, and Dan had transformed the gym's health bar into a cocktail counter.

Despite the crowd, Ruthie spotted Shane in an instant. He stood by the bar, looking devastatingly

Kiss Shot

handsome in a black shirt, tie, and pants. Her heart skidded. Maintaining the façade and separating her head and her emotions was becoming more difficult with each passing day. She was no spy. Not really. Her training at the agency had been intense, but it had primarily focused on self-defense, which was a pity, because that was the area in which she already excelled. A part of her had wondered if she was being set up to fail, but why would they do that? Training a new recruit cost them a lot of money. Surely they'd want to make good on their investment?

Shoving these doubts and worries aside, she turned back to Gen and Emma. "I'm going to go over to Shane. Catch you later?"

"Sure," Gen said. "Have fun. In the meantime, I'm going to steer Emma past Dan and make sparks fly."

Emma turned beetroot. "You will not. If I want to talk to Dan, I'll find him. I don't want it to look like I'm running after him."

Gen rolled her eyes. "You said that last weekend at the pub. By closing time, you still hadn't moved from your bar stool. There's a world of difference between throwing yourself at a man, and acting like he has the plague if he comes anywhere near you. Spoiler alert: the latter won't encourage him to ask you out."

"Dan's over in the corner, staring broodily our way." Ruthie nudged Emma. "Go on. I'm pretty sure it's you he's looking at."

"Dan's talking to Max," Emma protested. "He's not even looking in our direction."

"Not now he caught all of us staring at him." Gen looped her arm through her sister's and propelled a squawking Emma into motion. "See you later, Ruthie. I have some unsubtle matchmaking to take care of."

When the sister's had disappeared into the crowd, Ruthie cut a path through the throng and made for the bar and Shane Delaney. His face lit up when he saw her, and he gave her an appreciative once-over. "Wow. Some dress. You look gorgeous."

"You don't look too bad yourself." She fingered the tie—silk and expensive. "I don't think I've seen you in one of these before."

"I try to avoid them whenever possible." he grinned. "I was about to order another drink. What are you having?"

"Anything that's not a cocktail."

He chuckled. "That can be arranged."

"In that case, I'll have a glass of white wine, please."

Shane gestured to the barman. "A glass of dry white and a Guinness."

While the barman was readying their drinks, she took the opportunity to scan the crowd. Most of the guests weren't wearing designer clothes, but they were dressed in their best high-street gear. Siobhan, the birthday girl, looked stunning in a midnight blue dress that came down to her knees. Ruthie spotted her father standing near Siobhan, an expression of admiration on his face.

She waved over to him and smiled at his blush. Her dad deserved some happiness in his life.

A mental vision of her brother clouded her sunny thoughts. If her deal with the agency became public knowledge, any hope of her father finding happiness with Siobhan would be extinguished.

"Siobhan must have invited half of Kilpatrick," she said to distract herself from negative thoughts.

"My aunt loves a good party."

"I joined forces with Gen and Emma and bought her bath bombs and a silver bracelet. I hope that's okay."

"I'm sure she'll be delighted," Shane said, "but you needn't have gone to the trouble of getting her a present."

"I couldn't come empty-handed to her birthday party. I helped Dad pick up a gift certificate for a massage. He's clueless when it comes to shopping for women, and I don't know Siobhan well enough to buy anything more than a generic go-to gift."

Shane regarded her thoughtfully. "Are you okay, Ruthie? You look stressed."

In other words, she was babbling. His perceptiveness jolted her. At that moment, their drinks arrived. Ruthie grabbed her wineglass, relieved to have something to do with her hands. "It's nothing. I'm just a bit tired."

"How's Kevin?" Shane asked carefully.

"He's fine. We left him binge watching *The Walking Dead*."

Shane laughed. "That should keep him out of trouble for a few hours."

"That's the plan."

She'd asked her neighbor, Mrs. Cotton, to give her a call if she saw Kevin leave the house. While Ruthie felt uncomfortable leaving her brother unattended, she couldn't babysit him twenty-four hours a day. If she were to have any chance of repaying his debt, she needed info on the Delaneys, and Siobhan's party provided her with an excellent excuse to chat with the Delaneys and their friends. It also gave her the chance to persuade Shane to take her back to his apartment, where he hopefully kept his laptop and key for the Triskelion Team's offices. If she couldn't hack them remotely, she'd have to try to do it on the premises. Her stomach churned at the thought. She took a swig of wine to calm her nerves.

"How's Flash?" she asked. "Has he stopped chewing up your apartment?"

Shane pulled a face. "Hell no. He ate my underpants this evening."

She roared with laughter. "I love that dog."

"*And* he dug up two potted plants. My upstairs neighbor has already threatened to tell our landlord." He rubbed the back of his neck. "I'm scouring the property pages for a new home before we're evicted."

"Any luck?"

"Not so far, but I'm going to view another house next Tuesday. Four bedrooms, two bathrooms, big garden.

Kiss Shot

That sort of thing." He reddened and cleared his throat. "You wouldn't want to, ah, come along? Give me a woman's opinion on the place?"

Her breath caught. She'd like nothing more than to help Shane hunt for a house, but she'd be back in Geneva on Tuesday. Back to tell the agency all the dirt she'd discovered on Shane and his cousins... What a fucking joke. A flash drive containing Shane's expanded file was burning a hole in her handbag, and she couldn't bring herself to open it. She'd had no problem scouring Lar's complete file—a few eyebrow-raising facts, but mostly what she'd expected. However, when she'd seen the folder with Shane's name, she'd switched off her laptop.

Frowning, she glanced up at Shane and froze. He was watching her, his expression inscrutable. "I suppose you want to talk about what happened the other night."

"Not particularly. As long as you promise me you've stopped tailing Reuben, that man is a topic I'm happy to avoid."

"He makes my skin crawl. I haven't gone anywhere near him." At least she could be honest with Shane about one thing.

A man brushed past, almost spilling his drink over Ruthie. He held his palms up in apology. "Sorry."

"No worries," Ruthie replied and turned back to Shane. "How do you cope with such large parties? I mean, I know a lot of these people are your relatives, but I get nervous having to talk to so many people at once."

"I'm not a party person," he admitted. "If it's a party with people I know and like, that's fine. But something this big isn't my cuppa. Siobhan often throws family dinners and only invites the people she likes. In other words, not my dad. But for her birthday, she's gone all out and invited everyone she ever knew."

Ruthie laughed. "It certainly looks like that. How many people are here anyway? There's got to be a few hundred."

"More like a couple of hundred." Shane grinned. "Dan put his foot down when the list got too long."

"It's good of him to host it. I would've expected the party to be held in Frank's place."

Shane smirked. "I don't think Siobhan wanted her birthday party in a strip club, even if she works there. And she definitely wouldn't be able to persuade Frank to close the place down for a night in order to host a private event."

"Your dad doesn't do favors?"

"My father is too fond of money to sacrifice an entire night's takings. And there's no way he'd offer Siobhan a decent discount to hire the place. It's not how he operates."

Yeah, Ruthie knew all about Frank Delaney. The man was ruthless. On the other hand, she could understand why he wanted to know what had happened to his son in

Kiss Shot

Boston. Why Frank's curiosity in the case should arouse such interest at the agency was a mystery. And Ruthie didn't like mysteries. She liked to know where she stood, especially with people who employed her.

She drained her wineglass and stretched. Time to mingle. She touched Shane's arm and smiled. "I'm going to go over and talk to my dad." This was a lie. She intended to accidentally-on-purpose bump into Frank on her way over. She didn't recall ever talking to the man before, and she doubted she'd be able to pump him for information. However, getting the measure of the man in person could prove useful, and this party might be her only chance.

"Will you dance with me later?" Shane asked.

She raised an eyebrow. "You dance?"

"Not well," he replied with refreshing candor, "but I can shuffle around the dance floor for a bit. Besides," he gave her a cheeky grin, "it's a great excuse to feel you up under that dress."

"I should have known your mind was in the gutter."

He chuckled. "Where you're concerned, always."

"In that case, I'll dance with you later, but only if you promise not to step on my toes."

"I think I can manage that," he said dryly and dropped a kiss onto her hand.

A frisson of sexual awareness shot through her, and seconds later, it was followed by the all-too-familiar stab of guilt. She was playing games with him, toying with his emotions and her own. She hadn't planned to seduce Shane, or at least this was what she kept telling herself. Once Kevin's debt was repaid, she'd leave Kilpatrick forever and never see Shane again. The thought burned a hole in her stomach. Taking a deep breath, she banished thoughts of Shane from her mind and maneuvered her way through the crowd toward Frank. When she reached him, she sent a silent thanks to the careless man who'd given her the idea. She casually looked over the crowd in the other direction and jogged Frank's elbow, causing him to spill whiskey on his shirt.

She opened her mouth in mock horror. "Oh, I'm so sorry." She pulled napkins off a nearby table and pressed them ineffectually to his stained shirt.

Frank eyed her with distaste and gave her a cursory once-over. "Clumsy little thing, aren't you? No wonder you get along well with my son."

Her chest swelled in indignation. This man was a complete and utter prick and he treated the only son who was worth anything like crap. Quashing her real feelings, Ruthie forced a smile. "It's so crowded in here," she said. "Someone bashed into me, and I bashed into you. I'm very sorry about your shirt. I'm happy to pay the dry-cleaning bill."

Frank snorted and glowered at her. "You're Big Mike's girl, aren't you?"

Ruthie maintained her friendly demeanor. "Yes. I was just on my way to talk to Dad."

"Well, don't let me stop you. Try not to cause any more damage on your way, eh?"

So much for turning on the charm with Frank. She didn't let his taciturn manner deter her. While Big Mike didn't generate quite the amount of terror in the local community as Frank "Mad Dog" Delaney did, she was pretty sure Frank wasn't going to mess with Big Mike's daughter. With a parting smile and a cheery wave, Ruthie melted into the crowd. The next chest she bashed against was accidental. Greg Delaney barred her path, a drunken leer across his face.

"Well, hello there," he said, staring down at her with bloodshot eyes that were currently fixed on her breasts.

She tried to move past him, but he held her arm in place. Many things had changed in Kilpatrick since she'd left. Greg Delaney's odious personality wasn't one of them.

"We haven't met," he said. "I'm Greg."

"Actually, we have. On that occasion, I gave you a black eye and knocked your brother's tooth out." She glared at him. "I regret the tooth, but not hurting you."

"Well, I'll be damned." Greg's examination of her person was more thorough this time. "You're Big Mike's girl, the lesbian. Dad told me you were Shane's new girlfriend. Guess he got that wrong."

Ruthie rolled her eyes. No point in getting into an argument about gay rights with a dickhead like Greg Delaney. In his world, women didn't take up martial arts, and they certainly didn't beat the crap out of men. If Greg wanted to believe she was a lesbian, whatever. "I've known Shane for years," she said. "We reconnected recently."

Greg smirked. "Yeah. He used to be friends with your druggie brother."

Ruthie's hands balled into fists, but she held her temper in check. Punching Greg Delaney in front of his father—and her father—wouldn't be a smart move. She yanked her arm free from his grasp.

"Hey, where do you think you're going? I'm not finished talking to you yet."

"I don't think we have anything to say to one another." Again, she attempted to walk past him.

Again, Greg grabbed her arm, this time twisting it painfully. "No one walks away from me."

"This woman does," she snarled. "Take your hand off my arm, or I'll break it."

He laughed whiskey fumes in her face. "Go ahead and try, sunshine."

"That's enough, Greg," said a voice behind her. Shane prized his brother's fingers from her arm and glared at him when he saw the marks Greg had left on her skin. "Do you have to hurt every woman you meet?"

"I was only being friendly. I wanted the chance to get to know your new girlfriend. What's wrong with that?"

"I thought you said I was a lesbian," Ruthie pointed out.

Kiss Shot

Greg shrugged. "Maybe you swing both ways."

Ruthie placed her hands on her hips. "If you're referring to my right and left hooks, then yeah."

"Getting to know someone doesn't involve leaving marks on their arm," Shane snarled. "Stay away from Ruthie."

Shane took her hand in his and tugged her forward and out of Greg's reach. "I'd like to knock that prick's block off."

"So would I. How come no one's killed him yet in a neighborhood this dodgy? All those gangland killings making the papers, and Greg is still prowling around."

"Keep your voice down," Shane said, but he was smiling. "Greg doesn't have many friends, true, but most people are too afraid of our father to take him on."

"I'd heard he treated women like crap."

"Oh, yeah. He takes pleasure in terrorizing the girls at the club."

"What's his problem? If you wiped the smirk off his face, he wouldn't be a bad-looking guy. Why does he need to get aggressive with women?"

"It's not just with women. He's like that with everyone he feels superior to. As for his treatment of females, I'm guessing it's in part to do with our mother leaving. And Frank is no saint where women are concerned, so he's set a bad example."

Greg's interruption had rattled Ruthie more than she liked to admit. "One of these days, he's going to get what's coming to him."

"Probably," Shane agreed. "But I'd rather it didn't come from you." He ran his fingers over her cheek, making her skin tingle. "Now can I have that dance?"

"I haven't had a chance to wish your aunt a happy birthday yet," she said, the desire to stay with him warring with the pressing need to get valuable information for the agency before tomorrow morning.

"There'll be plenty of time to do that later." Shane leaned closer, and the spicy scent of his aftershave teased her senses. "Come on, Ruthie. A dance with you will make my evening."

"If a stagger around the dance floor is all it takes to make you happy, then you're easily pleased."

He laughed. "In my arms, you'll glide. It's a promise."

"You think highly of your dancing skills."

He snorted with laughter. "My mother was an Irish dance teacher. We all had to learn it. And if you learn one style of dance, it's easy to pick up others. I'm no pro, but I can get us around a dance floor, feet intact."

"Do you ever hear from her?" Ruthie asked, genuinely curious. She had only the vaguest memories of Chantelle Delaney.

"No." The syllable was laden with emotion. He looked away before adding, "The last I heard, she was sunning herself in Marbella with her latest toy boy."

Kiss Shot

"Do any of your siblings have contact with her?"

"Kaylee visited her a few years ago but feels no pressing need to go back. She said Mum was her usual self-absorbed self and uninterested in getting to know her adult daughter."

"Some people aren't cut out to be parents," Ruthie said.

"True, but it doesn't make their rejection any easier." ABBA's "Dancing Queen" came on over the speakers, and Shane's serious expression vanished. "This song is terrible."

"So terrible that everyone knows the words and sings along," she said dryly. "Looks like all the party guests are hitting the dance floor."

Gen swung by in Lar's arms, laughing at something he'd said to her. Over by the bar, Emma swayed to the music. She winked at Dan and held out her hand. He hesitated for a moment before a hint of a smile broke through his taciturn demeanor. Even her father had been persuaded to hit the dance floor and was currently showing the birthday girl his limited moves.

Ruthie hated dancing. But somehow, being in Shane's arms felt right. She laid her head against his chest and inhaled his scent: a mixture of washing detergent, aftershave, and something male. His heart beat against her cheek, and his strong arms wrapped around her in a heavenly embrace. For a brief moment, she forgot about her worries. Kevin and the money, Travers and his ultimatum, Dad and his heart problems—everything faded into the background. She wanted to bottle this moment and revisit it when she was alone in her sterile apartment in Geneva.

"Do you want to get out of here?" he murmured. His breath tickled her ear, sending a wave of molten desire searing through her body.

Ruthie looked Shane in the eye and ran her palm over his short beard. "Yes," she whispered. "I'd like that very much."

TWENTY-TWO

They took a taxi back to his place and rode the elevator up to his apartment. Flash, thank goodness, was asleep and didn't wake up when Shane and Ruthie tumbled through the door, leaving a trail of clothes in their wake.

"You're so fucking beautiful," he said when they lay on his bed naked. "My balls ache every time I see you."

"I'll take that as a compliment."

"It is, trust me."

Her eyes darkened and she ran the tip of her tongue over her upper lip. "I want you inside me this time, Shane. Will you do that?"

Shane laughed. "Hell, yeah." He touched the soft skin of her thighs and skimmed the back of her knees, tickling them and noting the sharp intake of breath as she reacted. Before their encounter in the shower, he'd only come close to sleeping with her on one memorable occasion five years ago, yet he still recalled her erogenous zones and where she liked to be touched as if they'd been screwing for years.

"Don't stop," she whispered against his cheek.

"I have no intention of stopping, Ruthie. Not unless you ask me to."

"Oh, I won't tell you to stop. I want this, and I want you. Maybe I shouldn't, but I've never been very good at doing what's good for me."

"That's something we have in common," he murmured, bringing his hand to her upper thigh and stroking her slit. She gasped when he touched her, turning him even harder.

No, they shouldn't be doing this, but right at this moment, Shane couldn't recall the reasons why. All he saw was the beautiful, sexy woman in front of him, begging for his touch. He was more than happy to oblige. He played with her for a few minutes, gently at first, then increasing the pressure. He let her guide his hand, show him exactly where to touch her and how much pressure to use. She was slick and wet and ready, her breathing shallow and her eyes dark with lust.

"I want you, Shane Delaney. I want you inside me."

"Not so fast. I intend to torture you a while longer."

"You're an evil man."

He chuckled. "I take great pleasure in torturing you, Ruthie. When you come, I want it to be the best damn orgasm you've ever had."

"After the one you gave me in the shower, that's a tall order," she teased, licking her lips. The sight made his hard-on throb.

"It's an order I intend to fulfill." He leaned down and put his head between her legs. She arched her back and gasped the instant his tongue made contact with her clit. He teased her with light licks, slowly working up to sucking on her. She tasted so fine. Like strawberries and cream and all his favorite things rolled into one. Shane massaged her thighs with one hand and cupped her buttock with the other, relishing the heat of her silky soft skin.

"Oh, Shane," she moaned. "This feels so good."

It felt pretty damn good to him, too. He liked giving women head, and Ruthie was especially responsive. There was no practiced artifice in her reactions. What she experienced, she displayed. Every moan, every expression, every movement came from the heart. That was what had made the experience in the gym's showers so memorable.

Growing up with a lap dancing club-owner as a father —not to mention the brothel in the basement—Shane had lost his virginity early and spent his teen years getting laid by lap dancers and pros. He'd grown bored by the practiced professional moves before he'd hit twenty, preferring a laywoman's natural reactions.

And man, did Ruthie react. Everything she experienced was displayed on her face, in her sounds, and in her movements.

"Oh, God," she gasped. "If you don't stop, I'll come."

He stopped long enough to laugh and tickle behind her knees. "That's the whole idea."

"I know, but I have plans for tonight, and they include me coming while you're inside me." She pushed herself up to a sitting position and ran her palms down his chest. "How does that sound?"

"Amazing," he conceded with a chuckle. "I like a woman with a plan. But you know you can come more than once, right?"

For a moment, uncertainty flickered in her eyes. "Uh, sure."

He raised an eyebrow. "Haven't you ever had multiple orgasms before?"

"Not exactly." She flushed a becoming shade of pink.

"Well, then." Shane's stomach contracted in anticipation and he brushed his lips against her cheeks. "Let's make tonight a first."

"Okay. As long as you let me tell you what I like and what I don't like."

"Hey, if you want to boss me around, I'm game." He pinched her bottom, laughing at her squeal of outrage. "Just don't knock any more of my teeth out."

Kiss Shot

* * *

Ruthie cupped Shane's face in her hands and kissed him. His warm lips meshed with hers. The kiss deepened and her breathing grew shallow. She'd come so close to going over the edge, but if she only had one night with Shane, she wanted to do it right. For years, she'd fantasized about having sex with him and wondered what it would be like to be his girlfriend. She'd never get to experience the latter, but she could, if just for one night, make her sexual fantasies come to life.

Tonight was all about pure seduction. She was willing to do whatever it took to bring Shane Delaney to his knees. This wasn't just about the job. This wasn't just about her family. This was about her own needs. Everything she'd done over the last few months had been for someone else. She'd accepted the Jarvis Agency's offer to salvage her pride. Accepting that her dream to become a top MMA fighter would never happen had been gut-wrenching. The last thing she'd wanted to do was crawl back to Ireland with no degree and no job prospects. The agency's proposition had seemed a godsend.

And then Kevin had contacted her, and events had spiraled into a knot of complications.

She pulled back from Shane and hauled in a deep breath. What had she been smoking when she'd agreed to this mad scheme? She was no spy. And as for playing the role of the femme fatale, what a bloody laugh. Ruthie could barely get it together to flirt with a guy, never mind seduce one. The not-so-small matter of her brother's debt to a violent drug kingpin called for drastic measures, even if those measures included faking a sexual confidence she didn't possess.

Ruthie met his gaze and exhaled. She could do this. She pulled Shane into a kiss and ignored her racing thoughts.

Feeling his warmth melted the last of her reserves and reminded her how good they'd been together. They were both at least a little drunk, but she didn't care. Before the night was over, she'd intended to get good and shitfaced. She'd also intended to get laid.

Without breaking the kiss, Ruthie slipped a hand between Shane's legs and cupped his balls. She drew a finger along his hard shaft, marveling at the smoothness of his skin. When she teased the tip, he pulled away from her. "Ruthie, you're killing me."

She stared at him for a long moment, taking in the dark eyelashes most women would kill for and the deep blue eyes she'd never been able to forget. Her throat constricted. Once upon a time, she'd loved this man. Now she was about to seduce and betray him. "Do you have condoms?"

He grinned. "A whole box. Brand new, just for you."

"I'm touched." She shoved him back onto the pillows and took him in her mouth. Tentatively at first, then gaining confidence. The idea of giving a man oral sex had grossed her out, but the reality was an unexpected pleasure. The skin of his shaft was smooth and taut. Her tongue glided upward and paused to tease the tip of his cock. Shane guided her gently, and showing her what he liked, but always making sure she was okay with it. From a sex guide she'd read as a teenager, she remembered a few tips and tried them out, enjoying his gasp of surprise when she pulsed her mouth over the top section of his erection. "God, Ruthie," he groaned. "You're incredible."

At that moment, she believed him. Being with Shane made her feel invincible.

Shane placed his hands on her shoulders and stilled her movements. "I want to be in you, Ruthie."

Her heart skipped a beat and, for a second, she couldn't breathe. "I want that too."

He rolled her over onto her back and ran his palms over her thighs, and then over her slit. "You're wet."

"Oh, yeah." She smiled up at him. "You made sure of that."

With a wink, he reached into a drawer and produced a foil wrapper. She watched in fascination as he rolled it over his erection. Pulse pounding, she squeezed her eyes shut and basked in the moment. She could do this. She'd faked confidence in many situations in her life. Surely sex wouldn't be any different? And at her age, what was the likelihood he'd even notice she'd never done it before?

And then he was between her legs, pushing into her. He paused at her opening before entering her in a single thrust.

Ruthie gasped, and squirmed in pain. Ow, that hurt. A stinging pain ripped through her, subsiding only when he stopped moving.

"What the hell?" He stared at her, his face a tableau of horror. "Ruthie—?"

"It's fine," she said through gritted teeth, and forced a smile. "Keep going, and we'll talk after."

He blinked for a moment, then shook his head.

"Please don't stop," she said, her voice rising a notch. "I want to do this. Honestly. I want to have sex with you."

"Hang on a sec." Shane withdrew his cock, and she instantly felt empty. A wave of humiliation washed over her. Of course she hadn't been able to pull this off. Naturally he had no interest in having sex with a virgin.

But then he was back again, brandishing a tube of lubricant. "Condoms can be a bit dry. I'll put this on, and it should make things easier for you."

Moments later, he slid into her again, and the rawness ebbed away. His movements were gentle at first, only gaining in speed and depth when she pulled him deeper into her. "Faster," she whispered.

Shane obeyed. Each thrust made the memory of her initial discomfort hazier and brought her orgasm closer. He explored her body while he moved within her, kneading her buttocks and massaging her breasts. Ruthie returned the favor. She explored the contours of his back, marveled at his arm muscles.

As her need grew, the room receded around her, leaving only her, him, and mounting ecstasy. Her breathing became labored, and waves of pleasure built inside her. Each movement pushed her need nearer to the edge, receded, and then built again. Over and over. When her climax hit, Ruthie cried out, not giving a damn if she woke the entire building. Shane came seconds later. When the last wave subsided, Ruthie collapsed onto the bed in a state of exhausted bliss. "That was even better than the one in the shower," she gasped. "I didn't think that was possible."

Shane kissed her on the cheek and snuggled against her. "Why didn't you tell me you were a virgin before we started having sex?"

She froze in his arms and her cheeks burned. "I didn't know how to tell you," she said. "I was embarrassed. Most women my age have had multiple partners, and I hadn't even had one."

"All you needed to do was say the words." He stroked her shoulder, and the tenderness of his touch nearly undid her. "I would have been more careful."

"It was fine. Really. Okay, I was sore at first," she amended, "but that soon faded."

He pulled her around to face him. His creased brow and worried expression brought a rebellious giggle to her lips. "Do you mind telling me why you waited?" he asked. "You're a lovely-looking girl. You're funny, confident, and fit. What man wouldn't want you?"

She gave him a wobbly smile. "When I look in the mirror, I see the gawky teenage girl I used to be. I find it hard to talk to guys. Hard to talk to people in general, I guess. After my mother died, I could have become the woman of the house. Instead, I became one of the boys."

"There's more to this than you feeling awkward with men. You're not disinterested in sex, that's for sure."

"No, I..." She squeezed her eyes shut for an instant to block the memories, then forced them open and looked straight at Shane. "When I was a teenager," she said in a shaky voice, "something happened. It made me wary of guys in general and hard to let down my defenses when one got close."

He sat up straight, horror and trepidation written on his face. "What happened?" he asked hoarsely. "Did someone hurt you?"

She tasted bile but swallowed past her fear. "Two of Kevin's friends tried to rape me. If my father hadn't come home early that night, they would have succeeded."

"I'm so sorry, Ruthie. That's an awful thing to experience." He slipped an arm around her waist, tentative, as if waiting for her okay to touch her. "Did you see a counselor?"

She shook her head. "I preferred to deal with it by taking up martial arts. I couldn't tell Dad what had

Kiss Shot

happened—he'd have killed them and ended up in prison. So I did the next best thing. I asked him to arrange for me to have self-defense classes with a friend of his. I said I'd feel safer at night."

"I'd say Big Mike was all over that idea."

Ruthie laughed. "He was. Only he didn't expect the classes to spark my interest in learning taekwondo and kickboxing."

"I'll bet." Shane's expression grew serious. "I hurt you tonight. I hate that your first experience of sex was painful."

She smiled past her embarrassment. "It was more pleasure than pain, Shane. I'd definitely do it again."

His mouth quirked with amusement. "I'd be honored to be the man you choose to do it with."

"I don't want to do it with anyone else," she said softly. "I trust you." *Just as much as you shouldn't trust me...*

He kissed her lightly on the cheek and stroked her hair. "Why did you wait so long? What held you back from getting help after what happened to you?"

"Even before the assault, I found it difficult to talk to boys."

He frowned. "You never had trouble talking to me."

"Yeah, but you were different. You treated me like a cherished younger sister."

This made him laugh. "Hey, you were willing to play Settlers of Catan with me for hours on end. That totally deserved a bit of cherishing." They fell silent for a moment until he said, "And what about when you left Ireland? Did you not feel able to put the past behind you and have boyfriends?"

"When I left Ireland, I thought it would be easier, but I found it was better to keep my distance from men on the mixed martial arts circuit. As a woman, it's hard to be taken seriously. If I'd slept with any of them, I was afraid it would be used against me. Even once I got past that fear, I still couldn't do it. I can joke and banter with guys, but I can't flirt. I'm not girly and I don't fawn."

"That's part of the reason I like you," Shane said. "You're not like other women I know."

"Yeah," she said, hearing the bitterness in her voice. "I'm unfeminine."

"Hardly." His hand skimmed her breast, making her shiver. "You're not the only woman in the world who prefers casual clothes and no makeup."

"I enjoyed dressing up for Siobhan's party. I didn't expect to, but I did. I can imagine doing that every once in a while, including the makeup, but it's not what I want to do every day."

"You should dress to please yourself, not anyone else. And as you know—" his clever fingers tickled her belly, "—I find your sports bras adorable."

"Just as well. The lacy bra and knickers combo is the only lingerie I own. And, frankly, they itched. I don't know how women wear underwire bras all the time."

Kiss Shot

Shane laughed. "They look like torture devices to me." He trailed kisses over her shoulder. "Thank you, Ruthie."

"What for?"

"For trusting me enough to tell me all of this."

Guilt crawled over her skin. She hadn't told him everything. Not even close. "I'd hoped you wouldn't notice I was a virgin. I'd read that the hymen often breaks on its own by the time a woman reaches a certain age. I guess mine didn't."

"Are you very sore?" He trailed kisses along her collarbone, making her laugh.

"I feel a little...used...in that area, but it's not painful. I expect the discomfort will have gone by tomorrow."

"It's already tomorrow," he said with a laugh.

"Oh?" She leaned to the side and glanced at the bedside clock. "Shit. I need to get up in four hours. I guess we'd better try to get some sleep."

"Yeah..." He sighed. "I guess we should. I'd rather make love to you all over again, but I'll be sensible and try to sleep instead. Why don't I save the next seduction for tomorrow?"

A tomorrow they'd never have...She gave him a wobbly smile and stroked his face. "Sleep well, Shane."

TWENTY-THREE

Ruthie checked Shane's breathing for the fifth time. He was asleep. Slowly, she pushed back the sheet and climbed out of bed. Her heart pounded against her ribs and she had to wipe her sweaty palms down her T-shirt twice. She'd spotted his laptop earlier that evening while he'd been removing her clothes. Taking a deep breath, she snuck out of the bedroom.

She tiptoed across the open plan living space and retrieved her clothes. When she was dressed, she fetched the flash drive she'd concealed in her handbag and crept to Shane's desk. Like the rest of the apartment, the desk had a modern but lived-in look. In other words, it was untidy, but in that bachelor-pad manner of minimalist furniture and dark décor.

She'd barely had time to sit down when Flash woke up and padded over to lie at her feet. *Shit.* She needed him to stay quiet. A quick search of the dog's basket revealed a couple of toys. She gave them to the puppy, and he seemed content to chew on them as long as he was permitted to hang with her. As long as the dog stayed quiet, Ruthie could roll with having a canine witness to her crime.

With unsteady hands, she opened the laptop. Her heart was in her throat, and a wave of nausea rolled over her. All she had to do was walk away. Walk back to the bed and to Shane and pretend this was a bad dream. Seize the moment and take a chance on happiness and stability. Her stomach churned. Who was she trying to kid? The Jarvis Agency wasn't likely to let her walk away without consequences. She'd signed a contract. And whatever about Travers and company, the Kowalskis weren't about to forget Kevin's debt. Without Ruthie's help, he'd have no choice but to ask their father for the money. She squeezed her eyes shut. Dad had looked happy tonight, dancing with Siobhan. Theirs was a fledgling romance that should be nurtured. Ruthie had vowed that she'd look after the boys and Dad after Mum died, and she'd already broken the promise by leaving. She didn't intend to break it again.

The flash drive slipped into Shane's laptop without protest, but hacking into the computer took thirty tense minutes. Ruthie blinked when the machine decided to perform an unprompted restart. This wasn't a good sign. She bit back a groan of frustration. Fifteen minutes and two restarts later, she was finally in and browsing through Shane's files.

She drew her brows together to form a frown. Why did he have so few folders and applications on the laptop? Did he store all his stuff in the cloud, or on an external drive? While she could imagine him backing up files on an external hard drive, he struck her as too paranoid to trust cloud storage. Her fingers flew over the keyboard, searching for anything related to Shane's research into the attack at The Lucky Leprechaun. Finally, she struck gold. She clicked on a file labeled "Lucky" and bit back a curse when a GIF of a leprechaun danced across the screen. What the hell?

"Didn't find what you were looking for?" asked a deep voice.

Ruthie's heart leaped and she spun around to face Shane.

He stared back at her, expressionless, his arms folded across his chest.

Oh, shit.

"I...can explain," she stammered. But she couldn't. She had no words to explain away the treachery of hacking into his computer while he slept.

"I'm sure you can come up with a clever excuse on the fly," he said, the tenderness from earlier replaced by a note of steel. "You're smart enough to invent a thousand plausible stories on the fly. Only they'd all be lies, wouldn't they?"

Kiss Shot

A ball formed in her throat, making it difficult to breathe. "Did you suspect I'd try to break in?" she asked. "The folder—"

"It wasn't set up for you in particular." Shane moved closer, and she slid the chair back until it hit against the desk. "I don't trust anyone, Ruthie. Did you really think you'd be able to hack into my files that easily?"

She took a shallow breath. "Shane, I—"

"Can explain?" He raised an eyebrow and crossed his arms over his bare chest. "You've said that already. If you do intend to tell me why you've been using me to get information on what I've been investigating, say it fast before I lose my temper. Or worse—" he leaned in, and she felt his warm breath on her face, "—call my father and Lar. Seeing as they're the people I'm doing the investigating for. But you already knew that, didn't you?"

Ruthie wracked her brain for clues. Learning that Lar had done a deal with Irish intelligence had come as a shock, but she couldn't recall anything else in his uncensored file that could indicate what Shane was referring to, and she hadn't been able to bring herself to open Shane's complete file. What she was afraid of finding in the file, she couldn't say. Perhaps her trepidation lay in not wanting to violate Shane's privacy any more than she already had. And now she was paying the price for her cowardice. "Wait," she said. "I'm confused. Are you saying you work for both your father and the Triskelion Team? I thought that joining forces with Lar and Dan was supposed to be a fresh start for you?"

His bitter laugh sent a shiver down her back. "That was the idea, but it didn't go according to plan."

He didn't elaborate.

Ruthie exhaled in a shudder. Any chance she'd had of saving her brother's arse from the Kowalskis had been shattered to smithereens. She'd have to tell Dad. Her limbs turned to ice and her mouth wouldn't cooperate. "Fine," she said hoarsely. "Call Frank. Call Lar. Call whomever you damn well like. It makes no difference now. I tried and failed, and you caught me. There's nothing more to say."

"Oh, there's plenty more to say." He moved closer, lethal as a panther. "I want answers."

"I can't give you answers," she said in a broken voice, staring at the man she'd slept with and betrayed. "I signed confidentiality agreements."

His snort of laughter grated on her frayed nerves. "Fucking confidentiality agreements. They're haunting me."

So he knew about Lar. Was that why there was tension between the cousins? Aloud, she asked, "Why are you not getting on with him? Is it because of his... arrangement?" She was cautious in her word choice in case he didn't know.

Shane's nostrils flared. "Never mind my cousin. I want to know whose pocket you're in. Who's paying Kevin's debts?"

She met his glare but didn't reply. There was no point in denying that she'd sold her soul to bail out her brother. Shane wasn't stupid.

"I asked you a question." His voice was harsher now, and the hurt showed on his face. "Who hired you to hack into my computer? Was it the Kowalskis?"

"What? Oh, no. My only contact with them is over Kevin's debt."

"I'm sure it is," he said smoothly. "What concerns me is the deal you struck with them to repay the second part of Kevin's debt. Are you paying in cash or information? Have you told Reuben that I helped Kaylee and the boys hide?"

"Don't be ridiculous. I would never put Kaylee and her sons at risk."

Shane shrugged. "So they hired you to dig for information of a different sort."

"Why would the Kowalskis want to know what you and your family do?" she demanded in exasperation. "I thought Frank had an agreement with them."

"He does. However, I wouldn't put it past them to hire you to spy on us. Reuben is psycho, but Adam is ambitious. Expanding his little empire is exactly the sort of thing he'd try to do. And now that Jimmy Connolly is out of the way, I hear Adam has struck a deal with

Connolly's sons. His next logical move is to try to encroach on my father's territory, deal or no deal."

Shit. Much as she'd love to make the Kowalskis the fall guys for her current predicament, she couldn't in all conscience risk a misapprehension sparking a turf war in Kilpatrick. Innocent people would get hurt. "Shane, I can't tell you who asked me to hack into your computer, but I will say it wasn't the Kowalskis."

He took a step back, nostrils flaring. His fingers curled into fists. "That leaves only one other possibility. Lar."

Ruthie did a double take. "Why the hell would he want to hack into your computer? You work for him. Surely he knows what you're looking for."

"If he's discovered I'm spying on him, he'd have every reason to want to return the favor." Shane's mouth twisted. "Him or his MI6 girlfriend."

"Okay, hold on a sec." She put a palm up to stop him when he opened his mouth to interrupt her. "This is getting out of hand. Lar didn't hire me."

Shane frowned. "My cousins in Boston? Max in Berlin?"

"No," she shouted. "None of your family or friends had anything to do with me hacking into your computer—or trying to hack in." She regarded the laptop pensively. The mad leprechaun was still dancing across the screen, showing her his arse.

"That makes no sense. Why would a total stranger spy on..." He trailed off, and she could see the wheels turning in his head. "The police. Or Irish intelligence."

Closer, but no prize.

He bounded over to a drawer and drew out a gun.

"Whoa," she said, heart pounding. "Simmer down."

He turned to her, and she read the hurt in his eyes. "This has got to be Lar and Gen."

"I have no idea why you keep thinking they're involved..."

"The intelligence connection," he said in a rough voice.

"They didn't send me here, Shane. Listen to me, for heaven's sake, before you rush off and cause a family feud. Lar and Gen had nothing to do with my being sent to Dublin. The Kowalskis didn't hire me. In fact, no one in Kilpatrick hired me. Beyond that, I can't say any more."

"Because it's confidential?" He sneered and pushed past her to the laptop. "Let's see how far your hacking got you."

His fingers flew over the keyboard, and the contents of the flash drive appeared on the screen. Ruthie gasped and reached for the flash drive, but Shane was too quick for her. He pinned her wrists behind her back. "Why do you have files with my name and Lar's?"

The uncensored file with his name on it that she'd been too shit scared to read. "No, Shane—"

But it was too late. He'd clicked on the file icon.

"What the hell?" He drew back as if he'd been electrocuted. "What is this shit? They've got every fucking part-time job I ever did listed here, legal and illegal."

She swallowed. "I don't know what's in your folder. I read Lar's, but I didn't look at yours. I was supposed to, but I...I couldn't do it."

He rounded on her, breathing hard. "Did your conscience get to you, Ruthie? What the fuck is this file? Did the Kowalskis ask you to plant this crap on my computer?"

Ruthie pushed past him and scanned the screen. And frowned. The first page of Shane's file listed a date and place of birth and all the other basic facts she'd expect to find. Something nagged at her memory, some piece of a puzzle that didn't quite fit. "Wait a sec. Your birthday is in January. Why does this say you were born in April?"

"It also says I was born in Kildare. That's bullshit. I was born at the Rotunda hospital in Dublin. The Kowalskis, or whoever put together this nonsense, are idiots. Or they're trying to fuck with me."

"May I?" Ruthie took the mouse and scrolled down the file. Page Three contained a scanned copy of Shane's birth certificate. She frowned. "Weird. The birth certificate they scanned also gives your date of birth as the fourth of April. Did they scan someone else's birth certificate by mistake? Your father's name is correct, but

Kiss Shot

they have your mother down as Theresa Delaney, not Chantelle."

Shane's tanned face turned chalky white. "What the fuck? Let me see that."

Ruthie stepped to the side to give him a better view of the screen. "See? The name is wrong. Unless your mother chose to go by Chantelle instead of Theresa. Can't say I'd blame her. Your father's name is correct, though. Maybe that's where the mistake occurred."

Shane stood frozen, his features immobile.

"Shane?" Ruthie prompted. "What's up?"

"Theresa was Lar's mother," he said in a hollow voice, "and Francis Malachy is not my father's name."

TWENTY-FOUR

Shane stared at the screen, unseeing. Malachy was his biological father? Malachy, the person who'd offered him refuge whenever things got bad at home.

Ruthie stared at him, her brow creased in confusion. "Your dad's called Frank. Did they get his middle name wrong?"

Shane swayed before regaining his balance. After taut seconds of silence, he said, "All the boys of my father's generation had Francis as their first name, but only Francis Michael was called by his first name."

"Francis *Michael*, not Francis Malachy?" Slowly, realization dawned on her face. "Oh my God. The priest."

He pinned her in place with a glare. "How accurate is the rest of the information your source gave you?"

She fiddled with her rings, twisting and turning them in a frantic fashion. "I've never found a single mistake."

Kiss Shot

"In that case, I have to assume the birth certificate is correct." His exhale of breath was audible. "And if that's true, Malachy has a lot of explaining to do."

"Assuming the Theresa Delaney listed is Lar's mother," Ruthie said, "that makes him your half-brother."

Shane nodded stiffly. "If this is accurate, yes."

"Where does this leave us?" Ruthie asked and shifted her weight from one foot to the other.

"Us? There is no us. Everything you told me was a lie." He slammed his fist down on the desk, relishing the pain that shot through his arm.

"Shane, you'll hurt yourself."

He rounded on her. The rage burning its way through his body must have been reflected on his face, because she blanched and took a step back. *Shit.* He flexed his shoulders and uncurled his fingers. No matter what lies Ruthie had told, no matter what she'd done, Shane didn't harm women. "I don't care if my hand hurts," he ground out. "The pain feels real, unlike your bullshit stories and all the lies my so-called uncle and cousin have told me. Was any of it true, Ruthie? Were you a virgin? Did you even come, or did you fake that too?"

"Yes," she said in a small voice, "I was a virgin, and I didn't fake orgasm. Almost everything I told you since we met in Power's Pub was the truth."

"Ah, yes. Our meeting." He sneered at her, not bothering to disguise his contempt. "How convenient for you to bump into me like that, just when Lenny had canceled our night out. Lenny, who hadn't been in touch with me for ages." Shane's jaw hardened. "How much did you pay him to arrange to meet me?"

Her expression was a mix of guilt and anguish. He didn't give a fuck. Her hand fluttered to her throat. "Yes, I asked Lenny to arrange for you to be at Power's that night. I figured I'd bump into you at some point, but I needed to speed it up."

Shane crossed his arms across his chest. "Why? I want the truth."

She sighed. "As you've guessed, I was paid to ferret out information on you and your family. In return, I'd receive the money to pay off the rest of Kevin's debts."

"The Kowalskis. I'll fucking kill them."

"No. I told you it's not them."

"Then who?"

"I can't say."

"*Won't* say, you mean." He pointed to the door. "I want you to leave."

"Shane, please—" Her tears only hardened his resolve to see the back of her. He'd never dealt well with crying females, and Ruthie meant more to him than any other weeping woman.

"Just go," he growled, "before I do something we both regret."

Wiping her eyes with the back of her hand, Ruthie gathered the rest of her stuff and went to the door. She hovered in the doorframe. "I know this is lousy timing,

Kiss Shot

but I love you, Shane Delaney. I've loved you since I was eight years old. I've fucked up big time, but I'm going to find a way to make this right."

In that instant, his rage deflated, replaced by resigned regret. "There's nothing you can do to make this right, Ruthie. I'm done caring about people who stab me in the back. First Lar, then Malachy, and now you. All I want is for you to get out of my life and stay gone this time."

Her look of devastation cut through him like a knife.

After she closed the door, he slumped onto the sofa. Flash took this as an invitation to join him and leaped onto his lap. The puppy nuzzled Shane's chest and whimpered.

"Come here." Shane cradled the dog in his arms. "You wreck my apartment and cost me an arm and a leg in vet bills, but you don't lie to me. You can stick around."

He drummed his fingers on the edge of the sofa and glanced at his watch. Malachy had still been at Siobhan's party when Shane and Ruthie had left. The priest would probably be home by now. Shane got his feet, decision made. Time to pay his beloved "uncle" a visit.

* * *

Malachy answered his front door on the second ring. "That was quick. I only called the taxi— " He broke off and stared at Shane. "What are you doing here? Is something wrong?"

Shane crossed his arms over his chest and glared at the priest. "Hello, Uncle. Or should I say, Father?"

Malachy's craggy features froze in a snapshot of horror. "Did Francis tell you?"

"No."

The priest drew his bushy gray eyebrows together. "Then how did you find out?"

"Does it matter? Fact is, I know. What I don't know is why you've lied to me all these years."

Malachy looked up and down the street and then stepped aside. "You'd better come in."

Shane marched into the house and almost brained himself by tripping over a suitcase in the hallway.

"Sorry." Malachy rushed to move it out of the way. "I was on my way out when you rang the bell. I thought you were my taxi."

"At this time of night? Surely you don't need a suitcase to give someone the last rites?"

Raw pain flickered across Malachy's face before his protective shutters slammed down concealed his emotions. "I have to go to a conference. My flight leaves in a couple of hours."

Had it not been for his initial expression, Shane might have believed him. He eyed the man skeptically. "Funny, you never mentioned leaving for a conference at the party."

"We didn't have a chance to talk much there. I was trying to keep my sisters from tearing each other's hair out, and you were busy flirting with Ruthie Reynolds. How did that go, by the way?"

Fantastic...until the night imploded in lies and deceit. Shane unclenched his jaw. "Don't change the subject. I've just found out you're my father. I want answers."

"Fair enough." Malachy led the way into his cramped living room and gestured for Shane to take a seat. In an ironic echo of Frank's actions in his office the other week, the priest opened his liquor cabinet and poured two generous shots of whiskey. "I think we could both do with a drink," he said, handing a glass to Shane. "How much do you know?"

Shane took the glass. He wasn't in the mood for whiskey, but he needed to do something with his hands that didn't involve punching a priest. "I saw my original birth certificate. I was born on the fourth of April in Kildare, not on the fourth of January in Dublin. My mother is listed as Theresa Delaney, and Francis Malachy Delaney is down as my father."

Malachy ran a hand through his silver-gray hair. "I wasn't a priest when you were conceived. Not that that makes having an affair with my brother's wife any better."

"No," Shane said coldly. "It doesn't."

The priest knocked his whiskey back in one and looked Shane straight in the eye. "You have to understand. Theresa was stuck in a miserable marriage. Patrick was in prison for most of their marriage. When he wasn't locked up, he was busy getting drunk and chasing other women. By twenty-five, she was stuck at home with three kids under the age of five, no money coming in, and a husband who'd just been sent down for a five-year stretch."

Shane snorted. "And you offered a convenient shoulder to cry on?"

Malachy had the grace to flush. "It wasn't planned, Shane. I was back in Dublin after a stint in Boston. I was having doubts about the life I was leading, and I wanted to get out. For years, I'd convinced myself we were doing the right thing by fighting for a free Ireland. Part of me still believes that. But I never signed up for the drug smuggling and the gun running and all the other stuff we did to finance our cause." His smile was bitter. "Most of us, me included, lined our pockets with some of that money and told ourselves it was okay. Everyone else was doing it, so why shouldn't we?"

"Going from a paramilitary-come-drug-smuggler to a priest is quite a jump."

"Yeah, I know." Malachy rubbed his stubbled jaw. "Getting Theresa pregnant was the last straw. We thought we were doing the right thing by keeping you in the family. Chantelle had just lost a baby, and she and Francis agreed to adopt you and raise you as one of their own."

"Theresa could have left Patrick, and you could have stood by her."

Kiss Shot

Malachy shook his head sadly. "It wasn't that easy in those days. Divorce was still illegal in Ireland, remember?"

"You could have gone abroad," Shane insisted. "If you'd wanted to keep me, you'd have found a way."

"We considered all our options, believe me. Theresa wouldn't leave her kids."

"If Patrick was the waste of space you described, which I totally believe, why the hell didn't you just leave and take the kids with you? You could have gone to America and stayed with Theresa's family."

"We went over our options for months." Tears filled Malachy's eyes and his voice developed a warbly quality. "All the time Theresa was down in Kildare, waiting for you to be born, we talked of little else."

"Ah, yes. Kildare. I suppose she headed off to hide and give birth." Shane sneered, anger swelling in his chest. "What a fucking cliche."

"Patrick would have killed her if he'd known." Malachy cleared his throat and stared imploringly at Shane. "That's why we changed your birth month, just in case it ever came out that Theresa was your mother. With the timing of Patrick's stint in prison, a baby born in January could have been his."

"Whereas he'd have known an April baby couldn't be," Shane finished, his nails digging into his palms. "I can't believe you gave me to Frank to raise. Chantelle was useless, but Frank's a bully."

Malachy hung his head, his usually erect posture slumped. "Francis wasn't a great father substitute for you, I admit, but he's loyal. He knew Patrick's temper, and you were family. We protect our own, even from our own." The doorbell rang again, and Malachy drained his whiskey glass. A muscle flexed in his cheek. "I'm sorry, Shane. I have to go. I know it's terrible timing, but I don't have a choice."

"A conference for Catholic priests is a matter of life or death?" Shane didn't even try to keep the bitterness out of his voice.

Malachy opened his mouth as if to say something, then shook his head. "Trust me when I say it's urgent. I'd cancel if it weren't."

"Where is this urgent conference being held?" Shane asked. "If I'm being brushed aside for a bunch of dudes in dog collars, you can at least tell me when you'll be back."

"Switzerland," Malachy said after a long pause. "My return flight is booked for Tuesday. I'll call you when I land."

The doorbell sounded for a second time, this time longer than the first. Shane grabbed his jacket and strode down the hallway.

"Shane?"

He turned and faced Malachy, eyebrow raised. The man appeared older than he had when Shane arrived, and wore his weariness like an ill-fitting coat. "Go and talk to Lar," the priest said. "Please. Let some good come of this discovery. Until recently, you two were close. Now you know he's your brother, you need to patch things up with him."

Shane's stomach flipped. A few weeks ago, gaining Lar as a brother would have been a dream come true. With the current strain on their relationship, he didn't know how to feel. Outrage? Elation? A weird mixture of both? In contrast, the news that Kaylee was his cousin, and not his sister, didn't change his feelings for her one iota. And he didn't give a damn about losing Tom and Greg as biological siblings—they'd never been close.

"Promise me you'll go see him?" Malachy's eyes pleaded with him, but all Shane felt was numb.

"I'm making no promises to you. As far as I'm concerned, you can rot in that hell you preach about."

"Shane, please—"

But Shane shrugged into his jacket and left the house without a backward glance.

TWENTY-FIVE

Ruthie leaned her forehead against her bedroom door and warm tears spilled down her cheeks. How had she managed to mess up her life quite so spectacularly? Shane, Kevin, the Kowalskis...they all jumbled together to form one massive vortex that threatened to suck her in and never spit her out.

She grabbed a tissue from her nightstand and blew her nose. Now that Shane knew she'd been spying on him, any chance she'd had of getting the money to pay the Kowalskis had vanished, along with Shane's affection. Her failure to keep her cover secret would end her career with the Jarvis Agency, but she didn't give a damn about them. Her chest rose and fell with simmering resentment. If Travers hadn't put pressure on her, she'd have been more cautious. But even if Shane hadn't caught her in the act, she'd still have betrayed his trust. Ruthie collapsed onto her bed and buried her head under the pillow.

Kiss Shot

A knock on the door interrupted her litany of self-recriminations. When she'd arrived home, she'd been too upset to notice whether or not her father's or brother's bedroom doors were closed. "Yeah?" she said between sniffs.

"Ruthie?"

She sat upright when she heard her father's voice. Dad was wearing his favorite pair of button-up pajamas, the ones she and Kevin loved to tease him about—red polka dots that time and multiple washings had faded to pink. They would have looked ridiculous on any man, but Big Mike's bulky frame lent them a particular absurdity.

"What's wrong, love?" he asked, stepping into the room and closing the door behind him.

"Nothing. I'll be fine, Dad. Don't worry."

"You're crying, love. That's not nothing." He came over to sit on the edge of her bed. "Please tell me what's going on. I know you've had something on your mind. Maybe I can help."

"Oh, Dad." She allowed him to envelop her in his strong arms and leaned into his broad chest. For a moment, she was a child again, confident in the knowledge that her father could right all wrongs and heal every pain with a single kiss.

He stroked her hair. "What's up, Ruthie? Why are you so upset? Is it Shane?"

"Partly. I've made a mess of my life and I don't know how to fix it. I tried to help someone, and it backfired. I ignored my conscience and got sucked into doing something I knew was wrong, and I justified it by telling myself it was for a good cause."

"Care to give me the specifics?" her father asked. "I don't care what you've done or why. Just tell me, and we'll try to fix it."

She shook her head. "It's too late to fix most of it. I messed up big time."

"Shane?" he prompted again. "You two were getting cozy at the party."

"As were you and Siobhan," she countered with a small smile. "How's that going?"

Her father's broad face flushed. "I'm taking her out to dinner next week. To a proper restaurant."

Ruthie swallowed a laugh. Big Mike's idea of a proper restaurant left a lot to be desired. Left to his own devices, he'd take Siobhan to Nando's. "I can recommend a couple of places she might like."

"That'd be great. Thanks, love." His gaze grew shrewd. "But before we worry about my dinner date, I want to know if I need to knock young Shane's block off."

Ruthie rolled her eyes. "No, Dad. Shane behaved like a gentleman." A very sexy, very naked gentleman, who'd taken her virginity a couple of hours ago. Yeah, better leave that part out.

Kiss Shot

"Why won't you tell me what's bothering you? Seriously. I want to help, if I can."

She squeezed his arm. "I know you do, Dad. Maybe tomorrow. I have a decision to make and I need to sleep on it."

"Fair enough. You know where I am if you change your mind." He patted her on the head and dropped a kiss on her forehead. "Get some sleep, love. You look exhausted."

"I'll try." She squeezed his arm. "Thanks, Dad."

"What for? I didn't do anything. I only wish you'd let me."

"You were here for me. That means a lot."

"Of course I'm here for you. I'm your dad." A slow smile spread across his broad face. "Want some hot chocolate?"

"Only if you spike mine with Bailey's."

He laughed. "No problem. I'll bring it up to you in a few minutes."

After her father had left, Ruthie lay back on the bed and stared unseeing at the ceiling. Tomorrow—today, actually—she'd have to decide which truths to tell and which to leave unsaid. Whatever she decided, someone would get hurt, and she'd have to live with the consequences.

* * *

For the second time tonight, Shane rang a doorbell at an unsociable hour of the night.

A minute later, the intercom crackled into life. "Yeah?" Lar stifled a yawn.

Shane waved at the security camera. "Hey."

"Shane? Hang on a sec."

Lar answered the door in his underwear, clearly half asleep. He scrutinized Shane. "Jaysus, man. You look like hell."

"It's been quite a night," Shane said dryly. "Can I come in?"

"Sure." Lar stood aside and Shane stepped into the house, leaving Lar to lock up.

"Drink?" Lar asked when they reached the kitchen.

"I just had one at Malachy's. A coffee would be great though."

His cousin grinned. "One sickly sweet coffee coming up."

Shane dropped onto a seat and leaned back. "I can't believe you've started stocking caramel syrup. Go on, admit it—you're secretly a fan."

"Hell, no." Lar chuckled. "Tammy likes it. I keep it on hand for when she comes to stay."

"Shame she couldn't come to Siobhan's party." Shane had a soft spot for Lar's daughter, even though he didn't know the girl well. Fairly or not, Tammy's mother limited the time she spent with her ex-con father, and Shane suspected Lar wasn't keen on Tammy hanging out with her extended family.

"Tammy will be coming to stay with me in July for part of her school summer holidays," Lar said, shaking coffee beans into the machine. "You'll see her then."

The familiar whir of the grinder and the scent of freshly ground coffee soothed Shane. He'd spent many happy evenings at Lar's house, watching bad porn and crappy movies, or cheering on their favorite football team. It felt good to be here, despite the shitty circumstances. "Sorry to call around so late," he said belatedly.

Lar placed a frothy latte in front of Shane. "No worries. From your expression, I figured it was important."

To Lar's credit, he was uncomplicated in that regard, and always willing to drop everything to help the people he cared about, including Shane. Why had he lost sight of Lar's everyday actions and focused on the words he hadn't shared? *Frank.* He'd allowed himself to be manipulated by the man, temporarily forgetting Frank's talent at spotting weaknesses in others. And he'd gone straight for Shane's Achilles' heel—Lar.

By the time the coffees were ready, Shane had slipped Ruthie's flash drive out of his pocket. "Got your laptop?" Shane asked, taking his latte from the coffee table. "There's something you need to see."

Lar raised an eyebrow. "Sure. It's in the office. I'll go get it." He slipped into the home office that was located just off the kitchen and emerged with his laptop under his arm. He keyed in his password and handed the device to Shane.

With Lar leaning over his shoulder, Shane inserted the flash drive. The two file icons appeared on the screen.

"What's this?" Lar growled. "Who's keeping files on you and me?"

"Ruthie." Shane failed to keep the bitterness out of his tone. "Or whoever it is she's working for."

Lar whistled. "Well, shit. You know Gen doesn't trust her, right? Emma does, but she's more gullible."

"I hadn't picked up on that vibe, but it doesn't surprise me. Gen trusts no one."

"No one is an exaggeration, but yeah, she's cautious. She was in the spy business a long time." Lar crossed his arms over his chest. "So...what's in our files?"

"Everything." Shane clicked on Lar's. "It lists your time in prison, the deal you made to get out early, every woman you've ever fucked. The usual." His eyes slid to meet his cousin's.

Lar swore in a mixture of English and Irish. "I'm sorry, Shane," he said after he'd drained his swear word vocabulary. "I couldn't tell you about the deal. If I had, I risked going back to prison."

"What did you tell them about us?" Shane asked, his voice raw. "What did you tell the spooks about our family?"

Lar leaned back in his chair and pulled a face. "More than I wanted, less than they'd hoped for. They were mostly interested in Frank. Where his money came from, who he met, that sort of thing. They didn't give a shit about him running a brothel. After I got sent to Boston, they wanted to know all about The Lucky Leprechaun. Who worked there, who the regulars were, and if Con and Frank were receiving payments on behalf of the paramilitaries."

"And were they?"

"Of course." Lar rolled his eyes. "All of Frank's clubs cook the books. He's laundered a ton of money over the years." Lar took a sip from his espresso cup, a belligerent jut to his jaw. "Listen, Shane, I know Frank's your father and I understand you feel loyal to him, but he fucked me over. Him and my father. I didn't kill the security guard. I wasn't even fucking *there* the night of the robbery. I should never have listened to them. I should never have taken the blame. They hired a slimy lawyer who told me I'd be out in a few months, tops. I was seventeen and stupid enough to believe him."

"I understand." And, for the first time since he'd discovered Lar's deal with the government, he did. On a rational level, he always had, but in his heart, he'd wanted his cousin to be able to come to him and tell him everything, even if it made no damn sense for Lar to do so. "I've never kept secrets from you. Whatever there is to know about me, you know. Finding out that the trust wasn't a two-way street cut deep."

Lar rubbed his jaw and sighed. "I do trust you, Shane. I trust you with my life. My not telling you about the deal had nothing to do with a lack of trust. You have no idea how many times I came close to spilling the whole sorry story to you. Keeping something that big from you hurt."

"So why didn't you tell me?" Shane demanded. "You say you wanted to, and you had ample opportunity over the years."

A pained expression passed over Lar's face. "Apart from the confidentiality part, I didn't want to cause problems between you and your dad. We've always been close. I was reluctant to put you in a position where you felt you had to choose between us. If I'd told you the truth, it would have put you in an awkward situation with Frank. He's a dickhead, but he's still your father."

"Actually, about that—" Shane broke off and shook his head. "No. There's something I need to tell you before I show you my file. A few weeks ago, I installed bugs in your house. I also hacked your security cameras and your and Gen's phones."

Lar stared at him open-mouthed. "Uh, okay...why?"

"One word. Frank."

Lar's expression hardened. "The conniving bastard. So *that's* what he has you doing as your final job for the family 'firm'?"

"Yeah." Saying it was a relief, like a weight being removed from his shoulders. "When Gen came on the scene around the time Dan and I told him we wanted to join you in forming the Triskelion Team, Frank started getting suspicious. An MI6 spy with a connection to the attack that killed his oldest son? That triggered alarm bells. He's not aware of your get-out-of-jail-free deal, but he knows damn well you don't like him."

Lar snorted. "No one likes him. Even Malachy doesn't like him, and he's a priest."

This made Shane laugh. "I don't think being a priest and liking dickheads is synonymous."

"So where are these creepy crawlies?" Lar asked, more incredulous than annoyed.

"All over the house, but I drew the line at installing them in your bedroom or the bathroom."

A brief silence descended as Lar registered his meaning. Then he grinned. "You sly dog. Only you could have gotten away with it. I'm paranoid about checking for shit like that."

"I know." Shane cleared his throat, struggling not to laugh. "Can I also say how grateful I am that you and Gen don't send each other naked pics? 'Cause, seriously, I don't think I could have dealt with that. The lovey-dovey text messages were more than enough."

Lar's eyes widened and then he burst out laughing. "Crap. I didn't even think of that. But no, we don't do naked selfies. Gen worked in intelligence for way too long to trust the security of mobile phones."

"Smart woman."

Lar grew serious. "Does Frank know about my deal?"

Shane shook his head, and relief flooded Lar's face. "For what it's worth, I've known about it for a couple of weeks and I haven't said a word to Frank. And I don't intend to."

"Thanks. I appreciate it. I'd cope if I had to, but I'd rather not have the hassle of Frank losing his shit on me." Lar pointed at Shane's file. "Okay. What dirty secrets have you been keeping from me? A secret penchant for dressing up in animal costumes?"

"No, but you're not going to like it." Shane opened his file and zoomed in on the scanned birth certificate.

"Holy fuck," Lar said after an infinite pause. "You're my brother?"

"Half-brother," Shane corrected.

"Don't split hairs. You're either my brother or you aren't." Lar's face split into a wide grin. "That's awesome news. Not as entertaining as you bugging my house, but I'll take it."

"Wait, back up. You understood the part about your mother and Malachy doing the dirty, right?"

"Uh-huh. At least she got some action. It's not like Dad was faithful to her." Lar shook his head. "Man, you get all the lucky breaks. Why couldn't I be Malachy's son instead of being lumbered with an eejit like Patrick?"

"This isn't a cause for celebration. My biological father is a *priest*."

Lar shrugged. "Shit happens."

"They gave me up for *adoption*. To *Frank*, the greatest arsehole in Dublin."

Lar considered this for a moment. "To be fair, Reuben Kowalski is a strong contender for that title."

Shane crossed his arms over his chest. "Why do I get the impression that you're taking this all in your stride? Why aren't you freaking out?"

Lar rocked back in his chair and laughed. "Dude, my girlfriend came back from the dead; my cousin, who's apparently my brother, has been spying on me; and our investigation into The Lucky Leprechaun has developed so many subplots that I don't know what the fuck went on, and *I was there*. I gave up being serious weeks ago."

"Point taken." Shane massaged the back of his neck. "The news is too fresh for me to know how I feel."

"I can understand that," Lar said, eyeing him shrewdly. "I wish you'd told me what you'd dug up about my deal. I knew you were on edge about something, but you went into lockdown mode every time I tried to talk to you. I didn't know what the hell was going on."

"It's been on the tip of my tongue for weeks. I regret not punching your lights out and solving the whole problem with a fight."

"You have an excellent right hook. I'm glad you kept your fists and elbows to yourself." Lar's expression grew serious. "What's the story with Ruthie? Why's she been spying on us?"

"The *why* part is easy. Her brother owes money to the Kowalskis, and neither Ruthie nor Kevin want Big Mike to find out about it in case he shoots the fuckers and causes a civil war."

"I have no objection to Big Mike shooting the Kowalskis," Lar said dryly, "but I can see why Ruthie would like to avoid that scenario. I'm guessing the loved-up impression you two were giving tonight is at an end?"

Shane's heart thumped against his ribs and his jaw clenched. "Yeah. How can I trust her after this? She set me up, Lar. The whole bumping-into-me business was planned down to the last detail. All she wanted was to use me to get info about our family."

Lar frowned. "Who, exactly? All of us? Frank? Or the Triskelion Team?"

"I don't know. I threw her out and stormed around to Malachy's before I could pump her for details."

"*You* lost your temper?" Lar whistled. "You must have been pissed. You're the most placid of all of us."

"Yeah," he muttered. "Too damn placid. And too damn trusting."

"Dealing with the info about me must have sucked," Lar said. "And then Malachy and Ruthie...that's fucked up."

Shane gave a bitter laugh. "You know what's totally crazy? Finding out about Ruthie and then Malachy put

Kiss Shot

the situation with you in perspective. Yeah, you should have trusted me. I understand your reasoning for not telling me, but I'm still mad as hell. But Malachy? He's lied to me my whole life."

"And Ruthie?"

His jaw clenched. "She took my heart and stomped on it. And then went back to add one of her excellent roundhouse kicks."

"I'm sorry about Ruthie. I thought you two were a good fit." Lar shook his head. "And as for Malachy, I always knew he had a soft spot for you, but I thought it was because of your shared love of books. What did he say when you confronted him?"

Shane snorted. The dissatisfaction of that encounter still rankled. "Not much. He didn't deny it. Just made the expected excuses of wanting to protect me. Protect himself, more like. He cut the conversation short when his taxi arrived."

"Taxi?" Lar glanced up in surprise. "Where was he off to in the middle of the night?"

"The airport and a conference in Switzerland."

Lar frowned. "He didn't mention that to me at the party."

"I guess I'll have to tackle him again when he gets back."

"Listen, Shane..." Lar hesitated before continuing. "I'm sorry to hit you up with yet another revelation tonight, but there's something you should know about Malachy, Jimmy Connolly, and my—*our*—mother's death."

"Go on. Frank is still insisting you killed Connolly, by the way."

His brother grimaced. "I very nearly did."

"Whoa, back up a sec. Why would you be stupid enough to carry out a hit in your own neighborhood?"

Lar examined his knuckles, then focused his deep blue eyes on Shane. "Long story short, Jimmy Connolly ordered the hit on Theresa because he believed she was about to rat him out to the police about a kid he killed during a shootout. When I found out, I went ballistic."

Shane's stomach lurched and a cold horror settled in his bones. "The dickhead," he growled. "If he wasn't already dead, I'd kill him myself. Wait...if you were going to kill him but didn't, then who shot him?"

Lar's steady gaze didn't falter. "Malachy."

Shane exhaled in a whoosh. "Seriously? Malachy shot a man?"

"And not for the first time, judging by the way he handled the rifle."

"Malachy," Shane said in a hard voice, "has some explaining to do when he gets back from his conference."

An understatement on a grand scale. Shane balled his hands into fists. If the priest didn't cooperate, he'd pummel the information out of him.

Lar nodded. "I agree. However, until Malachy returns, we have to concentrate on the Ruthie situation."

Shane swallowed hard. "We need to tell the rest of the team she's been spying on us."

"I'll call a meeting for first thing in the morning. Which—" Lar glanced at his watch, "—is in a couple of hours."

Shane stood. "I'll let you sleep."

"Want to crash in the guest room?"

"Thanks, but I'd better get back to Flash."

At the door, they circled each other warily. Finally, Shane closed the gap between them and enveloped Lar in a bear hug. "Unlike those jackasses Greg and Tom, I'm proud to call you brother."

Lar slapped him on the back and grinned. "Right back at you. Trig and Davin are going to be stoked when they find out," he said, referring to his older brothers. Shane's older brothers too, it seemed.

"Yeah. Don't tell them yet, okay? I need to wrap my head around the situation first. And talk to Kaylee. I don't give a shit about Greg and Tom, but I still consider her my sister."

"Gotcha. Deal with it in your own time." Lar pulled a face. "Speaking of telling people stuff, if you know about my prison deal, I'd better tell Dan."

"Of course. You can rely on both of us to keep the information under wraps."

"I know. And I appreciate it." Lar grinned. "Go get your beauty sleep, *bro*. I'll see you at nine."

TWENTY-SIX

When Shane took a seat at the Triskelion Team conference table at nine the next morning, his eyes felt like he'd attacked them with sandpaper. He'd spent what was left of the night tossing and turning and unable to sleep. The double whammy of discovering Ruthie's betrayal and Malachy's deception had left him reeling. Flash licked his hand. Shane stroked the puppy on instinct, enjoying the warmth of the dog snuggled against his chest. As if sensing his master's distress, Flash had insisted on sleeping in Shane's bed last night, and had accompanied him to this morning's team meeting.

Lar sat at the head of the conference table, twirling a pen between his fingers. A frown was etched on his forehead, and his good humor from a few hours ago was gone. "Thanks for coming in on a Sunday. Something's come up, and I figured it was better discussed in person."

Kiss Shot

Gen's expression was impassive, but when she met Shane's gaze across the table, she gave him a reassuring smile. Lar must have told her all about Ruthie, Malachy, and the whole damn mess.

Only Dan wore a *what the hell?* expression on his face. He dropped a soluble painkiller into his water glass. He looked as tired as Shane felt, with the added joy of a hangover. "It had better be important," Dan grumbled. "I dragged my arse out bed for this meeting."

"And did you leave someone in that bed by any chance?" A hint of a smile played at the corners of Gen's mouth. "Only Emma's not answering her phone this morning."

Dan flushed. "I, uh..."

So Shane hadn't been the only member of the team to get lucky last night. He grimaced. Hopefully, Dan's night with Emma Reilly had ended better than his had with Ruthie.

"Oy," Lar said, rescuing Dan from further embarrassment. "I wasn't screwing around when I said we had an important issue to talk about this morning. Time to focus. Shane, I'll let you start."

Shane blew out his cheeks. "You all know Ruthie Reynolds. And you probably guessed she and I were seeing each other."

"Were?" Dan interrupted with a frown. "You two looked nauseatingly happy at the party. What the hell happened?"

What, indeed? "I caught Ruthie attempting to hack into my laptop."

"Whoa." Dan's eyebrows shot up. "Why the hell would she want to do that? Is she some kind of stalker?"

"Worse." Shane cuddled Flash, gaining comfort from the little dog's presence. "Ruthie was sent to spy on us."

"Who by?" Gen demanded. "The Kowalskis?"

"She says it wasn't them, but I don't know what to believe. Her brother owes Adam and Reuben a shit load of money." Shane shot a glance at Lar. "Another possibility is Frank. What Lar hasn't mentioned yet is that Frank asked me to keep tabs on Lar's activities as part of the family 'firm' exit deal. It's not a stretch to imagine him hiring Ruthie to spy on me."

Dan whistled. "The conniving weasel. You know he wants to send me to Berlin, right? And he's being vague as fuck about what he wants me to do. It wouldn't surprise me at if he's yanking all our chains."

"You mentioned the Berlin business," Shane said, "but you didn't say when it was happening."

"July, allegedly, but I'm not holding my breath." Dan pulled a face. "I think Frank likes keeping me dangling."

"I'm hoping it is July," Lar interjected. "With Tammy coming to visit, I'll be in Dublin for the entire month, but Gen and I will have to make a trip to Boston before the summer is over."

"Can't Trig follow up on the information I dug up?" Shane asked. "He's on site after all."

Kiss Shot

"He's the manager of The Lucky Leprechaun now," Lar said, "but he wasn't working there the summer of the attack. He doesn't know all the people involved. If Gen and I want to track down former colleagues and pump them for clues, we're better to do it ourselves."

"Fair enough." Shane's grip tightened around his coffee cup and his stomach heaved at the thought of Ruthie. "What are we going to do about my pet spy?"

Before anyone could answer, a rap sounded on the door and Imelda waltzed in on impossibly high heels. "You have a visitor, Shane. *Ruthie Reynolds* wants to see you."

Shane had a shrewd notion that Imelda liked to listen at doors, and the distaste with which she emphasized Ruthie's name confirmed his suspicion. Despite her brash manner, Imelda knew how to keep her mouth shut. If she didn't, Lar would fire her, family or not. He cast a look around the table. Dan, Lar, and Gen wore matching grim expressions. Shane tasted bile. With the memories of last night fresh in his mind—both the good ones and the bad—Ruthie was the last person he wanted to face this morning.

With a sinking sensation, he shoved his chair back from the table. "I'll go and see what she wants."

TWENTY-SEVEN

The morning after Siobhan's party, Ruthie stood on the pavement outside the Triskelion Team's offices, staring at the door. She wiped her clammy hands on the front of her cargo pants and pressed the buzzer.

A cheerful voice answered. "Triskelion Team Headquarters."

"Ah, hi. This is Ruthie Reynolds. I'd like to talk to Shane or Lar or whoever's in."

An ominous silence. "Hold on a minute." Whoever the speaker was, her friendliness vanished the moment Ruthie said her name. She blew out a sigh. What had she expected? They'd all hate her now, and it was no more than she deserved.

The seconds passed, each one longer than the next. Finally, when Ruthie was sure she'd sweat through her T-shirt, the woman's voice returned. "I'll buzz you through. Take the elevator to the fourth floor."

Kiss Shot

Ruthie obeyed. The ride up in the elevator took forever. And then the doors slid open. Her stomach churning, Ruthie entered the reception area of the Triskelion Team's offices.

Her heart leaped. Shane leaned against the reception desk, talking to a dark haired girl that Ruthie recognized as Imelda, one of the many Delaney cousins. Hers, then, had been the hostile voice on the intercom.

Pulse racing, Ruthie went up to the reception desk. "Hey."

Shane's expression darkened when he saw her, and his stance radiating displeasure. "What do you want?" he demanded in a low growl. "I thought I told you to get lost."

"You did, but I owe you an explanation. You and your cousins."

The receptionist gave a derisive snort, but Ruthie ignored her. "Shane? Please. You need to hear what I have to say."

A muscle in his cheek flexed but he didn't respond. After staring her down with an intensity that made her wish the floor would open and swallow her whole, he straightened and strode to a door. "Come on," he grunted.

He led her into an office where Lar, Dan, and Gen were seated around a glass table. They all looked up when she walked in, and their combined hostility could nuke a nation.

Ruthie took a deep breath. "I signed a confidentiality agreement when I took the job that led me to spying on you, but I've decided I owe you more than I owe them, so to hell with the consequences."

Gen treated her to an arched eyebrow and a wintery smile. "You'd better take a seat."

Ruthie hesitated for a second before taking the only free seat left—beside Shane. He stiffened when she sat beside him, but raised no objection.

"So," Lar drawled. "Spill. Who hired you?"

"An international intelligence agency," she said without preamble. "My job was to find out what you knew about the attack on The Lucky Leprechaun five years ago and, specifically, why you were looking into it now."

"My brother and my cousin died in that attack," Lar said coldly. "Isn't that reason enough to want to know what happened?"

"Sure, but the timing of your investigation raised alarm bells."

"Alarm bells? Why?" Gen demanded, peppering her with questions. "Who do you work for? Why are they so interested in us digging up the past? Do they want to stop us?"

"I don't know if they want to stop you." Ruthie paused, mulling over the conversations she'd had with Travers. "I got the impression that they were concerned about what you *knew*. I never received instructions to disrupt your investigation."

"You didn't say who hired you," Shane muttered, avoiding eye contact. "An international intelligence agency is vague."

"Gen asked me a lot of questions at once," Ruthie replied, jutting her chin in defiance. "I dealt with her questions regarding motive first." She turned to Gen. "They call themselves the Jarvis Agency. Does the name ring any bells?"

Gen frowned and shook her head. "No, but that isn't surprising. There are a number of secret intelligence groups, many of which are collaborations between the intelligence services of several countries. I can call a contact and find out if he's heard of them. How did they recruit you?"

"I lost a fight due to a bum knee and I knew my fighting career was over." She glanced at Shane. "No fight fixing. I lied to you about that."

He fixed her with a cold stare. "Indeed? What a surprise."

She'd expected he'd hate her, but the reality of being faced with his icy disdain hurt more than she'd anticipated. Ruthie blinked back tears and clasped her hands in her lap to stop them from shaking. When Shane had left for Australia without saying goodbye, she'd thought her heart would never mend. Sitting next to him now and witnessing how much her betrayal had hurt him was a million times worse. If she could rewind the clock and go back to that first night in Power's Pub, she'd have spilled the whole story to him and asked for his help. Maybe he'd have cooperated and helped her feed the agency enough info to keep them satisfied, but not enough to disrupt what he and his cousins were doing. But playing the *what if?* game led nowhere.

"How did they approach you?" Gen asked, her elegant fountain pen poised to take notes. "Did they do so directly, or use an intermediary?"

"Directly. Straight after a fight I'd lost." Ruthie's smile was grim. "These people know how to find weak spots. I was stressed over Kevin's phone call and upset that my career had crash landed. Anyway, the agent explained that he worked for an off-the-books international collaboration between several western nations. Ireland is one."

Shane whistled. "Holy fuck. What do they want with us?"

"They asked me to spy on you and your family. Inveigle invitations to Delaney family events, that sort of thing."

"Which you've done rather successfully," he said dryly.

"Yeah." She bit her lip. "I'm sorry I lied to you, Shane. You have no idea how many times I wanted to confide in you, just blurt it all out."

"Why didn't you?"

She blinked back tears and held her trembling hands in her lap. "Because, for better or worse, I signed a contract with the agency, and I agreed to take this job."

Shane and Lar exchanged significant glances that Ruthie couldn't interpret.

"And in return, they agreed to cover your brother's debts?" Lar asked, eyebrow raised.

"More or less. I'm being paid my regular salary, plus expenses. However, I was offered a substantial bonus if I uncovered information that they considered useful. That bonus would cover the second installment of Kevin's debt."

"Doesn't that strike you as an odd arrangement for an agency to make?" Gen asked. "I don't recall ever being offered a bonus of that nature, and I worked for MI6 for years."

"This is my first solo assignment, so I can't say. I thought the incentive of a bonus might be because my situation was unique. I'm from Kilpatrick and I was already known to you and many members of your family. They didn't even need to create a legend for me. They knew I was the ideal person for this assignment and were therefore willing to make an unusual deal with me."

Shane shifted in his seat. "Was the deal your suggestion or theirs?"

"I..." Had it been her suggestion? She'd been flabbergasted to be called into Travers's boss's office and stunned to be informed her first real assignment would be in Dublin. She screwed up her forehead, replaying the interview. "No, I brought up needing a specific amount, but they didn't seem surprised. Mind you, they probably already knew all about it if they'd researched my family."

"It's an odd scenario, though," Lar said. "I can see why they might feel you were ideal for the job, but I don't understand why an international agency wants to spy on my family. What, exactly, are they hoping to discover?"

She took a deep breath and looked at them each straight in the eye. "I don't know why they want certain information about you and your family, but I do know *what* I was sent to discover. They want to find out how far you've gotten with your investigation into the attack on The Lucky Leprechaun."

Shane scrunched his forehead. "Why? Apart from it being a personal tragedy for the families who lost loved ones, why would some anonymous international agency care whether or not we find who was responsible?"

"Why indeed?" She sighed. "Look, I'm sorry for the subterfuge, Shane. For what it's worth, I regretted accepting the job the moment I met you at Power's."

"That's not much consolation to me, Ruthie," he said in a low voice that exuded a resigned hurt. "You lied to me, repeatedly. You let me care about you, and you fucking lied to me."

Her throat constricted and she could barely squeeze the words out. "Shane, I'm sorry. I truly am."

"When was this?" Dan asked, drawing her attention away from Shane. It was the first time he'd spoken since she entered the room.

"Last November. I had several months of training. This is—was—my first solo assignment."

"November, eh?" Dan drew his brows together. "That was long before we started taking another look at what happened at The Lucky Leprechaun."

"I don't think her recruitment was connected," Gen said. "Ruthie is the type who'd interest an intelligence agency. She's smart and she has fighting skills."

"But when the agency discovered we were digging for info," Lar added, "they decided Ruthie would be the ideal person to infiltrate the team."

Gen nodded. "Exactly."

"For what it's worth, I haven't told them anything yet. I haven't had enough time to find out anything of relevance."

Shane snorted. "You would have if I hadn't caught you trying to hack my laptop."

A tense silence descended, and Ruthie's cheeks burned with shame. "I'm sorry, Shane. Truly I am. I'd never have agreed to the assignment if I wasn't desperate."

"I can't believe *you're* a secret agent."

She gave a rueful laugh. "You've stripped the secret part out of my job description. The agency must have been desperate to send me here. My training concentrated on fighting, not actual spying."

"That makes sense," Gen said. "There are different types of agents. Not all create legends and conduct undercover work as I did."

"In other words," Shane bit out, "you were prepared to sell us out for money."

"If I could have found the money any other way, I would have done it. Involving Dad would have led to disaster. Settling the first part of Kevin's debt wiped my savings. I was desperate."

"I understand the impulse to protect your family," Shane said, "but—" At that moment, his phone rang, cutting short whatever he'd been about to say. He stared at the screen. "Shit," he said. "It's Kaylee. I have to take this call." He held the phone to his ear. "Kaylee?"

Shane's eyes widened as he listened and his knuckles turned white from the force with which he was holding the phone. "You fucking bastard. If you hurt her—" He held the phone in front of his face and groaned.

The others were all on the alert. "What's happened?" Lar demanded. "Is Kaylee okay?"

Shane turned to face Ruthie, riveting her in place with the intensity of his gaze. "That was Reuben. He says Kevin is holding Kaylee hostage."

TWENTY-EIGHT

"What the hell?" Ruthie leaped to her feet and stared at Shane in disbelief. "Are you sure? Kevin has his issues, but I've never known him to be violent to women."

Shane glared at her, and all the anger and resentment that had been building since yesterday came tumbling out. "If you hadn't come sniffing around, none of this would have happened. If you hadn't made me trust you, I wouldn't have let my guard down. You made me *love* you, Ruthie. You made me imagine a future with you in it."

Tears streamed down her cheeks. "I'm sorry, Shane. I never meant to hurt you."

Aw, crap. He hadn't wanted to make her cry. "Look, Ruthie, I—"

"Enough," Lar said, standing. "You two can fight another time. Where is Kevin allegedly holding Kaylee?"

"At the cottage, but I don't buy it." Shane looked at Ruthie, and then back at Lar. "Ruthie's right. Kevin is mentally ill, but he wouldn't do something like this. I think Reuben is setting a trap for us."

"Trap or not, we can't leave Kaylee in the lurch," Lar said in a grim tone. "We have to find out what's going on."

The thought of Kaylee in danger was like a blow to the solar plexus. She might not be his sister by blood, but she was in every sense that mattered. "How fast can we get there, Dan? I don't give a shit if we break the speed limit."

Dan, the logistics specialist for the Triskelion Team, checked his watch. "If we floor it, we can be at the cottage within an hour."

"I'll call my father," Ruthie said. "Check if Kevin is missing."

Shane frowned. "Was he there when you left the house this morning?"

"His bedroom door was closed, but that doesn't mean he was in there. I thought I heard the front door close when I was in the bathroom, but I assumed Dad had gone out to buy a newspaper."

"Okay," he said. "You call Big Mike and try Kevin's phone as well. I'll try reaching Kaylee."

"And I'll phone the security team at the cottage," Lar added.

The next few minutes passed in a tense round of phone conversations and attempted calls. Neither Kevin nor Kaylee answered their phones, and Big Mike confirmed that Kevin wasn't at home. Ruthie gave him a truncated version of events, and he agreed to gather his troops and meet them at the cottage in Wicklow. To Shane's alarm, none of the bodyguards on duty were answering their phones.

After stocking up on firearms and ammo, they donned bulletproof vests and piled into two of the Triskelion Team's SUVs. Flash stayed behind with Imelda. Shane sat in the back of one of the vehicles, next to Ruthie. She sat stiff as a board, oozing tension. Being this close to her stung. Part of him wanted to kiss her worries away, and the other part of him wanted to scream and roar at her for making him feel emotions he didn't want to have and then ripping his heart out. Neither kissing her nor shouting at her was a smart move. He settled back in his seat and counted bullets for the nth time.

The journey down to Wicklow was a blur. No one spoke. Shane checked his weapons, the routine helping to calm his nerves. By the time Lar turned into the narrow road that led to the cottage, Shane could barely breathe. If Reuben had hurt Kaylee or the boys, he'd rip his fucking throat out.

* * *

Ruthie fought nausea for most of the journey. By the time Lar pulled up beside a black SUV and killed the engine, she was ready to hurl.

"Big Mike's not here yet," Shane said. "I'm assuming that's Reuben's car."

Sure enough, Shane's loathsome brother-in-law emerged from the side of the house, gingerly stepping over the prone figure of one of Kaylee's bodyguards and dragging two little boys behind him. Shane leaped out of the car, and Ruthie tumbled out after him.

"Finally," Reuben snarled. "You lot took your damn time."

Shane ran to the boys, and they hurled themselves into his arms. "We got here as quickly as we could," Shane said, picking up his nephews and scanning his surroundings. "Where's Kaylee?"

Ruthie followed the direction of his gaze. Apart from Reuben, she couldn't see anyone. A shiver went down her spine. The whole business stank. No way would Reuben hightail it to a hostage situation without backup. Heck, he'd dragged four flunkies with him to tackle Lar and Shane the other night.

"Kaylee is still in the house with that lunatic." Reuben turned on Ruthie. "That fucker invaded the cottage and took my wife and kids hostage. He only let the boys go when Kaylee agree to stay."

Ruthie ran a hand through her hair. "What do you want me to do? Talk him down? If Kevin is holding them hostage, isn't this a job for hostage negotiators?"

"No police," Reuben was up in her face. "You call them, and I'll make damn sure your brother dies."

Kiss Shot

Burning rage scorched her throat. She was in no mood to let a psycho wife-beater bully her. "Threaten my brother one more time," she snarled, "and I'll rearrange your face."

"Your brother is holding my wife prisoner, and you're threatening *me*? He's a deranged lunatic. He's been stalking Kaylee for months."

Ruthie locked eyes with Shane. "This is the first I've heard of Kevin bothering Kaylee. You?"

Shane shook his head. "She said nothing about Kevin to me. The person she's afraid of is you, Reuben. How did you find the cottage, anyway?"

"Because I'm not stupid." Reuben glared at his brother-in-law. "I'm not a model husband, but I wouldn't threaten my wife with a power drill."

What the hell? "That doesn't sound like something Kevin would do," Ruthie said to Shane. But how well did she know her brother? Or rather, his illness? Would he be capable of hurting people while high on drugs and a bout of paranoia?

She turned back to Reuben, who was impeccably dressed as always. Even in the midst of a crisis, the creep didn't have a hair out of place. "If you think your wife is in danger, we need people with professional experience in dealing with these situations." She reached into her pocket and took out her phone.

"I said no fucking police." Reuben grabbed her phone and hurled it on the ground, where the screen shattered.

"You dickhead." Ruthie went for him, and he twisted her arm. She bit back a scream of pain and kneed him in the balls. The man fell back, roaring. "Touch me one more time, and I'll shove your balls so far up your arse that you'll need surgery to remove them." She turned to the Delaneys. "The prick broke my phone."

Shane hauled Reuben into a sitting position and held him by the scruff of his neck. "Have you not learned your lesson yet?" he growled. "Never hurt a woman. Not on my watch."

With those words, Shane's eyes met Ruthie's, and her heart performed a flip. She loved this man. She loved him with every atom of her being. And judging by the haunted expression on his face, he felt the same way. If only she'd pushed past her fears and confided in him days ago, while there was still a sliver of hope that he'd understand.

She drew in a shaky breath and turned to the others. "I'll deal with Kevin. Out of all of us here, he's most likely to talk to me."

Lar nodded. "Fair enough, but take a gun with you."

She bristled at his words. "I'm not shooting my brother."

Shane released his grip on Reuben and stepped closer, so that only she could hear his words. "It's not Kevin we're worried about. Do you have your gun with you? I'd feel better knowing you're armed."

"I have my pistol in my holster. I can look after myself."

A tentative smile broke through his grim expression. "Oh, I know you can." He pointed to his teeth. "I've seen you in action."

Her eyes met his and, for a brief moment, the familiar spark was there, the sense of mutual longing. He stepped back and the spell was broken. "Be careful."

Her vocal chords didn't seem to want to cooperate. "I will."

Ruthie trudged over the gravel to the front door, feeling the weight of the world on her shoulders. Surely Kevin wouldn't threaten a woman and her children? But how well did she know her brother, truly? She'd been away for years, and there was no denying that Kevin's condition had deteriorated. No, this had to be a trap set by Reuben. And if so, she was walking straight into it.

Ruthie rang the doorbell. "Kevin, it's me. Please open up."

Beyond the closed door, she heard a shuffling sound. "Ruthie?"

She placed a hand on the door. "Yeah. Let me in, Kev. It's just me. No one else is coming in."

The door opened a crack. "Just you?"

"Just me. Come on, Kev. Let's talk."

Her brother grabbed her arm and pulled her inside, slamming the door behind him. He held the infamous power drill in one hand and a piece of plywood in the other. "Where's Reuben?" he demanded, looking around him furtively, as if the man had somehow snuck in. "What's he doing?"

"He's outside with Shane and his cousins."

Kevin frowned. "Anyone else with him? He didn't come alone."

"Is that a question or a statement? Apart from the unconscious bodyguards, I didn't see anyone but Reuben."

"Where are they?" Kevin asked, more to himself than directed at her. "It makes no sense."

She put her arms around her brother, felt his trembling body stiffen. "It's okay, Kev, I'm here now. But there's something I have to ask you. Reuben says you're holding Kaylee prisoner. Is this true?"

Kevin pulled out of the embrace and gave a violent shake of his head. "Of course not. It's all wrong, Ruthie. Don't you see? It doesn't add up. Where are they?"

"Where's who? Who did you see?"

Kevin wrapped his arms around his thin body and rocked back and forth, his eyes unfocused. "They're hiding, but they're watching us. I know they're there."

Ruthie took a deep breath and willed calm. Whether Kevin's mysterious *they* were real or a figment of his fractured imagination, she couldn't tell. "I agree with you that something's off, but before we deal with Reuben, I need to know that Kaylee is safe."

Kevin pointed to a closed door. "She's in the living room. I didn't touch her, honest. Go see for yourself."

Ruthie stepped up to the door and knocked before entering. Sure enough, Kaylee huddled on the sofa, her arms wrapped around her legs. Her head jerked up when Ruthie entered the room, but her panic subsided when she registered who it was—or rather, who it wasn't.

"Hello, Kaylee. Do you remember me? I'm Ruthie Reynolds, Kevin's sister." Ruthie took in the other woman's fading bruises and the stitches above her eyebrow and sucked in a breath. Even if Reuben hadn't set up this hostage situation, he deserved to get his arse kicked. Only an animal would batter his wife.

"I remember you," Kaylee said. "You were a skinny kid, but well able to give the boys hell if they pissed you off."

Ruthie laughed and perched on the edge of an armchair. "That sounds about right. Listen, Kaylee, can you tell me what's going on? Reuben called Shane and said Kevin was holding you hostage."

"I don't know what's going on," she said. "Reuben burst in here a couple of hours ago and grabbed the boys. He was ranting and raving about Kevin trying to kill us. I tried to stop Reuben leaving with the boys, but Kevin tumbled into the house, causing a commotion. During the confusion, Reuben legged it with RJ and Robbie. Kevin was in a terrible state, shaking and crying and saying we needed to protect ourselves because *they* were outside. I've tried to pump him for details, but he's too wound up to make any sense. All he wants to do is board up all the windows and doors."

"But he hasn't hurt you? Kevin, I mean?"

Kaylee's look of surprise lightened the weight on Ruthie's head. "God, no. He's more scared than I am. Of what, I don't know. I believe him when he says he didn't hurt the bodyguards, so I've got to think Kevin's right—Reuben's using Kevin to get to me."

As if on cue, Kevin lurched into the room and checked the boarded-up windows. "Secure. That's good. They're still out there. I can feel them watching us."

"The only people out there are Shane, Lar, Dan, Gen, Reuben, and the boys," Ruthie repeated gently.

Kevin rocked back and forth on the balls of his feet. "He's not getting back in here. The man's an animal. What sort of husband puts cigarettes out on his wife's body? People say I'm sick, but I'd never do that to anyone."

Ruthie's stomach clenched. Seeing her brother in such a state broke her heart. She exchanged a glance with Kaylee. "Okay, Kevin. Calm down. Let's talk about this. Why won't you let Kaylee leave?"

Silence.

"Please," Ruthie continued. "Talk to me, Kev. What's going on? Who are you afraid of?"

"The men in the trees," he said finally. "They're waiting for us."

Kiss Shot

Ruthie went to the window and peered through a crack in the plywood. The hill above the cottage was dotted with trees, but she couldn't see any people. "I'm going to search the house. Stay here with Kaylee, Kev. And put down that drill, okay?"

Kevin hovered nervously, unsure whether to object or obey.

"Please?" Ruthie led him to a chair and shoved him gently onto it. "Why don't you let Kaylee have the drill for now?"

He was instantly alert, and clutched the drill to his chest. "No. It's mine. I—"

"It's all right, Kevin," Kaylee interjected. "I don't mind you having the drill."

Ruthie cast her a grateful glance and slipped out of the room.

A preliminary search of the cottage revealed nothing unusual. Kevin had been busy boarding up windows, and only the downstairs bathroom window was left in its original state. Ruthie walked into the kitchen and searched cupboards and drawers, making sure to remove all the sharp knives in case her instincts were off and Kevin was about to melt down.

She closed the last of the drawers and scanned the kitchen. The only place she hadn't searched was the microwave—hardly a likely hiding place for knives. Nonetheless, Ruthie's training at the agency had instilled thoroughness. She opened the microwave door.

Oh my God. She leaped back, pulse racing, stomach in her throat. It was a remote-controlled bomb.

TWENTY-NINE

Shane paced the perimeter of the cottage. What was taking so long? Courtesy of the boarded-up windows, he couldn't see inside. Sweat beaded under his collar, and he undid the top button of his shirt. Letting Ruthie go in alone had been a mistake. Every second she was gone seemed like a year. All the things he should have said to her played in his head on repeat. He'd spent weeks feeling betrayed by Lar. He was still feeling bruised over that business, but the conversation last night gave him hope that they could heal their friendship. Malachy taking off like a bat out of hell effectively put that conversation on hold.

And Ruthie? Could he truly fault her for being willing to do anything to protect her family? How many times had he been guilty of doing a bad thing for a good reason? Let's face it, his own behavior toward Lar had hardly been honorable. He'd allowed Frank to bully him into undertaking surveillance on his best friend. Shane sucked in a breath. The instant Kaylee was safe, he was telling Ruthie how he felt.

He reached for his phone to call her and remembered that Reuben had broken Ruthie's phone. "I don't like this," he muttered to Lar. "It's too quiet in the house, and Reuben's acting shifty."

"Reuben always acts shifty," Lar said. "It's who he is."

Shane opened his mouth to protest, but closed it again when he picked up the sound of approaching vehicles. Two cars bounced over the rough path that led from the road down to the cottage. They screeched to a halt, and Big Mike and a few of his lackeys piled out.

Big Mike marched over to Shane. "What the hell is going on? Ruthie called me, and now I can't reach her or Kevin on their phones."

Shane jerked a thumb at Reuben, who was standing at the far edge of the property with the boys, under the watchful eyes of Dan and Gen. "Reuben claims Kevin is holding Kaylee hostage."

The vein in Big Mike's neck bulged. "That's bollocks. Kevin wouldn't hold someone against their will."

"Ruthie said the same. She's in the cottage, trying to reason with Kevin and find out what's going on."

Big Mike ran a hand over his bald scalp. "This is my fault. I should have listened to my daughter. She told me to force Kevin into treatment, but I refused."

"It's too late for recriminations," Shane said in a low voice. "For all we know, this is some scheme of Reuben's, and Kevin is a sitting duck. Either way, we have to be careful. I want everyone out of that house."

The older man grunted. "I agree, but how? I don't want to barge in and spook Kevin."

"No barging. We're going to divide and conquer. Lar, Dan, and Gen can keep an eye on Reuben outside. Your men can patrol the perimeter, and you and I will approach the cottage."

"Okay," Big Mike said. "I'll go tell them."

They split up, and Big Mike jogged over to his guys and began to relay instructions. Shane strode over to Gen and his cousins.

"Something stinks," Dan said when Shane had repeated what he'd said to Big Mike. "This whole situation gives me the creeps. How did Reuben find the cottage?"

"I don't know," Shane said. "Either we have a leak and one of the bodyguards let something slip, or Reuben had them tailed when they changed shifts."

"How would he have discovered who works for us?" Lar said. "We kept it on the down-low."

"All it takes is one slip-up," Shane replied. "A hacked phone. An indiscreet word here and there. And, as Reuben pointed out, he isn't stupid. He has the money and the means to tail us twenty-four-seven. We knew hiding Kaylee and the boys was a risk."

Despite the mild weather, Gen shivered and pulled her jacket around her chest. "Let's get moving," she said. "Good luck, Shane."

"You, too."

Shane left the others and headed for the cottage, where his path converged with Big Mike's. "Ready?"

Big Mike grunted. "Yeah, but I'd still prefer to beat the crap out of Reuben."

"All in good time," Shane said with a grim smile. "All in good time."

* * *

Ruthie raced back into the living room. "Kaylee, where's your phone? I need to call Shane."

Kaylee shook her head. "Reuben took it with him."

"Shit." Ruthie gulped for air. "Kevin, do you have your phone on you?"

"What?" Her brother looked distracted. "No. I left it in Reuben's car."

It always came back to Reuben. She punched her palm and bit back a scream. That prick had broken her phone deliberately, making sure they had no way of contacting Shane and the others once they were in the house. Meanwhile, Reuben was prancing around outside, armed with a phone that could detonate the device he'd left as a parting gift for his estranged wife. And with all of them dead, who would believe that Kevin wasn't responsible? When she got her hands on him...Ruthie blew out a breath. *Focus.* It was time to come up with a plan. "Kevin, you said you saw men outside. Did they travel down with you in Reuben's car?"

He nodded. "Yeah."

"Kaylee, Did you see anyone else when Reuben came into the cottage?"

The other woman shook her head. "Just Reuben and Kevin."

Ruthie turned to her brother. "How many men were there?"

"Four," Kevin said without hesitation. "Two came with us in Reuben's car, and the other two came in a second car."

Four men... Ruthie would bet good money that they were the same four eejits who'd tried to beat up Lar and Shane. She returned to the crack in the plywood. Yeah, the trees were far enough away to conceal men hiding behind them, but not far enough away to prevent them from having an excellent shot at the people outside the cottage. *Shit.*

She drew back and took a deep breath. "Okay, listen to me carefully. We're going to go outside the cottage—"

"No," Kevin shouted. "The men in the trees—"

"I'll deal with them," she said grimly. "Now shut up and listen. We'll all walk outside the cottage together. When we get outside, we run like hell. And here's the key part. I want you to run *toward* Reuben, not away. Got it?"

Kaylee blanched. "Why?"

"Just trust me to know what I'm doing. Please, Kaylee. Kevin, I want you to protect Kaylee. Stay with her and guide her toward Reuben and the boys."

Kevin nodded, apparently relieved to be told what to do. "Got it."

"Okay, come on. Time to get out of here."

Kevin and Kaylee followed Ruthie out into the hallway. Her heart rate kicked up a notch when she slipped her gun from her pocket.

"Is that necessary?" Kaylee asked, horrified.

"Better safe than sorry." Ruthie opened the door a crack and peered out. Reuben was about a hundred meters away from the cottage with his sons, well out of blast range. Meanwhile, Dad and Shane were walking straight toward the house. *Damn it.* "We gotta move. One the count of three, run like hell. One...two...three..." She threw the door open and began to run, waving her arms at Shane and her father. "Bomb. Reuben. Remote control."

Shane and her father froze for half a second, their eyes widening. Then Shane glanced at the cottage and back at her. "Come on, run."

They all legged it as fast as possible. Ruthie had almost reached the shed at the far end of the property when shots rang out. A cry sounded from behind her. She spun around to see Kaylee fall on her face, clutching her leg. They weren't far enough away from the cottage for it to be safe.

Kiss Shot

The others were further ahead and wouldn't reach Kaylee in time. Ruthie turned back and sprinted to Kaylee.

"My leg," the other woman moaned. "Some prick shot me."

"Kevin was right about the men in the trees." Ruthie put Kaylee's arm around her neck and pulled her up. "I know it hurts, but we've got to keep moving. And keep your head down."

Kaylee nodded. "I know."

Ruthie was dimly aware of shouts in the distance and the sound of running feet, but she focused on moving them forward, one slow step at a time, pushing them closer to safety. Shane came into view, sprinting hard in their direction. Even from a distance, she recognized the panic on his face. Ruthie quickened her pace, ignoring Kaylee's cry of pain. She'd almost caught up to Shane when a loud noise ripped through her consciousness and she was hurled through the air. And then the blackness claimed her, and she knew no more.

THIRTY

When Ruthie regained consciousness, she was in a hospital room, hooked up to a machine. Shane sat in a chair beside her bed, snoozing. His beard was unkempt and he wore the same clothes as he had at the cottage. She tried to sit up, and fell back on her pillows with a groan. Her head felt like someone was trying to hammer through it from the inside.

Shane was awake in an instant. "Ruthie?"

"Hey," she said in a croaky voice. "How's Kaylee? Is she okay?"

"She's fine. She had to have surgery to remove the bullet and fix her leg, but she'll make a full recovery." He touched her face with his fingertips, and his brow creased in concern. "How do you feel?"

She gave him a wan smile. "My head hurts like a mofo. Apart from that, I'm okay. What do the docs say?"

Kiss Shot

"You have concussion and a few scrapes and bruises. You took a nasty blow to the head when the bomb went off."

"Ugh. That explains the headache."

He took her hands in his and kissed them. "I thought I'd lost you, Ruthie. When the bomb exploded and you went flying, it was the worst moment of my life."

"I'm hard to kill." She tried to sit up and winced. Shane helped her to arrange her pillows. When she was comfortable, she peppered him with questions. "What was Reuben's motive? Apart from being a dickhead psycho, I mean."

"Life insurance." Shane's lips twisted into a bitter smile. "We've done digging into Reuben's affairs since yesterday. Apparently, he took out a policy on Kaylee's life several months ago. Not necessarily for a nefarious reason at the time, but when she wanted to divorce him, he was livid."

"So he decided to get rid of her and claim the settlement?" Ruthie asked, incredulous. "It's like something out of a bad thriller."

"Real life is often more twisted than fiction," Shane said. "Setting Kevin up as the fall guy was the perfect solution. Who'd believe a mentally ill man who's off his meds and talks about imaginary enemies?"

Ruthie shuddered. "That's diabolical. Poor Kevin."

"It's a diabolical plan that very nearly worked." Shane pulled her into his arms. "I'm sorry, Ruthie. Not that I was angry with you because you'd lied to me, but for shutting you out. I should have listened to your side of the story, maybe waited until I'd had time to simmer down before reacting."

"You'd just caught me trying to hack into your computer, right after we'd had mind-blowing sex," she said dryly. "I don't blame you for being upset."

"Mind-blowing?" He grinned. "I like that description."

She blushed. "I was kind of hoping you'd had a similar experience."

Shane leaned over and brushed his lips over hers. "Oh, yeah. It was the best night of my life. That's part of the reason it felt like you'd ripped my heart out when I found you on my laptop."

"For what it's worth," she said softly, "I ripped my own heart out too. I hated the subterfuge. The reason I took a risk and tried to get into your laptop while you were asleep was that the agency was putting pressure on me to produce results. For whatever reason, finding out what you knew about The Lucky Leprechaun attack had become a matter of urgency."

"About that..." Shane said. "I had a meeting with Gen and the guys earlier. Gen says the Jarvis Agency is legit, but even her contact didn't know much about them. We're going to do more digging to see what we can find out about them and why they're so interested in our investigation. In the meantime, we have a proposition for you."

She squinted at him through the pain of her throbbing head. "You do?"

"You know the Jarvis Agency. You know the people who work there, and you can put faces to names."

"Well, I know some of them," she amended. "It's on a strictly need-to-know basis."

"We—the Triskelion Team, that is—want you to go back there and find out why they're so interested in us."

She frowned. "You want me to go back to Geneva and spy on the agency?"

"Yes." He leaned forward. "And I want you to take Flash and me with you. I'm getting kicked out of my apartment soon anyway. I'll need somewhere to live, and a change of scene would do me good."

Her heart leaped. Was he serious? "What about your job for the Triskelion Team?" she asked. "You guys just started your business."

"I'm still working for the Triskelion Team. Security and internet research is stuff I can do anywhere. Besides, I'm hoping that living in Geneva won't be a permanent solution—for either of us."

Her heart beat a little faster. He couldn't mean...but no. That wasn't possible. Not after what she'd done. "Do you want me to tell the Jarvis Agency I'm stringing you along for info?"

"Tell them whatever works. As long as we know it's real, that's all that counts."

For a moment, she forgot to breathe. "Wait...I thought you wanted to use me to spy on the Jarvis Agency. Do you mean—?"

He grinned, and her heart melted. "Yes, I want you to spy on them, but I have an ulterior motive—you. Almost losing you put everything in perspective. You screwed up by not telling me why you were back in Dublin, but I understand why you did it. I can respect wanting to protect your loved ones."

"I didn't do a very good job at protecting anyone."

"You saved Kaylee's life." He squeezed her hands. "Don't ever forget that. I know I won't. I owe you one, Ruthie."

This made her laugh. "And I owe you two thousand euros. I'll give you the money when we get to Geneva."

"Never mind the money." He dropped a kiss on her forehead. "All I want is to be with you. If yesterday taught me anything, it's that I can't live my life being afraid to trust the people I care about. And that includes you. I want to start over with you, Ruthie. I want us to be a proper couple."

"And I want to be with you, Shane. You have no idea how much. But first, I need to sort out Kevin's predicament."

His expression softened. "Your dad took care of that. After the police were done questioning everyone, Big Mike persuaded Kevin to check into a psychiatric clinic. He seemed to take it quite calmly."

A wave of relief washed over her. "I can only hope he stays. What if he changes his mind and checks himself out?"

"Take it one day at a time, Ruthie. At least he won't need to worry about his debt to Reuben anymore."

She raised an eyebrow. "Reuben is letting it slide?"

A sly smile crept over his face. "Reuben is in police custody and has no say in the matter. Adam came to a deal with your father. He agreed to drop the matter in exchange for five thousand in cash and Big Mike's promise not to torch every premises he owns."

Ruthie squeezed her eyes shut. "Shit. Dad went ballistic, didn't he? I knew he would if he found out. His blood pressure..."

"Big Mike is fine. Siobhan talked him down and suggested the deal. Those two are good together."

Ruthie opened her eyes and blew out a breath. "Thank goodness. And yes, they are good together. I'd better make sure Dad's booked a good restaurant to take Siobhan for their date. I have visions of somewhere like Burdock's Fish and Chips, or Nando's for a chicken dinner."

Shane laughed and leaned over and kissed her, properly this time. When they broke apart, he looked her in the eyes and smoothed her hair back from her face. "I don't know what's going to happen in the future, Ruthie. You're not long back in Kilpatrick, and we're just starting to get to know one another again. What I do know is how being with you makes me feel. When we're together, I feel whole. I hadn't realized I had a chunk missing until you walked back into my life. Will you take a chance on us?"

Her chest swelled and she pulled him close. "Yes, Shane. Yes."

EPILOGUE

Two Year's Later

Shane raced into the emergency department and charged up to the reception desk. It was unoccupied. *Shit.* Heart pounding, he spun around and pounced on a passing nurse. "I'm looking for Ruthie Delaney," he said breathlessly. "I was told she collapsed."

The nurse surveyed him with a dubious expression. "One moment. I'll check the register."

The woman slipped behind the counter. While her fingers clicked over the keyboard, Shane tapped his foot with ill-concealed impatience. What the hell was taking her so long? After what seemed like an age, the nurse glanced up. "Mrs. Delaney is in consulting room 12. She's with the doctor now. Do you want to go up to her?"

"Yes, please."

The nurse gestured to the ominous looking door that separated the reception area from the hospital beyond.

"Go through the door and walk to the end of the corridor. Room 12 is on right hand side."

"Thanks," Shane called over his shoulder, already barging through the door. He ignored the nurse's squawk that he should slow down. When he'd received Dan's text message to say that Ruthie had been taken ill, he'd been out walking Flash while the others finished the preparations for Shane's birthday party. The walk had turned into a sprint back to his car and a mad dash to the hospital, breaking several rules of the road along the way.

Room 6. Room 8. Room 10. And, finally, Room 12.

Shane knocked on the door and entered without waiting for an invitation.

His stomach relocated to his throat. Ruthie lay on an examination table, deathly pale and hooked up to an ultrasound. "The baby?" he managed hoarsely. "Is the baby—?"

Ruthie turned to face him and her pale face lit up with a smile. "Everything's fine, Shane."

"Oh, thank God," he said in an exhale. "What happened? Are you all right?"

The doctor, a cool blonde in her early forties, stepped back from the ultrasound machine. "Your wife has low blood pressure. It's very common, especially in a multiple pregnancy. We'll keep an eye on it, but as she's otherwise fit and healthy, I don't think it will cause a problem."

Kiss Shot

Shane's mind reeled. "Back up a sec. Did you say *multiple* pregnancy?"

A mischievous glint sparkled in Ruthie's eye. "Yes, she did. We're expecting twins. Happy birthday, Shane."

—THE END—

OTHER BOOKS BY ZARA

THE BALLYBEG SERIES
Love and Shenanigans
Love and Blarney
Love and Leprechauns
Love and Mistletoe
Love and Shamrocks
Love and Snowflakes

BALLYBEG BAD BOYS
Her Treasure Hunter Ex
The Rock Star's Secret Baby
The Navy SEAL's Holiday Fling
Bodyguard by Day, Ex-Husband by Night
The Navy SEAL's Accidental Wife

DUBLIN MAFIA: TRISKELION TEAM
Final Target
Kiss Shot
Bullet Point (Spring 2017)

ABOUT ZARA

USA Today bestselling author Zara Keane grew up in Dublin, Ireland, but spent her summers in a small town very similar to the fictitious Ballybeg.

She currently lives in Switzerland with her family. When she's not writing or wrestling small people, she drinks far too much coffee, and tries—with occasional success—to resist the siren call of Swiss chocolate.

zarakeane.com